Behind the Courtesan

BRONWYN STUART

This book is for my girls.

Reach for your dreams and don't let anyone or anything ever hold you back.

One

What men and women of the ton neglect to consider is that behind every courtesan is a woman, who, given another opportunity, would have been a duchess.

Or perhaps a queen...

Somewhere on the road to hell

England, 1805

Lions have lionesses, Maharajahs have their many wives and sheikhs, their harems. It seems no matter what manner of species one belongs to, all males think it their gift and right to have more than one female at their beck and call. It is no different with the men of the ton.

Sophia Martin snorted and threw the leather-bound book to the damp carriage floor. It was all about sex. Family, duty, king and country all came second for males seeking sexual gratification.

Drawing a long deep breath, she held it for four counts and then exhaled. Whenever her anxiety grew too great, she would take a deep breath. So many times in her life it had worked. Not now. Not when she faced her largest hurdle to date.

Blake.

Brambles danced thorny cartwheels in her stomach until her breath once again came in short pants and her damp hands crushed the velvet of her lavender gown. What scared her most— being near a new baby, surrounded by happy families, or returning to the place where her life first fell to pieces? Already the condemnation reached out to greet her, to suck her in and spit her out, defeated and deflated. She half imagined sharpened pitchforks awaited her.

Why had Matthew requested that she attend the birth of her niece or nephew? Why had she said yes? The whole situation seemed a cruel reminder of that which she would never experience. Tears pricked her eyes and made them burn as her hand drifted to her abdomen. Too late to change her mind now and far too late for regret.

Once the carriage stopped rocking and creaking, the silence became oppressive. She waited for the driver to leap down from his perch to hand her down.

Nothing happened.

Sophia stood, her body stooped so she wouldn't hit her head, and opened the carriage door. The first thing she saw was the reason the driver hadn't done his job. The dirt yard of the tavern she remembered from her childhood was churned to wet, dark mud that would cover her soft kid boots and more if she were jump down on her own.

Not an option. "Johnson." She called the driver's name through clenched teeth.

"Yes, ma'am?"

"Get down here and do what I pay you for."

A snort reached her ears followed by his chuckled reply. "You don't pay me enough to slog through that."

Had she known her frugality would make the difference between assistance and abandonment, she would have loosened her purse strings somewhat. It's what she got for hiring the only man interested in driving a courtesan to the middle of nowhere during the wettest winter in years. Now she regretted not taking the Duke of St. Ives up on his offer of a carriage and driver but at the time, anonymity was foremost in her thoughts. No one could know where she had gone. "I'll pay you a further guinea if you get down here and help me."

Johnson snorted again and the carriage rocked slightly but still he didn't climb down. "Not for all the gold in London, lass."

"You can't expect me to...to..." Her bottom lip quivered. She closed her teeth down on it in an effort to remain calm.

"Don't much care how. I could sit up here all day."

"Drive around another way," she hissed.

"Ain't no other way. Rain's washed everything to the same kind of sludge."

Cursing under her breath, she looked to the door of the tavern where a small crowd gathered for what was turning out to be their morning's entertainment and wondered how they had all reached their destination. What she longed to see was boards or a paved walkway to the door but it seemed none of her wishes mattered that day.

"An ale she falls flat on her face," a voice cackled from the open doorway.

"Two she falls on her arse."

The pair roared with uncouth laughter.

The urge to huff and scream overwhelmed her, but she tamped down her fury for the moment. She gritted her teeth and said, "I'll buy you both three if I can get some assistance."

One dirty face looked to the other and for a moment hope blossomed. Then, "No deal, lass."

"Four?" Useless tears stung her eyes once again and exhaustion made her heavy skirts drag at her legs and back.

This time they didn't reply, only guffawed and continued to watch.

"What have we got, boys?" The voice that now echoed from the inn didn't laugh. She sucked in a breath and started counting. She hadn't expected to see *him* so soon. She wasn't ready.

Sophia straightened as fully as the low ceiling allowed. Slow drizzle made it difficult to see from where the voice would emerge, but before long, a man—familiar and yet not—emerged, his bulk filling the entire door frame.

"Little Sophie, is that you?"

Even from across the courtyard, she felt his gaze like a sudden pressure to her chest. It had been an age since anyone had called her Little Sophie. She pressed her lips together and tried to ignore the sarcastic tone to his question.

"I suppose you'll be wanting a hand, Madam?" he called from the dry stoop of the inn.

"If it isn't too much trouble." Sophia waited and watched as Blake slipped his worn leather boots from his feet and yanked his woolen socks off. He then rolled his rough work pants to his knees, revealing long muscular calves—much to the amusement of the cackling animals.

Sophia was so cold her lips wouldn't do what she wanted and her teeth began to chatter against one another. "You needn't undress. Just come and fetch me."

"I've already lost one pair of shoes to that mess and the stepping boards. I won't lose anything else to it. I don't know what the fuss is anyway. I'm sure your fine carriage is more comfortable than my inn."

The pits of hell couldn't be any more uncomfortable, though at least there she'd be warm.

As Blake took his first step into what had to be ice cold mud, Sophia gave in to curiosity and studied the man he'd become. Brown wavy hair cropped short, a hint of gold shining through as a lone ray of sunshine pierced the clouds overhead.

What drew her eyes more than anything else—and kept them fixed—were Blake's arms. A workman's muscles now bulged from shoulder to elbow where over a decade ago he had been skin and bones.

Instant and unexpected warmth curled through her torso as she imagined those strong arms holding her close.

Sophia shook her focus free, disgusted at herself.

"Your chariot, Madam." Blake held those arms out in front of her and waited, yet to meet her eyes with his.

"I don't think this is a good idea. I'm really heavier than I look." Would his fingers curl about her back and legs? Was he as warm as he looked?

Blake raised one dark brow, his gaze contemptible as he took in her grey half boots, her ruined, travel-stained gown, lingering on the swell of skin rising above her neckline to finally—*finally*—meet her eyes. The swirling color nearly swallowed his pupils whole, fairly stealing her breath away.

Until he spoke.

"If I can handle the cows in the paddock, I think I can handle you."

The guffaws of laughter and back-slapping made Sophia's cheeks hot. Her anxiety made her words harsher, more childish, more defensive. "You cannot speak to me like that!" she huffed. "Where is the owner? Perhaps he will be a gentleman and rescue me."

"I doubt it, Duchess. Now will I carry you or would you like to go over my shoulder?"

She lifted her chin. "You wouldn't dare." Blake's mouth curved into a grin to rival Lucifer's and he took a menacing step forward. Too late she recalled the words *wouldn't, couldn't or can't* only ever served as a challenge. Clearly what occupied the space between his ears hadn't developed as much as his body had.

"Make your decision."

But Sophia didn't really hear his words. She was caught up imagining what those long fingers and strong hands were capable of. She must be delirious. There was no other explanation. Surely a decade and half away from the place she once called home made them veritable strangers?

Within a breath the world around her tilted and she found herself upside down, her cheek rubbing against the ratty wool of Blake's hard back as she struggled and tried to slip from his shoulder.

His hold tightened. "Cut that out, or we'll both be swimming in filth."

With his command, Sophia struggled in earnest until a large, warm hand closed over her bottom. Shock held her immobile, unable to utter a syllable, unable to tell him to remove both of his hands, the other of which now gripped her thigh to hold her legs still. His touch wasn't harsh, it wasn't repulsive or lecherous, but it was unwanted and unasked for. It had been years since a man had touched her without her permission and be damned if Blake got away with it either.

Gritting her teeth, Sophia tried to find somewhere to put her hands, tried to find some purchase in case the buffoon decided to drop her. She looped her thumbs into the top of his worn trousers. If he let her slide into the mud, she was going to take some of his pride with her.

"What are you doing?" he yelped and jumped a little, his deep voice no longer gravelly. "Your hands are like ice."

"If you drop me, Blake, your trousers are coming too." If he wanted to put on a show for those watching, she would ensure she wasn't the only clown in the act.

The back beneath her cheek lurched with poorly concealed laughter.

"This is not amusing," she fumed, scrabbling to hold on.

His body shook. "It has been the highlight of my day."

She protested with a violent wriggle to shore up her position. But then the unthinkable happened. The body beneath hers went rigid as she started to slide. Blake's grip became bruising with the effort to hold her. She was jostled as he fought to keep his footing, but it was no use. One moment one of London's most sought after courtesans hung over the shoulder of a brute, her hands tucked indecently into the waistband of his trousers, and the next they were both flailing for purchase, uselessly sliding, slipping, until they landed in the mud only two short feet from the doorway. Only one thought hovered in her mind in that indescribable moment...

Mud was infinitely softer than stones or pitchforks or condemnation, but the sting was just as sharp.

Laughter built inside Blake's chest until he could no longer contain the guffaws. It was the last sound she would want to hear but the situation was just too ridiculous.

The noises she made suggested her mouth had filled with something even fouler than her disposition, which made the men in the tavern wild with hoots and calls of a lewd nature.

"You did that on purpose," she cried, flinging mud from her hands with a wild, angry shake.

"I did not," he replied, but a smile still stretched his face. He knew she wouldn't believe him but he truly hadn't intended to drop her. "The last thing I needed today was to go traipsing through the mud with your royal highness."

"Cease your taunting and help me up."

Had she no use for manners in London? She hadn't said please once since he'd glimpsed her fine carriage through the tavern's window. He had thought, since she had fled one black night without a word, that she would slink back with her tail between her legs to beg forgiveness and acceptance. But then she had probably forgotten all about him the second she stepped into her new life as a prostitute.

Blake's laughter died as he looked at her—really looked at the woman the girl had become. Night black hair still framed a familiar face, but that's where the distinctive marks she used to have stopped. The handful of freckles Blake had teased her about mercilessly were gone, no laugh lines creased her eyes, no dimples marked cheeks so pale the skin was nearly transparent.

Well, that's what happens when you laze abed all day and indulge only in night-time activities.

The sour thought brought him up short and instantly brought with it anger. This wasn't the Sophie Martin he used to fish with as ten-year-olds. The girl he had known would have laughed in the mud until she couldn't breathe. She certainly wasn't the same young girl he'd fallen in love with, only to be betrayed and left without a word or thought. Now she was a woman whose choices made her a pariah.

"Since you have already soiled your gown with my mud, help yourself."

She attempted to wrestle herself free but sagged back into the mire awkwardly. "Blake, why are you doing this to me?" she whispered.

Damn it. Were those tears she worked so hard to disguise? Even now, as hate warred with the familiar sound of her voice, he still couldn't bear to see her upset. Cursing under his breath, he hauled himself to his feet and offered her his hand.

"No tricks?" she asked, her voice low, her eyelashes glittering with moisture.

"You have my word."

Hesitantly, Sophie placed her hand in his, and for a moment, shame washed through him. The shock of seeing her again had obviously muddled his senses.

Blake scooped her into his arms and juggled her against his chest, both of them dripping with foul mud. He carried her inside, ignoring the men crowded in the doorway making suggestions about what he could do with 'Her Highness'. He tried to ignore her feeling of insult that hardened her like pine in his hold, though he knew he was to blame.

"I'm sorry, Sophie." He set her on her feet outside the private dining room.

"Do you think coming back is easy for me, Blake?" The naked emotion in her voice and downcast eyes only made him feel worse. He was despicable.

He'd waited in tense anticipation from the moment Matthew had announced she might return, and now he'd made a right mess of it all.

His apology was lost as she forged on. "When I left here, I promised I would never, ever return."

She made it sound as though the village was plagued. "Why did you come then? If it's so hard, why didn't you stay in London?"

"I came because Matthew asked."

"You've never answered his summonses before." The accusation was out before he could catch it. It was none of his business.

Her face fell and she turned away from him, hand on the door. "Things are different now."

"You could at least appear happy when he arrives." He didn't want to know how things were different. They were still the same for him. Same tavern, same work, same existence, same everything. Blake turned to leave and send word to her brother, but then she spoke again.

"I was nervous. Worried, if you must know. Perhaps even scared."

"Oh?" he said, her admission paling in the light of years of being ignored. Now she wanted to pour her heart out? Now she wanted to confide in him? Pent up anger spurred him to say yet more things he didn't mean. "Were you scared of me? Of facing your brother? Or returning to the country without your maids and footmen?"

A sharp intake of breath made her shoulders rise in outrage. "Have you forgotten where I came from? I am perfectly capable without servants, thank you very much."

As if he could ever forget. There were only two women in his life he had loved unconditionally and they had both abandoned him without word or regret. That kind of betrayal wasn't likely to ever be forgotten. Or forgiven. "You were a girl then.. What happened to her?"

"The same thing that happened to the bastard son of a duke. We grew up."

He gritted his teeth hard, the pain easing the urge to hold his hand over her mouth so she wouldn't utter another word. "I grew into what my life should have been. I was born a nobody and I will die a nobody just as the circumstance of my birth decreed."

"And my birth?" She crossed her arms over her chest. "What did my first breath mean to the world? Was it written on Destiny's tablet that I would become a courtesan?"

"No." Sadness weighed him down. The kind of sadness he'd only ever known in connection with her. "You made your decisions. No one else."

"Yes, I did. Regardless of what you think you know, my life is full and happy. I learned to accept my lot a long time ago."

If she looked him in the eye and told him she was happy again then he would know she had become a liar as well as a nobleman's plaything.

Fury reddened his vision until he saw only the woman she could have been. The wife she would have made. The love they could have shared. He blinked and this dream Sophie vanished into Sophia. He didn't have to be nice to Sophia. He didn't have to respect or like her so she could break his heart again when she left. Let her go to her brother's. "Is that what you call lying on your back for pretty things?"

The crack of her palm across his face echoed off the walls. Then she opened the door at her back and fled into the warmth and safety of the parlor.

He sagged there in the dim light as he rubbed a hand over his stinging cheek and cursed his tongue. He as good as called her a whore. Despite what he told himself in his mind, she was still Sophie. Little Sophie he'd carried on his back when the walk was too far or the river too deep. He'd wiped blood off her skinned knees, held her up so she could pick the sweetest apple from the highest branch, had his first kiss with her in a field of spring flowers, but he could never forgive her for leaving without a word. He couldn't forgive the fourteen years of silence that followed or the rudeness now.

And to be honest, he didn't want to.

Two

Sophia still sat in her filthy dress an hour later—although now at least she was dry—and cursed her rash behavior. She really should have sent word that she was returning to the village, perhaps then she could have continued directly to her brother's home instead of waiting for him at the only inn in town. But the events of the last few weeks had seemed to happen so quickly and Matthew's letter had arrived at a time when her future and direction was uncertain.

She had thought time in the country, away from the pressures demanded of her particular type of lifestyle, would help to return some form of balance even though the prospect terrified her. She should have followed her initial instincts and traveled to the coast or Bath, somewhere she didn't have a history, somewhere a stranger with a made-up past could find her place.

Her former protector had offered her a little house in Dover, a place to rest and recuperate, but buried deep in sorrow, she had turned him down. She did not need charity. She yearned for safety, comfort and, most of all, security. The only option she had was to return to her first home, to the family and village she had fled.

Her turbulent thoughts drifted back to Blake. She knew their first meeting wasn't going to go well, but she hadn't envisioned it would go as badly as it had. Once upon a time they had been the best of friends, more. If only he knew the truth about why she had run away in the first place, he might have understood her anxiety. But she'd promised herself not to tell a soul. Not her brother and certainly not Blake. She could not handle the revulsion she knew would surge before any sympathetic emotion.

Where was he anyway? He hadn't even offered refreshments. Perhaps he would ride out to her brother and deliver the message himself just to be rid of her all the quicker.

She smoothed her skirts, giving them a shake which loosened dirt all over the floor before the fire. A small smile of satisfaction lifted her lips.

Before she could have any more thoughts of how much dirt she could be rid of by jumping up and down, the door flew open, slamming against the wall behind it with a bang.

"Sophia?"

The tall man staring at her through eyes the color of her own didn't wait for an answer to his question. He rushed forward and drew her into his arms as though fourteen years was only a number and not half a lifetime.

"Matthew, it's so good to see you." She tried to disguise the involuntary flinch that came whenever she was touched, but soon hugged him back.

"I can't believe you came," he said quietly, his voice muffled by her hair..

Was that relief or hesitation she heard? She pulled back, but he wouldn't let her go.

"I've missed you," he said when finally he released her.

She turned away from her brother. Deep emotion was not something Sophia could handle in that moment so when Blake entered the room, she was almost relieved.

Looking back to Matthew, she asked, "Is Violet with you?"

Now it was Matthew's turn to look away. "I left her at the house. She is not feeling well today."

Blake stepped further into the room with what looked like panic written on his face. "She was well enough this morning. Should she be alone?"

Matthew glared at him before he turned back to Sophia, who watched the exchange with dismay, although she tried to hide it. "She is not so happy that I am here, is she?"

"It's not that. We hadn't heard from you and the only spare room we have has been turned into the baby's room.

Violet, that is, we, thought you might be more comfortable here."

The only sound to penetrate the sudden tension was the crackle of the fire. It was Blake who recovered first.

"What?" he said. "She can't stay here."

Matthew glared at him again. "This is an inn, is it not?"

Sophia shook her head and interrupted the argument. "I think it would be best for Violet if I return to London." She gathered her skirts in her hands and turned towards the door. "I shouldn't have come."

"But I want you to stay," Matthew said blocking the doorway.

Just not in your house. That much was abundantly clear. So she couldn't stay but neither could she go. Her back ached from the jarring carriage ride she had already endured and she was tired beyond reason. Then there was the fact that she didn't have a house to return to in London. Her previous residence had belonged to the Duke of St. Ives, and they had since parted ways.

She looked to Blake to gauge his reaction. He hadn't said a word, but the set of his mouth and his crossed arms said he didn't like the situation any more than she did.

"There must be somewhere else I can stay? A hotel or boarding house?" She didn't mean for it to sound as though the inn was beneath her, but the thought of the laughing men in the tap and Blake's hostility was enough to almost make her ask if she could sleep in Matthew's barn.

"Not for miles," Matthew shook his head and looked to Blake. "Can you make up a room?"

"If she says please."

Sophia gritted her teeth until her head pounded. Seems there was little choice for any of them. She released her breath and forced a smile. "Please?"

"There," Matthew grinned, "I knew we could work it out."

As the afternoon waned, Sophia bathed and dressed in a wrinkled but clean gown and still she fumed.

She ran a silver-backed brush through her hair again and again in front of the banked fire, as her stomach growled. Refreshments hadn't been offered and Blake hadn't come to apologize. It was the latter that had her on her feet in front of the looking glass, pinning the hair from her face with quick, angry movements.

If he thought she was going to hide away and be ignored until her sister-in-law had her baby, then Blake had better think again.

Sliding the last pin into place to secure one errant black curl, Sophia drew a deep breath against her worries of pitchforks and cruel laughter and opened the door. She expected to do battle in the hall, yet there was not a soul around. Her steps were slow but sure as she made her way down the stairs and into the taproom.

With an hour until supper, the tap was relatively empty, the laughing group from earlier nowhere to be seen. Heads lifted, bored faces stared for a moment, curiosity quickly replacing tedium. She met their gazes one by one with what she hoped looked like confidence, inclined her head and started for a table in the farthest, darkest corner of the room. A cold shiver worked its way down her spine, but she ignored it. Even in her own mind she wouldn't admit fear and dread made her feel more vulnerable than she had in years.

"You shouldn't be down here," Dominic, the young man who had earlier filled her bath, told her from the bar.

She'd wondered how long it would take for him to notice her presence. "I'm thirsty and hungry, where else would I go?"

"Blake won't like it," he said with a nervous glance in the direction of the other occupants.

Aware of their audience, she bit her tongue against anger and smiled sweetly. "If he'd offered sustenance in my room, I would have accepted."

"I'll bring a tray up. Please, you can't be down here."

Sophia narrowed her eyes. "And why not?"

"It's not for ladies, miss."

"Then we shall count ourselves lucky that I'm no lady."

Dominic stared at her for a full minute as he fidgeted with a linen towel before rounding the bar toward her. .

"I'll buy her a drink, lad." One of the men finally spoke up before Dominic could form a suitable reply to her insult of herself.

Sophia swiveled in her seat to face him and worked hard to school her features to calm politeness. "No, thank you, good sir, I'll get my own."

"His coin not good enough fer ya?" Another joined in the conversation as he rose to his muddy feet.

Dominic groaned.

"Thank you, but I pay my own way."

"Was just bein' nice, lass," the third man grumbled.

"And I thank you," she nodded in their individual directions. "But since I am now a guest here, I believe my food is already paid for."

With nods of agreements from the men and only one slight brow rise from Dominic, she went ahead and ordered. "I'll have watered ale and whatever food you have, and then I'll leave."

"Ale?"

Sophia rather liked the taste. "Yes please."

"We only have cold stew from lunch and dinner won't be quite ready. I'll bring a tray up when it is."

"Stew will be fine, Dominic, thank you."

Cold stew was a better alternative to starving. She hoped. No sooner had she thought the thought then Blake appeared, a thunderous expression on his face. Perhaps he read her mind about his stew. She smiled again.

"You can't be down here."

"I have already been informed of that fact, but I am hungry and wish to eat."

"Dominic can serve you in the private parlor."

Sophia shook her head. "No, thank you. I'll eat right here." In London she was never obtuse; she didn't have to be. She was also not usually sarcastic, but Blake was beginning to make her feel it wasn't the taproom that was at fault so much as her presence in it. "Unless there's something wrong with the food?"

"There is nothing wrong with my food."

"Excellent." She linked her fingers on the tabletop and relaxed back in the chair.

"You still can't eat in here. You are a single woman with no chaperone and this will soon be a room filled with men."

Her sharp smile softened and for a moment she felt real humor. "A chaperone? I am almost thirty years old, Blake.

Well past needing someone to watch out for me."

"These aren't the nabobs you're used to, Duchess, these are working men--rough, uncouth, impolite to say the least. I can't have you in here with them."

"Oy, that's a bit harsh." The first man who offered to buy her a drink jumped to his feet and puffed his chest out.

"Sit down, Peter, this doesn't concern you."

"It does if you're insulting us, or saying that we'd be anything but perfect gennel-men to the lady. It's not every day one of her kind comes a callin'."

Sophia bristled. What happened to just being nice?

"This doesn't concern any of you," Blake told them again.

One of the men circled around to the back of her chair and gripped it between her shoulder blades. "If Blake here is going to be rude, you could always come stay wiv us."

So the heat from the stranger's hand wouldn't penetrate her dress, she leaned forward and shook her head slightly. "Thank you but I'm sure Blake will rediscover his manners at any moment."

"Murray, go and sit down."

Murray took a menacing step in Blake's direction. "Are you going to make me?"

"Do you want to be barred again?"

Murray thought about it, his bloodshot gaze switching from Sophia and then to Blake. He eyed her again, one last time, up and down with a look that turned her stomach, and then finally sat back down.

"I make the rules here and the rule is, no unescorted females, lady or otherwise, in my bar."

"The sooner you bring me something to eat, the sooner I shall return to my room." This time she meant it. Wounded pride and hunger had fueled her to impulsiveness, but now she longed for the solitary confines of her room.

Blake's hands crashed down on the table as he leaned over her. "Have you no use for manners at all?"

"I said please the first time I asked," she pointed out, his loud display only slightly frightening.

Just then the taproom door slammed opened, a healthy gust of damp cold air blowing across the scene inside. "What's going on here?"

Sophia peeked beneath Blake's arm. "Matthew?"

Blake muttered something beneath his breath that sounded a lot like another insult but Sophia ignored him, forcing him to step back as she rose to greet her brother and the woman half hidden in his shadow. "What are you doing back?"

Matthew folded her into his arms for a second time, squeezing her hard. "I wanted you to meet my wife and didn't want to wait for tomorrow. This is Violet."

Sophia took in the girl with a golden halo of curls framing a perfectly flawless face. She wondered what Matthew had said to his wife to prompt her visit, especially as they had not previously met. "It's lovely to meet you, Violet."

"And you," she returned, but made no move to embrace her or kiss the air by her cheek.

Sophia understood Violet's reaction and didn't press a situation that would make the heavily pregnant woman more uncomfortable. It was the same notion of scandal and propriety that had kept Sophia from attending their wedding. Or at least that's the excuse she had given at the time she declined their invitation.

Regardless of the rising tension now, she didn't want them to leave. "I was about to have an early supper, would you care to join me?"

"In the back parlor," Blake interjected through gritted teeth.

Sophia didn't want to surrender, but she couldn't suppress the excitement that infused her over spending a few hours alone with her family. "Very well, the parlor."

She turned her back before Blake's inevitable look of triumph could reach her. He'd won this round, but if there was to be another, she would fight with everything she had to show him she wasn't a woman to be ordered around or treated with fragility.

As Blake watched the trio wander off down the corridor, he was left with feelings he hadn't expected either. What rocked him to his core was seeing Sophie sitting in the bar where just two nights before a man had nearly killed another. This wasn't a sitting room where ladies took tea. It showed him she certainly did need someone to watch over her. The women who ate here came with their husbands, to be protected if need be. Even Violet, one of his closest friends after Matthew, wasn't allowed to eat on her own there. There was no way Peter or Murray's actions were protective. Why hadn't Sophie seen their leers?

There wasn't enough time in his day to warn every customer to stay away from the beautiful creature in the corner.

He nearly groaned out loud as he rubbed a hand over his forehead. He shouldn't think of her as beautiful. He shouldn't think about protecting her either. She'd already made it quite clear she didn't need or want his input. But what more could he do? Throw her to the wolves? No. Even *he* wouldn't do that and especially not now she was a guest at his inn. He had to keep her out of sight and out of the tap for the duration of her visit.

Anyone seeing the look on Violet's face upon meeting her sister-in-law couldn't mistake the discomfort there. As much he wished otherwise, Sophie would have to stay with him until the babe was born.

He pondered the dilemma as he went to the kitchen and heated the leftover stew she would have received cold. He poured ale into four mugs, watered down two of them, and then placed them on a serving tray for Dominic to deliver. By the time the food was ready and four bowls were full, he still had no idea how to keep her out of the way.

It was understandable that Violet didn't want a courtesan in her home even if said courtesan was family. She had her standing in the village to think about and there was the fact that her pregnancy had been a difficult one. He didn't think the women of the village would heap the sins of another onto Violet's head, but women could be crueler than men.

When Matthew had first warned him he'd asked Sophie to visit, Blake had been pleased for him, but then his brain started to work away in the frustrating way it did, and he'd remembered the betrayal and the hurt. His best friend had begged him to try to find a way to forgive. Matthew had known having his sister back in their lives would be difficult, even so he was determined to make everyone consider giving her a second chance.

Much easier said than actually done.

He finished the tray with a plate of bread and then headed with it toward the parlor still minus a way to keep Sophie out of trouble. It left a sour taste in his mouth that he would care that much anyway.

It wasn't that he was a monster, quite the opposite, but Sophie had devastated him when she'd left. Had they been a few years older, they would have had the bans read and been happily married, so sure he was of their future. Instead she'd disappeared in the dead of night.

Months later an envelope had come to him with another letter inside addressed to Matthew. He didn't even warrant a "Hello, how have you been?" Never had she sent a letter to him to say "Sorry for ripping your heart out." How could she do it? How could she forget him and what they could have had and turn to a life of prostitution?

He better be careful lest the question accidentally slip out over dinner.

With his foot, Blake pushed the parlor door open and then slowed as a wave of tension greeted him. Despite the laughter brother and sister shared, the scene seemed uncomfortable.

Though Violet managed a small smile, Blake had known her long enough to see she would rather be anywhere else. The woman usually chattered on about this and that constantly. Her silence was another obvious sign of her discomfort. Was Matthew ignoring his wife or could he just not see it?

"Blake, Sophie has been regaling us with the events of the afternoon."

He scowled in her direction. "She has, has she?"

"We did get off to a bit of a bad start," she said, the mischievous gleam in her eye extra bright in an otherwise shadowed room.

He put the tray on the table with a clang and crossed his arms over his chest. "A bit?"

Matthew cleared his throat. "Blake, please sit and eat with us."

Sophie's smile drooped just as Blake's lifted. "Don't mind if I do."

They ate in silence for a few moments and Blake was glad to have a moment to gather his thoughts. They were all over the place. On the one hand he was happy that

Matthew had reunited with his sister but on the other hand, Matthew had his wife to think of. A wife who was clearly stuck in the middle of this very awkward situation. These were the moments he wished he was a member of their family rather than a close friend. He wanted to speak his mind and tell everyone what he really thought, that they couldn't play at being a contented family after the damage her departure had left. But he wasn't family, and he'd already said too much to Sophie as it was.

He couldn't help watching her as she ate, her eyes closed and a small smile playing over her lips.

"Nice?" he leaned over and asked as he remembered her earlier jibe about his food being bad.

When Sophie opened her eyes her cheeks flushed having been caught in her moment of flavor rapture. "Very. You must have a talented cook."

"The vegetables are grown right here, in the field behind the kitchen."

He tried to keep the inflection from his tone, tried to keep it light and nonchalant, but aggression crept its way into his words, though he longed to take them back. She knew where vegetables came from. He wasn't sure why he felt the sudden need to remind her. Why did he continue to behave like a brute in her presence?

She ignored him anyway and turned to her sister-in-law. "Violet, I bought you a gift before I left London."

"You did?" Violet said, shock written all over her delicate face.

"A cradle for the baby. It's really very beautiful, I do hope you like it."

Surprise filled her eyes and then was gone, not quite replaced by hostility, but close. "We already have one."

Sophia hadn't thought of that. She'd only been thinking to get rid of another reminder of her London life before it drove her insane. That she purchased it for *them* was only a little white lie. She couldn't very well reveal over the dinner table that it should have held her own child

"I am a carpenter, Sophia. I already made us one. Two actually," Matthew told her with a forced chuckle.

"Of course you did." She couldn't meet his eyes nor anyone else's as her cheeks flushed. From the edge of her vision, something happened between Matthew and his wife.

Violet cleared her throat. "It was a lovely gesture."

Not by the tone in her voice, but Sophia gave her a half smile anyway and then returned to her meal. She would have to ask Blake to dispose of the cradle so she wouldn't have to endure the constant reminder. This was the first day in a long time that she hadn't given herself over to tears and grief over the miscarriage she had suffered some months before. She sighed. The day wasn't done yet.

"What are your plans while you are here, Sophia?" Matthew changed the subject with grace. She could have hugged him.

"I don't have any." She wouldn't admit her only plan had been to rest and try to find direction for her life. To try to find a way to accept her existence would never be the same now that she had come to realize what her choices had robbed her of. Matthew's invitation had arrived opportunely. She didn't regret decisions made when she was a scared fourteen year old but now she was an adult and had to take matters more firmly in hand. Yet another failed pregnancy had forced her to open her eyes and stop living in the moment, although some days she wished denial still cloaked her.

"You could venture forth and meet people. There's a dance organized for Sunday afternoon at the McFarlane farm."

"I don't think so." She shook her head to clear morose thoughts and painful memories. The second to last thing she wanted to do was be in a place where the women would scowl at her and the men would wonder at her availability. The absolute last was to be openly shunned.

"I'm sorry. Our little dance probably isn't sophisticated enough for you anyway."

"Blake." Matthew's warning tone rang out across the table, but Blake paid him no heed.

"You would especially hate market day. Your delicate hems would never stand up to the crowd, to the manure on the road, the dirty children brushing past your expensive skirts. Perhaps it would be best if you stayed in your room?"

Sophia's mouth fell open. She wasn't quite sure where this vitriol had come from but she wouldn't endure it. Not quietly anyway. "You think there is no manure on the road in London? No dirty children? What are you really saying, Blake?"

"I'm saying you aren't cut out for country life, you would only get in the way."

"I would not. You know nothing about me to make those kinds of assumptions."

"You are a delicate woman now." Blake picked up one of her hands and turned it in his. "Your pretty hands, your polished nails, one day of work and you'd be a mess."

"I would not." She repeated, doing her best to ignore the warmth that crept from his skin to hers.

"I don't believe you," he taunted.

Sophia wanted to punch him. This man who insulted her, who made her out to be some sort of aristocratic invalid, she wanted to make him hurt. What the hell had Blake Vale done that was so special anyway? Poured ale for dogs for twenty years? Scrubbed vomit off the floor occasionally? He had no idea what she'd had to face, how strong she'd had to be. She snatched her hand from his grip. Let him live through even half of what she had.

"I'll prove it," she said, pushing her chair out with a scrape of timber against timber.

"For one week?" Blake said, leaning back in his.

"I beg your pardon?"

He came to his feet, arms crossed over his chest. "It's all well and good for you to milk a cow or to prepare a single meal but could you do it for a week?"

"Certainly. But why would I want to?"

"That's right, Duchess. Why would you want to? You have servants to cook your meals and run your bath. Do you have a maid to dress you? Wipe your arse?"

He'd called her that name in the yard as well, that name that made her insides shudder with dread, and try as she might, it was impossible to ignore the jibe. "I dress myself, thank you and as to my other habits, they are none of your business."

"I thought so," he replied with a smug look on his infuriatingly smug face.

Instead of the physical harm she dreamed to inflict, she nodded and said just one word. "Agreed."

"What?" three voices echoed in perfect unison.

"I'll do it for one week--I might even do it for two." Perhaps then he would see her as more than a courtesan.

Blake snatched up her hand and shook it vigorously. "Two weeks then, Duchess. This is going to be fun."

As Sophia sat, fuming that he thought her useless, the realization sunk in that she had been goaded into spending her visit working. Alongside an insufferably judgmental oaf. He would probably have her mucking out stables or shoveling the very same mud she'd worn not four hours earlier and she had fallen headlong into his trap. At least keeping her hands busy might relieve her mind from its current state of anxiety.

Without warning, Violet dropped her spoon on the table and clutched her stomach with a groan.

Both Matthew and Blake shot to their feet, the silly challenge momentarily forgotten, but it was Matthew who got to his wife first. "Violet, are you all right? Do we need to call for the doctor? Is the baby coming?"

When Violet looked at her husband, she seemed furious. "'Tis just the baby moving. I do not need the doctor."

"You should be at home resting," Matthew growled.

"Yes, I should," she said with a pointed glance in Sophia's direction and then back to Matthew.

"You begged me to take you somewhere!"

"But not here," she hissed.

"Sophia is my sister and I wanted you to know her."

"I think perhaps I am a little more tired than I thought," Violet said into to the thick silence that followed the argument.

"Take her home, Matthew."

Matthew ignored Blake and turned to Sophia. She nodded her agreement. As much as she wanted them to stay, there were no words she could say to Violet. Apologies were sure to get her nowhere.

"If you'll excuse us?" Matthew helped his wife to her feet, cast Blake a scorching look of censure—to which Blake shrugged—and then they shuffled from the room.

As soon as the door closed behind the pair, Sophia whirled on Blake, murder once again on her mind. "What just happened?"

"What did you expect? Violet is a delicate woman." Blake kept his eyes on his plate, idly toying with his food.

"I think Violet would have survived a meal in the same room as me given the chance."

"You have no idea what Violet could endure. Is one dinner enough to take her measure? A dinner forced upon her at the last minute?"

"I would like to get to know her."

"Why now? You didn't want to know her before."

"Let's not pretend this is about Violet. You attacked me and then you challenged me in front of them. Are we to be as uncivilized as snarling bears?"

"You think folk here are."

"Where does all of this come from?" They did nothing but talk in circles. Sophia narrowed her eyes. "Are you drunk?"

"Would that I was," he muttered.

Sophia turned toward the door. Her appetite had disappeared and she found herself longing once again for the confines of her room. "I am tired of this. Perhaps tomorrow we can start afresh but if not, I will stay in my room as you suggested."

"Answer me one question before you go?"

She paused without wanting to at the anguish in his voice. Did he feel guilty about his behavior? "What is it?"

"Do you want to be a duchess?"

Her stomach gave a flip flop as she reached for the door handle. Is that why he called her duchess in such a derisive tone? He thought that's who she aspired to be? This was yet another conversation she wasn't ready to have. He clearly thought her a whore and a gold grabber looking to climb to one of the highest stations in the realm. Why should she make him think any differently?

Blake was no longer the boy she used to know, to love. He was now a hateful, spiteful man who was obviously going to make it his business to persecute and humiliate her. In his eyes she was a lowly courtesan, but she had worth. She would show him that she was more than a bed warmer to a duke and then he would have to apologize for his harsh treatment of her. For his assumptions that she would sell her soul for a title and servants.

She opened the door and took one step over the threshold, but paused for a moment to leave him with something to ponder. "I have never wanted anything less in my entire life."

Blake continued to sit at the dining table, the plates where they were, and felt he'd been blindsided by a mule cart. Only he wasn't the one who'd been led into a trap.

He'd needed a brilliant idea and had one too late. One he should have thought out a little better. Surely there were other ways to keep her safe from his patrons that didn't require keeping her at his side all day every day? He didn't believe her that if they continued to fight she would stay in her room. That would have made it too easy for him.

He grimaced. He was lying to himself if he thought it would be effortless to fight with her for the next few weeks, he wasn't normally so difficult to get along with. There was just something about her attitude since she had arrived that irked him in the worst way. She may say she didn't want to be a duchess, but already she had perfected the art of making him feel like a peasant.

Remorse began to dull the edges of his anger. He even considered going to her, to knock on her door and apologize, though his challenge did still serve a purpose. He would keep her at the inn so that Matthew wouldn't have to choose between his wife and his sister. In the process, he'd keep her busy and out of his bar. He'd also try to keep a lid on his temper now that he'd gone ahead and taken the responsibility from everyone except for himself.

In his mind he began to better formulate the plan. She wouldn't even be aware that he watched over her.

It sounded so simple. Why did it have to feel so complicated?

Three

S ophia had been sleeping the sleep of the dead when the banging started. First it was so soft she barely drifted to a level above unconsciousness. Then it got louder. And louder. And louder. Once she realized it was her door someone was trying to knock down, she leapt from her bed. Not bothering with a wrapper or shawl, she gripped the handle and threw the door wide.

"What?" she asked into the gloom. "What is it? What's the matter?"

"It's time to wake up, Duchess."

Sophia tried to comprehend just what had happened that would make Blake wake her in such a manner. He was dressed in a thick brown coat buttoned only halfway, a shirt the same color peeking from beneath. Navy breeches replaced yesterday's trousers and were tucked into high boots, mud already marring the dark surface. As her sleepy gaze traveled back up to his face, he also wore that smug look that clearly came as second nature. Most other people smiled, she thought sourly.

"Get dressed, we're already late."

Puzzled, she answered, "Late for what?" But Blake was already gone. His long strides carried him along the corridor where he thumped down the stairs and into the lower parts of the tavern.

Sophia closed the door and peered into the darkness overlooking the rear yard. It was pitch black out. Why did he wake her? For a moment she'd worried that something had happened to Violet through the night.

But then those anxious feelings sank to the pit of her stomach with a weight she did not like. Why would Violet need her help with anything? It was clear her sister-in-law wasn't enamored of her. She lit a candle and sat on the edge of her bed, staring at the cradle in the corner of the room. She should have left it in London with everything else she wouldn't need for the rest of her life. It would have fit next to the chest holding her ball gowns and crystal slippers. Right beside the tiny gown her own child would have worn had it been born.

With a shuddering breath, she tore her gaze away. Today was not a day for tears. Today was a day for taking her mind off London and what-should-have-beens. Today she was going to show Blake Vale that she was a perfectly capable woman.

The memory of last night's challenge almost sapped her will. Surely normal, everyday folk didn't rise before the rooster had the chance to crow his crow? She knew farmers rolled from their beds at god-awful hours, but not tavern keepers. What could possibly need doing before the guests or patrons had even thought of breakfast or their first ale for the day?

Sophia contemplated the comfortable bed. She could settle beneath the warm blankets and go back to sleep, but Blake would expect her to do that. He would expect her to quake at the first hurdle, and to get up before the sun definitely counted as a hurdle. She wouldn't give him the satisfaction so she threw a blanket over the cradle and then opened her dresser and rifled through the gowns hanging in the cramped space. Eventually Sophia decided a riding habit would have to suffice. She didn't have clothing suitable for mucking out stables. And she was sure that's what Blake had in mind. He wouldn't stop today until she begged for mercy. It wasn't the first time her stubborn pride had gotten her into trouble.

The next knock at the door startled her so much her hands shook and the shoelace she tied snapped off in her fingers. "Damnation," she swore beneath her breath. She didn't have another pair of shoes she was willing to sacrifice in the name of idiocy and her riding boots had a heel on them that would leave her with a limp by the end of the first hour.

With a muttered curse she tucked what was left of the laces into the top of her shoe and stalked to the door. She took a second to school her features and when she opened it, gave Blake the brightest smile she could summon. "Good morning, Blake."

"That's not going to work with me this morning, Duchess."

"What?" Feigned innocence was one of the best weapons she had at her disposal and she did it well.

"Your pretty smiles and feminine airs will not help you today, so stop looking at me like that."

Was she supposed to grunt her morning greeting as he did? "I was merely being polite. Next time I will scowl."

Blake opened his mouth to issue probably yet another insult but then obviously changed his mind.

"Come," he said with a gentler tone. "We are already behind."

Sophia hid her answering smile and hoped tomorrow morning's awakening wouldn't be quite so brutal since she hadn't muttered one protest.

But after two steps through the back entrance of the tavern, she hoped tomorrow morning would never come. A thin layer of frost covered the ground, and as she bit her lip against the cold, her breath fogged. She considered running back to her room for a blanket to wrap about her shoulders.

Blake must have noticed her hesitation on the stoop, because he called to her over his shoulder, "You won't be cold for long, Duchess. Now, keep up."

"Do you think you might call me by my name today?" she asked his broad back as she lifted her hems to keep up as requested.

He stopped so suddenly, she nearly ran into him. "And what name would that be? Sophie? Sophia? Grand, adventurous Madam?"

"My name is Sophia. Not Duchess. Not Sophie and definitely not Madam."

"Your name is not Sophia and we both know it. Just because you change a letter at the end does not make it so. And I like the ring of 'Duchess'."

"Very well." Sophia shrugged as she lifted her arms to rest her hands on her hips. "I shall call you swine."

"I beg your pardon?"

"As you should! You have done nothing but goad and insult me since I arrived. Your behavior is much what I would expect from a pig."

As anger flared to life in his eyes, she knew she had said something critically wrong rather than simply rude.

"I have insulted you, but you turn up your pretty little nose at everyone and everything. Do you think if you came to town with a friendly greeting and a smile, we might be in a different situation right now?"

Sophia rose to his bait in a heartbeat. She wondered if he stopped to consider the fact that she had nothing to smile about. She stepped forward but stopped short from poking him in the chest with her pointed finger. "And is that the only issue you take with my character, Blake? It has nothing to do with the fact that you hate everything about me and what I do?"

"I do not hate you. I merely feel sorry for you."

"Well, I don't need your pity. I am perfectly happy." And apparently not above lying just to prove him wrong.

"I don't pity you for sleeping with men for trinkets. I grieve the girl you once were. The woman you could have been."

He went to walk away, but Sophia decided in that moment that Blake needed to know a few truths about the woman she would have become if she hadn't fled Blakiston all those years ago.

She ran around him, the swirl of her skirts about her ankles letting the cold seep beneath. "Would you like to know what my father had planned for me? What price he put on my body to start the bidding?"

"What are you talking about?" His eyes rolled heavenward as though her excuses meant nothing to him.

Sophia opened her mouth, but then she snapped it shut again. Why should she defend her actions or her decisions to a man who would never understand them anyway? He wouldn't believe her. Her own brother wouldn't have believed her father's intention to sell her to the Duke of Blakiston in exchange for the neighboring farm. "Prime land for a prime filly," he'd laughed. Well, she hadn't laughed. She'd been terrified.

She bit her lip, welcomed the sting as she stepped out of his way. "Never mind. You wouldn't understand."

All was quiet for what felt like decades, and then he spoke. "I wouldn't understand because I am a swine or a simpleton?"

Sophia looked up into gray eyes narrowed in frustration . She could hear the hurt in his voice, but he could never comprehend her decision. She would have been foolish to tell him anything. "No, Blake," she replied with a sad shake of her head. "Because you are a man."

"That makes no sense."

"Men will never grasp the female mind and its intricacies."

"Nor do we want to."

Sophia forced a chuckle. It was a very good thing the males of their species were not perceptive in the least. It was also convenient that they were easily distracted. "What is first on your agenda, Blake? Chickens? Cows? Pigs?"

"I am not the one with the agenda, Duchess."

With a glare thrown over her shoulder, Sophia turned towards a low building at the rear end of the yard. "I am not going to talk about this anymore. Either we find a way to work together or I am going back to bed."

Mumbling beneath his breath, he passed her and made a track for the double doors at the far end of the barn. She almost called for him to slow down so she wouldn't have to trot to keep up but figured that wasn't worth yet another disagreement. She had to show Blake she could do anything he did. Keep up with his daily chores. Match him task for task. Otherwise he won.

She could not let him win.

As he threw the first door wide and then the second, heat washed over her along with the scents of hay and manure. It was an earthy, rich smell that didn't make her nose wrinkle as she'd envisioned. The moment was almost nostalgic. After all, she'd spent half her life mucking stalls, feeding horses, milking cows and collecting eggs.

Her first few steps into the barn made her think of her father and her brother in their happier years. Back to a time when her gangly limbs and freckled cheeks had been nothing more than a child's cuteness. The years before her breasts had formed, before her body had curved and filled out in all the wrong places.

"What are you thinking about?" Blake asked. He stood with his hands on a horse's bridle half lifted from its spike on the wall.

"Home," she admitted with a sigh.

"London?" His question broke the spell and Sophia grimaced. London was her home now. Thankfully there were no cows to milk at dawn and the only eggs she had to deal with were the kind one held up with a fork to put in one's mouth.

Ignoring his question— and the Pandora's box it would open if she were to dwell on her answer— , the curiosity in his eyes, she wiped her hands on her skirt and asked, "Where do we begin?"

Blake should have put her out of her misery. With every yawn she tried to suppress, he wanted to release her from their bargain and tuck her back into bed. He wanted to apologize and rescind all the hurtful words he'd said. But there was also a part of him that wanted to punish her.

Nothing he'd said to her so far was a lie. She needed to hear the truth, for surely she lived in a fantasy land. How else could she think she'd made the best decisions for her life?

He leaned against the side of the barn and watched as she hefted the heavy pitchfork fully laden with straw into the open horse's stall. He had to admire her gumption. Not once had she complained when clearing the muck. Not once had she surrendered or begged for mercy. Not that she would. The stubborn set of her shoulders, the tight grip she had on the timber handle, the spark of her eyes when their gazes happened to meet and clash, told him Sophie would endure.

Even though straw and dirt clung to her full skirts and God knows what sullied the hems, she still struck a magnificent view. Her black hair gleamed as it slid across the smoothness of her back, the fabric of her blouse pulling this way and that with her exertions. He was surprised to notice it was damp between her shoulder blades as her makeshift plait swung over her shoulders.

He wondered when the last time was she'd worked up a sweat, but then dismissed the thought. He didn't want to know what made her perspire. He didn't want to know about her life in London.

But she was still Sophie. The world hadn't ended when she'd lifted her skirts for the first nobleman to look her way. Her life hadn't ended when she'd made the worst decision a woman could make. And that was the one of the hardest parts of it. The world should have ended, it should have mourned the loss of an innocent girl the same way he had.

"Am I doing it wrong?"

Blake snapped his gaze from her back and looked into her eyes as she peered over her shoulder at him. "No." He shook his head.

"Then why are you staring at me like that?"

Blake shrugged his coat off and hung it on a hook. He wanted to hurl another insult her way and ask the question burning the tip of his tongue. He wanted to ask about her. The real her. The woman she'd become, but he couldn't. He wouldn't. So he told her the truth. "I was watching you work."

"Why?"

He shrugged again. "Why not."

Her curious glance turned suspicious and her lips parted as if to retaliate, but then she snapped her mouth shut and turned back to the stall.

Taking a deep breath against the urge to snatch the pitchfork from her and do the job himself like a gentleman would, he took a few steps away and instead took up a shovel.

"What are you doing now?" she asked when he returned to her side.

"I was going to help you. The lunch and evening meal will not prepare itself."

"Do we not get to break our fast?"

It was a simple question. She hadn't whined it. She hadn't huffed childishly. It made him feel like the bear he'd been since she'd arrived with her airs and orders. "I'm sorry," he apologized. "I don't take breakfast until the barn is tended, but it doesn't usually take this long."

She sighed and hefted the fork again. "Then it should my turn to apologize. I am slowing you down."

For a second his heart lodged in his throat. He liked her better when she gave him reason to be rude in return. "Let's just get it done. The day is nowhere near to being over yet."

With his back behind the shovel, the stall was mucked, cleaned and refreshed in thirty minutes. It could have taken her all day to do the simple task.

He had to remember that under her courtesan exterior and fierce glares, she was still a delicate woman not up to the tasks of a farmer. Despite her protests to the contrary.

"Can I have a moment to clean up?" Her voice cracked the hard shell of his thoughts. "It wouldn't do to enter a kitchen with this filth hanging from me."

"I don't want you entering my kitchen like that either," he chuckled. She now had straw in her hair and dirt smudged across one pale cheek.

Blake stepped toward her, his hand rising of its own volition. Sophie stepped back.

He paused with his fingers in the air. For a second she had been frightened of him. He'd seen the flash of fear skate across her eyes. "I wasn't going to do anything," he said defensively, as though he'd already laid hands on her person.

Her reply was a nervous laugh, her blue gaze darted from his face to the door of the barn behind him.

She gauged her escape. He knew it more surely than he knew his next breath would come. He lowered his voice. "I'm not going to touch you, Sophie. I was merely going to remove the field of straw you have in your hair."

"Oh?" She patted her hair until she located the offending stalks and dropped them to the ground, but not before her hands trembled enough to betray her. "I can do that myself."

As she whirled away from him, color high on cheeks that had been so pale, he wondered what the hell had just happened. How was it that she let men touch her for coins and trinkets, yet she'd been terrified to have her childhood friend approach? He meant no harm. She had to know that. Never once in their younger years had he raised a hand or even his voice to her. He'd loved her more than his own life in those fragile years when a boy becomes a man.

There were only two conclusions he could draw. Either she had been hurt at some stage of her sordid London life. Or she was repulsed by his callused hands. If he were to do more than slide a fingertip over her skin, he would probably scratch her. He was no gentleman, nor did he have the soft hands of one.

"Go and get cleaned up," he snapped, angry at each and every scenario that played through his mind. "I don't want one of my patrons to find flakes of horse shit in his soup."

He never resorted to these types of games with anyone else of his acquaintance. Even the men he hated with a bloodthirsty passion didn't receive the insults and scorn he heaped upon her. But then they hadn't hurt his heart the way she had. A heart he never knew he had until her disappearance had shattered it into a thousand pieces.

Four

Her body felt hotter than the blazing fire she stood in front of as cool, clean water dripped down Sophia's neck to seep into the edge of her gown. It was both refreshing and odd.

"That water is for washing the benches not your face," Blake chastised. He'd done nothing but tell her off since they'd left the barn. Now it was mid-afternoon and they'd only stopped to eat a piece of buttered bread. Lunch had been served and cleared away an hour beforehand, yet they ploughed on regardless of the hunger pains gnawing at her stomach. What she would have given to rest for an hour. To have a cup of tea or a sandwich.

"You have to keep stirring that or it will burn."

"No one would notice," Sophia muttered under her breath but moved the spoon in clockwise circles anyway. The stew appeared to contain every ingredient the kitchen had to offer, yet she couldn't define what color it was other than brown. Burning it would probably add to the flavor.

"And make sure you season it properly."

Her hands stilled. Season it? What was that supposed to mean? Summer or winter? A chuckle escaped her. Today had been the nightmare she'd known it would be, and the occasional satirical thought was about her only salvation.

Already they had been awake for ten hours and the day was only half done. Blake told her every five minutes how much work they had yet to accomplish. More than once she'd wanted to tip the pot of hot stew over his head and beat him with the spoon. But she hadn't. She wouldn't resort to violence or more insults. No matter how hungry and delirious she became.

When he'd railed that she couldn't cut through the large pumpkin he'd asked her to slice, she had merely smiled and asked him to show her how it was done. When he'd shouted chores at her as if she was the kitchen maid, she nodded and set to work despite how much her feet and back already ached.

The only way to make Blake treat her as a human being was to win his stupid challenge and smile the whole time she did his bidding. It grated. It gnawed on her senses until she wanted to tear at her hair and scream right back but she wouldn't give him the satisfaction. Perhaps if she showed him what she was made of, he would treat her less like a pariah and more like an old friend.

Already she'd given away too much, shown him more of the real her than she'd intended. In the barn when he'd reached for her, when she hadn't been able to discern the intent in his shadowy eyes, fear had lodged in her brain and held her immobile. It had taken her back to her days as a girl in London and before, in the days before she'd fled this place, when she had argued and pleaded with her father not to do it, not to sell her to the duke. Days she didn't want to recall. Her mask was very carefully, firmly in place to those who saw her, even if occasionally she was caught off guard.

It wasn't a nice feeling. When you didn't know what the man before you would do. What he was capable of. The scars he could inflict. But Blake was not his father and she had to keep reminding herself of that fact. Although they had the same eyes, the same aristocratic nose and full mouth, the same commanding tone, Blake was as far removed from the ton and walking in his father's footsteps as she was from being a lady.

"Stir the pot, woman!"

Sophia jumped. Damn him for scaring her witless again. She really had to stay with the task at hand. But she was exhausted. From the day and from the lies. For once she didn't want to be strong. She didn't want to be sensual or womanly. She wanted to be a petulant child and poke her tongue out at the oaf who ordered her about with a raised voice.

The spoon moved around the pot, occasionally hitting the edges with a clang and scrape, but Sophia had no real notion of what she was doing. Even if she did, she was sure he would tell her it was wrong. It's what he had done with the carrots, the fire, even boiling water. It's what he had done in the barn with that damned fork.

Hopping from one foot to the lean on the other, she nearly lost her balance and had to place a hand on the wall of the hearth to steady her body. Hearing Blake's heavy tread, she straightened and began to stir in earnest.

"Watch out," he warned, coming to stand beside her.

Sophia shuffled back and let him have access to the pot. When he tipped the green beans and corn into the stew, his elbow brushed her breast. Her cheeks heated but she refused to move, to acknowledge the accidental touch. A different kind of warmth—expected but unwanted— began to blaze its way through her body.

Blake stilled for a split second, a vein in his jaw throbbed just once, and then he stalked away, his bowl hitting the preparation bench with a thud.

She went back to stirring the stew, but she was so uncomfortable in her blouse. Every time she reached the far side of the pot, her top buttons threatened to choke her. With a quick glance to be sure Blake was occupied with his vegetables, Sophia undid her top five buttons.

Right away, she felt a difference and her neck finally stopped itching.

"Damn it, stir that pot!" Sophia jumped again. She turned half her body to snap and snarl the same way he did but then remembered her plan to show him she could keep up.

When she finished with the stew and it was off the heat of the fire, Sophia considered doing her buttons back up but she found her body temperature more comfortable without her blouse choking her. She also found Blake couldn't not stare. He tried valiantly and snapped his head this way and that whenever she happened to catch him in the act of ogling but still his gaze wandered back again and again.

When it came time to serve the evening meal, Sophia was surprised to find the table in the private dining room set for two.

"Are you expecting someone special for supper?" she asked Blake. Perhaps the man was meeting a lady friend and wished for privacy. There were no other guests staying in the upstairs rooms as far as she knew.

"No," he replied, his head resting against the door jamb.

"We are not having dinner together." That was his intent. It shone from his face.

"We can eat in the tap if you would rather," he shrugged and pushed away from the wall.

Yesterday he'd been adamant about her staying out of the tap. It took everything she had left not to narrow her eyes at his sudden change in attitude. "I'll take a tray to my room."

"Running away, Duchess?"

"What have I to run from?" she asked. The last few hours had been spent in relative peace. Were they to revert to mortal enemies once the hard work was done?

"I'm not sure. Why don't you tell me?"

"I've had enough games for one day. I wish to dine and then retire."

"I have to hand it to you, Duchess. I really didn't think you would make it."

Sophia shook her head rather than admit her own surprise. "You know nothing about me, Blake. Why don't you concede defeat and we can move on from this ridiculous contest of strengths."

"I will not concede. You have worked but one day. Not so hard for a woman used to physical exertion. I wonder if you can stand another?"

Physical exertion? He said the words as though they carried the plague and she knew exactly what he didn't say out loud. "Hmm," she murmured, if he was going to remind her of her occupation to make her angry, perhaps she would use it to spark his own temper in return. "It is true, I am capable of exerting a reasonable amount of stamina, but even I must go to bed at the end of the day."

She couldn't tell from his reaction, but Sophia had the feeling she had bested him once again. As she retrieved her dinner and skipped up the stairs, she didn't feel weary. She felt she had gained another point in their imaginary tally.

Sophia - two. Blake - zero.

Contrary to Miss High and Mighty's belief, Sophie had won nothing. Blake had been determined to ignore her siren's call, but as usual when it came to Sophie, he was an unarmed man. The first time she turned to him with the creamy expanse of her chest showing, his heart had quite honestly thumped against his ribs so hard, it was a wonder the next county hadn't heard the sound. Did she not know what that skin would do to the town's men already enflamed by her presence?

When he imagined her dining in the tap or even walking through the common room, his blood boiled and he thought of nothing other than violence, but for fourteen years she had looked out for herself. Blake doubted to the soles of his boots that she would welcome any interference from him.

It was why he had set the table in the back room. Dining with her would have been a torture, but he would have endured. He would have martyred himself if it meant keeping her from the prying eyes of his patrons.

Dominic had already warned him they were filled to the brim with punters come to get a glimpse of the famous London harlot. His fists had curled at his sides, but he'd bitten his tongue. He would not have Sophie turned into a public spectacle. Not only for her sake but for Matthew's and Violet's also. Once Sophie went back to her grand life, they would be the ones left to deal with the whispers over her visit. It would be Violet who would bear the gossip just for marrying into the Martin family and it wasn't fair to such a naive slip of a girl. As it was, they had tried to keep Sophie's improbable return as quiet as they could in the silent hope she wouldn't actually come.

Well, *he* had silently hoped.

So there he had sat, Dominic's statement about the men who waited for just one glimpse of Sophie heavy on his shoulders. He'd done the only thing he could. He set a trap and she'd walked straight in and predictably fought him, resulting in her eating in her room. He was beginning to see a pattern where she refused everything he asked of her if it meant they would be close to each other.

But what about tomorrow when the men came back? And the day after that? He couldn't trick her into staying in her room forever. How would he keep her out of sight? He did have to make a trip to Sheffield to purchase a few items that were hard to find around Blakiston, but he had intended to wait for a quieter day.

His shoulders lifted with a sigh. He would have to make the journey soon and convince Sophie to go with him. It hadn't occurred to him when he'd challenged her to walk in his shoes that she would have to step where he stepped and do what he did. Now he had an obligation to shield her.

This is why he should have taken the time to think before throwing down the challenge in the first place. There were loopholes and pitfalls in every action of his and hers. Would she see the Sheffield trip for what it was or would she wonder if the challenge wasn't all that important to him after all?

Why did everything have to be so complicated? This is what she had been doing to him since he was old enough to have an interest in her.

When she wasn't there, he wondered about her safety and happiness and when she was there, he worried even more. Why was it that whenever Sophie was involved, he had the feeling he would never win. Why was it that anything concerning Sophie made him feel as though he would always emerge the loser?

Five

When Blake knocked on Sophie's door the next morning, he expected to find her in that nightgown that hid nothing, her dark curls in disarray over her shoulders, and still half asleep. But when she answered his first knock bright eyed, dressed and wearing a vibrant smile, he wanted to close the door, knock again, hope she answered the way he'd wanted her to.

"Good morning, Blake."

"Good morning, Sophie. Are you ready to start the day?" he asked with a smile. This was one instance where he didn't want to spark her anger and cause her to do the opposite just to spite him. If he told her he needed to go to Sheffield and she declined to go with him, then he would look the fool and she would instantly know he staged the day.

Instead of walking through the kitchens and out to the barn, Blake put a hand on her shoulder and steered in the direction of the private parlor.

"What..." the softly spoken word died on her lips as eggs, ham and fresh bread came into view.

"I thought we could break our fast early today. We have to get the chores done and then hitch the wagon to make a trip to Sheffield."

"No milking cows and collecting eggs today then?" she asked with a heavy amount of suspicion.

"I was going to wait until next week but my...churner broke and I need to replace it. Don't worry, Dominic can handle the work for today, tomorrow it will be back to cows and chickens for us."

She didn't appear as though she believed a word he stuttered, but she didn't argue. Merely inclined her head and ate her breakfast as though it was to be her last meal ever.

When she flicked a glance in his direction, he couldn't help but keep staring.

With an odd look, she ran her tongue over her teeth, wiped her mouth with a linen and then stared back. "Do I have something on my face?"

Blake shook his head. "I haven't before seen a grown woman eat like you."

One dark brow lifted and he wished he didn't now raise her suspicion in every inconsequential comment. As a girl, she'd never been a particularly fussy eater. Those in the country couldn't afford to be. But he'd served many a titled gentlewoman in his private parlor, and more often than not, there were complaints about his menu options. As though he should have served only the finest of foods.

"I am hungry."

"That you are," he said with a laugh, trying not to think of her as fancy lady.

"If I am hungry, I eat. After yesterday's deprivation of breakfast and lunch, I thought to take advantage now."

And there it was again. Even though they didn't exchange insults, she was still mad. He was trying his hardest to be a gentleman now, but with retorts like that, it would be very difficult indeed.

Moving about the kitchen after breakfast, he washed the few pans and pots used to make a meal fit for a duchess and let his mind wander to the events of the day and their journey to Sheffield.

He planned to be his most charming self no matter her half remarks and reminders of the day before. He would let her chat away, listen when she talked, murmur the appropriate phrases when she drew breath and generally play the role of gentleman. It was the only weapon he had left now. Not in the sense of hurting her. No. He was beyond that. Seeing the hurt in her eyes did things to his heart that didn't feel comfortable.

Hanging his wet dish rag on a hook by the hearth, he took one last look around his kitchen with pride.

Everything was where it was supposed to be. Each pot had a shelf or hook, each plate, spoon, fork and bowl had been earned and lovingly cared for. He'd worked hard for every item is gaze roamed over. His was a good life, but he wished it had turned out differently.

When he was just five years old, his mother had left him on the doorstep of this tavern. She hadn't left a note. No explanation. Nothing. But his uncle had known why he'd gained an extra mouth to feed. A woman couldn't live alone with a child and not earn scorn and derision from her friends and neighbors unless she was a widow. It would have been so much easier for them all if she had been.

The only problem he'd seen through the eyes of a five year old child was that she'd abandoned him to a fate worse than derision or tomato target practice in the street. It had only taken twelve short months for Blake to become intimate with pain and humiliation. To dodge and duck the fists and slaps meant for his head and back. He'd missed his mother madly and held hope for a long time that she would come back and save him. That she would miss him so much, realize life was better when they were together and come back. After a few years, he'd forgotten the color of her eyes, how she looked when she smiled, the sound of her laughter. Resentment eventually had a way of shadowing the good times and turning them all bad.

His reprieve from the nightmare his life had become came in the form of Matthew Martin and a few years later his little sister.

Little Sophie who wasn't afraid of anything. Not even Blake's violent uncle.

But then just like his mother, she'd fled. Disappeared without a trace, without a goodbye or trail to mark the route she took. Slowly the days grew dull again, his uncle's beatings took their toll and he hardened himself to any kind of emotion that required he invest more than a kind word or smile.

It didn't mean he didn't long for a family or children, a wife to wake next to, to share his secrets with, the toll of the days or the happiness of a good harvest. He just didn't want them bad enough to put his soul on the line. Not again.

Never again.

"Well, that was...interesting," Sophia commented from the bench seat of Blake's cart.

That's not quite the word he would have used for the day they'd just had.

Nothing had gone wrong. He'd introduced her as his old friend, Sophie, and she had gritted her teeth and let him. He had towed her from market stalls to store fronts and then back to the market stalls. By the end of the day she laughed and smiled and even took care of some of the negotiations for his spices and fruits. Altogether it had been amicable, enjoyable even. But inside, Blake was torn and it made him angry and upset. It made him feel like roaring.

For years he had read far too many news sheets and heard tales involving courtesans and prostitutes, and for all of those years he had imagined her standing on some corner by the docks, displaying her wares for all to see. He imagined she had lost a tooth somewhere along the way, stacked on forty pounds and lost most of her hair. Clearly the stereotypes he read about were very far from the truth, and that made him angry as well.

She came home all this time later with confidence and her spine straight despite what she had run away to do. Despite what she had become.

"Blake, are you all right?"

His hands tightened on the reins and he had to bite his tongue. Hard. "I'm fine. Just tired."

"I'm not surprised," she chuckled. "Do you not have anyone at all to help you when you travel to Sheffield?"

Did she imply he had no friends? "I don't tend to go mid-week and usually Dominic comes with me while

Maria cleans the rooms."

"Maria?"

Why did she ask so many questions? Why could she not close her mouth and let him stew? He sighed. "Maria is Dominic's older sister."

"Why have I not seen her yet?" This was not a casual questions. There was a hint of outrage in her voice and he almost smiled.

"She only works one day a week, since she is only thirteen."

"Thirteen?"

Blake nodded. Dominic's father had died the year before and their mother struggled on her own, so the town's people helped where they could. Maria cleaned his rooms, dusted and scrubbed the floor in the bar once a week and he provided them with fruits and vegetables for their meals. Maria had said she preferred to be away from the gloom at home, and it gave her a sense of satisfaction to earn her way.

At least no one in that family had fled to London to warm beds.

He shook his head and closed his eyes for a moment. He had to stop doing this to himself. He had to stop seeing her in his mind. He had to start seeing her as she stood before him and that wasn't as a gap-toothed dove. The problem was that he had no idea where to start with this new Sophia. His body kept telling him to hate her but his brain longed for just one question to be answered.

"Why didn't you say goodbye?"

Sophie froze on the seat next to him and he called himself a dozen different kinds of idiot. He hadn't meant for the words to actually be said. Or had he?

It was the first question he would have asked his mother had she ever returned for him.

Even the horses felt Sophie's sudden panic as she gripped the edges of her seat. They strained at the bit and tugged on the reins. He applied a little more backwards pressure on the straps until the ancient pair fell into a smooth rhythm on the dilapidated road.

"This is neither the time nor place to have this discussion, Blake."

"You're wrong. This is the perfect time and the perfect place." She had nowhere to hide.

"Why do you want to rehash this? It was so long ago now. No good can come from going over it again and again."

That's where she was mistaken. He had never rehashed anything. He'd never gone over the truth again and again, because he'd never had it. All he did have were the stories his mind conjured to reason why she had left without a word. He needed this confrontation.

It wasn't even the fact that she had left that now infuriated him, because nothing could change what she had done or what she had become. He knew that as well as she did. But there were things he needed to know. Why hadn't she said goodbye? Why hadn't she come to him for help and most of all why he never rated a mention in any of her brief missives to Matthew.

It was never Matthew saying, "Sophie sends greetings and asked how you are." No, the only reason Matthew spoke of the letters at all was because he knew Blake fretted just the same as he did. The worry ate at Blake, sometimes so much so he couldn't function with her in his thoughts.

The silence lengthened, stretched, widened the emotional distance until he wanted to draw the cart to the side of the road and shake the truth from her.

"Perhaps you don't remember?" Immediately he regretted his snide tone, the sarcasm in his voice.

When her hands and fingers ceased their fidgeting, Blake worried she wouldn't speak. But then she surprised him. "I wanted to say goodbye to both of you. I really, truly wanted to tell you where I was going, but I couldn't."

"Why not?" It was easy for her to say that now. He would not make this easy for her.

"Because you would have done everything in your power to try to aid my stay rather than see me escape."

There seemed to be so much pain in her words. Or was it regret? "We were sick with worry. All of us."

The wry chuckle that slipped through her lips held disbelief. "My father lost no sleep with worry over me," she assured him.

"That's where you're wrong."

"How long after I went missing did he begin the search?"

"The very next morning. When you didn't come home he searched high and low. He paid men to dredge creeks and look under rocks for your body."

He saw from the corner of her his eye what appeared to be a huge sigh before she replied. "He paid men to find me and bring me home, Blake. I was of no use to him dead and even less disappeared."

"I still don't understand. You have to tell me why you left."

"You won't believe me. No one would have."

"I may not have understood, but I would have listened." He spoke softly even though he wanted to roar and shake her. He had been more in love with her than any other person dead or alive. She had been the anchor in the storm his life had become. Each time his uncle beat him, he'd closed his eyes and dreamed of Sophie, of the comfort she provided by simply being there. It had made her betrayal that much harder to bear.

"Do you remember the Mason farm?" Sophie asked.

"I do, right over the creek from your father's. Matthew owns the rights to it now."

For the first time since they had started to converse, her head snapped up, her gaze searched his face. "When did he buy the rights?"

"He didn't. Your father did. About two years after you left."

He thought he heard her curse, but he might have been mistaken. "Why is that so significant?"

She sighed, drew a deep breath and then told him the one thing he hadn't wanted to hear. Ever.

"My father was to sell me to Blakiston."

"I beg your pardon?"

"You heard me correctly."

"I don't believe it."

She laughed that same humorless chuckle that said so much more than her words. "I told you, you wouldn't. No one would have."

"How do you know?"

"I heard them making the deal. Father had asked a few questions in the weeks before that seemed rather innocent fatherly questions: was I seeing any local boys, did I plan to marry and who. All odd enough when strung together but on their own hadn't struck me as nefarious."

"A father would ask questions like that, Sophie. He had the right to know if you were thinking of boys."

"One night I was still awake when Blakiston's man came to the house. It was late, very late, and I snuck out to see what the commotion was, I thought perhaps the Duke had died or had an accident or some such thing. But no. He came to seal the bargain. To make my father sign a contract detailing that he would hand me over in return for use of the Mason land."

"Are you sure?" It wasn't that he didn't believe her. Mason had no sons, no family, and it wasn't as though fathers didn't regularly bargain their daughters away in marriage, but she had been so young. Fourteen years old was too little to have been just given away. Although not to a powerful duke who got everything he demanded.

He just didn't understand why. The old duke was charming enough that he had women falling over themselves to be his duchess without even considering his monetary worth. Blake imagined it was that charm that also first attracted his mother. She was not the type of woman to marry for anything less than a man who would treat her right.

So if his sire could have had anyone, why would he need a fourteen-year-old girl who wasn't willing? Then again, his father's problem had never been in attracting women, his problem had always been keeping them once they discovered his temper. His mother had left the estate because she had been beaten. His memories of her bruises would never fade in his mind no matter the time that passed.

"I had to flee. I had no choices then, Blake. No way to say no. To beg my father to see what he did was wrong. You and I both know how he coveted those lands. When old Mr. Mason was found hanging in his barn, the magistrate came to ask my father the first questions. No one actually accused him, but there were whispers that he tied the knot that killed that kind old man."

"You put too much stock in whispers. Mr. Mason was riddled with disease, dying a slow and agonizing death. Your dad didn't hang the man and if he did, Mr. Mason would have begged him to do it. There are two sides to every tale, and I think you've put all your faith in the only ones to reach your ears."

Her body stiffened, her chin rose and her eyes flashed fire. "Is that a kind way of telling me I overreacted?"

"That is not what I'm saying. And you haven't really answered the original question. You say you didn't want us to stop you. But that is not what I asked. In your first note, your hastily scrawled note to your brother, you didn't even mention my name. I never warranted a how-do-you-do in your second either." By the time the words flowed from his mouth like a flood of spring rain, he longed to take them back. At least ask them without a boy's insecurities driving them. But it was too late.

"I... I...don't know what to say. All of those letters were for Matthew. I had to let him know I was all right."

"The second letter came to me. Inside an empty envelope with my name on it was a letter to Matthew, but what of me?" Where did this all come from? And how could he dam the flow?

Six

The only sound for a full five minutes was the clip clop and squelch of the horse's hoofs against the dirt road, only slightly muffled by the slippery mud. Their rhythmic pace was a better distraction than Sophia's nervous fidgeting. Each time she opened her mouth to say something she just snapped it shut again.

What was she supposed to tell him? That she had sent the letters to him because she feared her father would intercept them at home, but knew Blake's uncle would be too drunk to notice the mail? That she hadn't fled until after she had been raped and beaten and locked in a dark room with only her own cries of help to let her know she was still alive, still there. Rationality had no place in her actions in those early days.

Or that's what she remembered. Thinking back was dangerous. All the pain, the fear. For two days she had traveled by foot, no shoes or stockings. Each step caused pain in so many places on her battered body, but still she didn't stop. Her hastily packed satchel held only one borrowed dress, a comb for her hair and a spare set of underthings that were far too big. She had nothing to sell if it came to it. All she could lay claim to in the world had been left behind. She dared not return to her father's house. She dared not tarry lest she be found and returned to Blakiston's home.

It was becoming more than apparent that while Matthew and Blake feared for her welfare, thinking she had disappeared, she had been in the area the whole time. Locked in a damp room without even a tiny window for fresh air or a sense of time. Screaming hadn't worked. Sobbing, begging, pleading to be set free hadn't worked either.

Every noise she heard behind and around her that first night in the open could have been the sound of pursuit: her father come to beat her for her insubordination, the duke come to take again what she hadn't freely given. She should have followed her initial instincts and run before the wax had a chance to dry on the documents.

Shaking her head, Sophia tried to dispel the memories that came unwanted to the forefront of her mind. She had no desire to rehash the past.

She stared at Blake, his eyes on the rough surface of the road ahead, his attention seemingly on the pair pulling the cart. "I'm sorry, Blake."

"Never mind." His answer was gruff, his gaze still on the road, but his shoulders seemed to drop a full three inches and the reins were somewhat released from the death grip he held on them.

Sophia resettled her skirts on the bench and hoped for a change of subject. She wanted no more attention to be paid to the night of her flight and there was something she still wanted to know, desperately. She half turned towards him and got ready for his anger.

"I don't like that look in your eyes," he said upon seeing the intention in hers.

"Why do you despise dukes so much? You almost could have been one." Only a few words exchanged before God made the difference between a bastard and an heir. Between legal and illegal.

"Apart from the obvious reasons?" he replied. "Would you tolerate me better? What would you have done if you'd arrived in the tavern yard only to be told that your old playmate was now a duke?"

"Well, for one, I'm sure I would have known before now. The old duke has been where he belongs for some good time has he not?"

Blake nodded.

"If I were a duke, we wouldn't be sitting like this."

"We wouldn't argue so either," she laughed. He skirted around the question but then she'd changed her mind when he'd asked if she would tolerate him better. She knew what he meant with those words and she wasn't sure how to answer.

The real puzzle wasn't if he would be a duke worthy of her bed, it was whether or not he would be a *man* worthy of her bed.

"I would like you just the same if you were a duke or a stable lad." They might battle with one another but she did respect him when he wasn't calling her names, even if they were mostly deserved.

"So you like me? Even as a bastard?" Blake leaned over and bumped her shoulder with his. It was the first glimpse she'd had of her childhood friend. Playful, fun, happy.

Sophia drew a theatrical sigh. "I suppose I must. It is still a long journey home."

Before he could catch her on her slip of an admission—home—the reins pulled sharply in his hands cutting into his skin as he attempted to bring Misty and Monster in hand.

Monster pulled hard and seemed to almost hit the ground but then a wild animal scream rent the air and the cart lurched violently. It happened so quick. He couldn't let go of the leather straps pulled tight in his hands. He couldn't even look to see if Sophie held on or if she was in trouble. Then she was gone. Her skirts didn't fill the edge of his vision, her cry a distant sound behind as he fought the traces.

And then the cart stopped dead and Blake was thrown over the drive board to land hard on the horse's warm flesh. The bones in his neck gave an almighty crack as his head snapped back. Beneath his shoulder and ribs, Monster screamed again and thrashed. The horse was down, but tried with every powerful muscle he had to right himself. Blake was once again launched through the air to land on the side of the road with an oomph, the impact knocking the breath from his body.

He jumped to his feet and ignored the sharp agony radiating from his left side. Monster still screamed in that way horses do when something is desperately wrong and only one glance told Blake he'd broken his leg, the bone visible through the blood and mud.

Damn Blakiston and his penny-pinching. The terrible state of the road was likely to blame for his horse's injury.

It took but a second to take in the scene and decide what to do. Misty kept launching herself at the traces, kept trying to drag the cart forward to escape the smell of blood, the fear from her companion and driver, the noise that scraped at your ears. She was going to turn the cart and drag everything straight into a ditch.

Climbing into the driver's seat, jerking this way and that with the horse's movements, he reached beneath the rough timbers. Blake took out two linen wrapped bundles. The first, a loaded pistol which he gripped tightly in his right hand, the second, a short knife which he held in his left. He wasn't sure what to do first. Put Monster out of his hysterical misery or cut Misty free.

Deciding it was more important for Misty to take off into the afternoon's fading light, he tucked the gun into the back of his waistband and approached Misty with a hand out, muttering soothing murmurs that she would only just hear over the still screaming Monster.

"Easy there girl," he said, trying to run his hand gently over the muscles rippling her hide. "I'm going to cut you loose."

If he released Monster from his pain first, Misty would still try to break free and they would all be in more trouble. He would rather be stuck on the road with a cart for shelter than lose everything including his last horse.

Within minutes, he had the lead ropes cut, still murmuring to a horse with wild eyes and a tension that told him she would be dangerous when finally unfastened.

He'd concentrated so intently that he hadn't noticed Monster's screams diminishing, the big horse now shooting breath from his nostrils in heavy gushes of wet, hot air. Reaching over Misty's back, he cut another rope. Only three left to do and she would be safe from the cart and ties. But not from her own terror. That could still undo her.

As he cut the rope stretching over her massive girth, he looped his fingers in the bit to keep her head still, but Misty wouldn't have it. She rose up in the air, blocking out the sky and everything else as she loomed over his head.

But even as Blake covered his head, he felt the edge of her razor sharp shoe skate over his shoulder, the pain immediate and searing, ripping through his shirt to graze down to his elbow. When she landed back on solid earth, he didn't hesitate. Sawing the knife against the leather took only seconds, but it felt like hours, the motions seemingly slowed to a point where he didn't think he even moved. Misty kept trying to thrash her head from side to side to dislodge the hand at her jaw. She was beyond help as she tried to bite, tried to dislodge the bit between her teeth so he would have no control.

And then he let her go, jumping back, landing heavily once again, Misty's beating hooves sounding for only two heartbeats before she was gone from sight.

Blake said a little prayer for her that she didn't find a hole in the deteriorated road or stumble in her haste.

Misty must have kicked Monster, either that or the big horse finally noticed he was dying, his screams of pain starting up again. Blake rolled to his feet, every inch of the pain inflicted on him by his own animals ached and throbbed at the same time.

There was nothing he could do for the other horse. He wasn't going to dodge yet more deadly hooves just to see if given the chance the horse would right himself. Reaching for his pistol, he found only the fabric of his dirty trousers. When he glanced back to see where he'd dropped it, Sophie was there, blood dripping down her cheek from her head. Her once beautiful gown was covered in mud and God knew what else. In her outstretched palm was the pistol he needed to silence the big black beauty.

"You might want to turn away," he warned as he took the gun from her shaking hand.

She nodded and turned her body, chin slumping to her chest.

"I'm sorry, boy," he whispered as he kneeled on the horse's neck. Monster renewed his struggle to stand as Blake's weight bore down. Placing the muzzle against Monster's head, Blake closed his eyes and pulled the trigger.

Seven

W hen Sophia saw Blake fall on his back, relief that he was alive warred with the panic that she didn't know what was happening. As she neared, one of the big horses ran off down the road sending divots of rock and mud flying in its wake. Before she could reach Blake's side, he was on his feet, resigned determination in the grim set of his lips.

Now one horse was dead, killed by Blake and his pistol, the other gone, terrified and panicked enough to never come back. Sophia felt...numb.

Should she mourn the dead animal? Thank God she was alive? Alone on the road, night encroaching, the scent of blood thick enough to attract nocturnal scavengers--should she worry?

And then Blake was at her back, his warmth a welcome reprieve to the cold nothingness descending. Strong arms encircled her, hugged her, held her. The reassuring weight of Blake's chin resting on her shoulder made her forget she didn't like to be touched. A childhood of memories stirred, lifted, swirled around in her mind until she turned in the shelter of his strength and cried against his chest.

"It's all right," he murmured, holding her tight.

His warm lips brushed against her forehead, her cheeks, her eyelid, first one and then the other, but it felt wrong. It had to be her decision, her instigating the contact, her in control. Sophia pushed against his chest, backed up until they no longer touched but then gasped when she saw the amount of blood on his ripped clothes.

"It's not as bad as it looks," he shrugged, a not quite contained hiss of pain giving his lie away.

Sophia arched a brow but didn't dignify his words with more. She stomped back to the carriage to see what they had in the way of bandages. There must be something she could use to clean the blood and dirt and then bind his wounds. Anything to take her mind off his kisses and the heat infusing her cheeks.

There was nothing suitable at all, only filthy old blankets to cushion supplies. Pretty soon, the top skirt of her ensemble—the one she hadn't wanted to sacrifice in the name of stubborn stupidity—was hiked up and out of the way as she ripped at petticoats until she had a handful of adequate strips to first clean and then bind.

"I'm all right, really, Sophie, don't fuss."

"Sit down," she demanded. For once he did as she asked and sat before he was pushed. The damage was extensive, but didn't seem life threatening. Down his left arm, an angry red graze already purpled as blood pooled beneath the skin. More blood trickled down his forearm to drip from his elbow. She started there, but was soon hampered by the torn linen of his shirt.

"Take your shirt off." She kneeled next to him in the dirt, waited for him to comply.

Blake shook his head and attempted to stand. Sophia wouldn't have it. Under the ferocity of her glare, hands on her hips, fire in her eyes, he finally pulled the shirt over his head and twisted his hands around it, dropping the bundle into his lap.

Her gaze followed the movement as she desperately endeavored to ignore rippling muscle now only covered by a sprinkling of dark hair. Her childhood friend had more muscle than all of the men at a London ball combined. Never had she seen such finely sculpted, individually corded, sinewy tone on another human being. On animals, yes. Men, no.

The thought of the dead horse, his screams permanently silenced, brought her back to the task at hand. When she looked up to gauge Blake's level of awareness, wondering if the shock had set in, he wore a smug grin of triumph.

"I was merely looking for more wounds," she squeaked, before any query was even voiced. It made her guilt all the more evident.

"You missed the one here," he said with a chuckle, pointing to his side where yet more blood dripped.

"You are in a bad way," she told him. She couldn't clean the wounds without water and binding open lacerations could invite infection, especially since her petticoats were hardly sanitary.

She wound a makeshift bandage around his shoulder and upper arm to the elbow and prayed for a miracle, that the flow of blood had largely removed any debris that may have lodged inside. Sophia placed the back of his hand against her shoulder so he wouldn't have to lift his arm. If his muscles were tensed while she wrapped the linen, it would become loose when he relaxed.

"Where did you learn to do this?" Blake asked.

Sophia wasn't sure if he sought to make conversation or if he really wanted to know the extent of her skills. A lump formed in her throat at the thought of sharing more of her life with him, but she gave him some of the truth. He could do with it what he wanted. "I have had some nursing experience in an infirmary of sorts." Her hands moved over the wound stretching over three of his ribs. As she gingerly probed the area, Blake hissed and flinched from her touch.

"You've broken a rib or two."

"I have not," he scoffed as if he were a child, but his tone lacked any real conviction.

She gave him another of her best glares.

"Very well, I may have bruised the bone, but I don't think anything's broken."

Silence fell as she did her best to pad the area. "Had we needle and thread, I would stitch this." Another length of linen came away from her petticoat to make a piece long enough to wrap around his torso more than once.

"Why do they let you tend this clinic of sorts?"

Sophia's hands stilled, her breath slowed, her eyelids fell. "Not all people think me lower than the dirt that mars their hems. And some don't have the luxury of being nursed by a real physician."

Warm fingers closed over her cold skin and squeezed just so. "I didn't mean to insult you. I merely want to know the kind of life you lead. The real life. Not the one you talk up to defend your actions. I want to know who Sophia Martin is, who Little Sophie has become."

A single tear escaped, rolled down her cheek to land on the mess that used to be her gown. When she met his frank gaze, she had to admit to a moment of terror even more frightening than being thrown from a moving carriage. It gave her a vision of the one person in the world who could know who she was. Who she wanted to be. Her deepest desires and darkest fears.

But he wasn't the one--this man who insulted, berated and belittled. He couldn't be the one to share her secrets with. She couldn't trust him. She couldn't trust anyone.

"You don't know what you're asking," she eventually replied, tying the bandage off just below his armpit, checking with a slight tug of pressure that the knot would hold.

"And you don't know who you are anymore." Lifting the shirt he held in his hands and holding it to the gash on the side of her head, Blake's voice held years of pain, emotion so familiar to her that she leaned away from his comfort and stood.

"Perhaps I don't want to know."

Blake could well believe she didn't want to know her real identity. It might scare her into doing something drastic. In her society world where the sun shone everyday on her happiness, had she lost sight of what it felt to be a real person? He wondered how long it had taken to talk herself into this level of veritable blindness. He wondered at the necessity for such an illusion.

There was a moment in her past that created that fear. He saw it in her eyes, in the tense line of her body, especially in the way she hesitated before getting close to him. Even before climbing on the bench with him in the cart, she'd eyed him warily as if to measure the chances he would grow a second head and attack her once they were out of town. But fear was nowhere to be found now as she tended to his injuries.

These tiny flashes of fear filled him with sadness, another factor that made her *Sophia*. Another stone of guilt to add to the pile that dragged at his shoulders. It was partly his fault that she'd run away. Not in any literal sense, no. His guilt came from her not knowing how deeply he felt about her all those years ago. Perhaps if she'd known the full extent of his love—that he would have laid down his own life for hers—she would have come to him, told him of her father's plans. He would have run away with her. He would have taken her all the way to freedom and safety if it meant she hadn't been alone.

A shiver worked its way through his body as the sun dropped lower behind the clouds. It was going to be a cold night.

Blake struggled to get to his feet. When he put his left hand on the damp ground, his ribs screamed pain and he had to bite his tongue against crying out. He tried with his right. When there was only a slight pull from his grazed skin, he pushed up until he was back on his feet. For a moment the countryside swayed around him, black spots swam in his eyes, but then the horizon settled and he took first one step, then another, putting his ruined shirt back on as he went. His body would be sore come morning.

Ensuring he made enough noise that she would know he was there, Blake approached Sophia where she perched on the end of the buckboard. He held out his right hand. "Truce?"

She sighed, lifted her watery blue eyes to meet his.

"Do you think we can call a truce?" He asked.

She shook her head and jumped from the cart as a blush tinged her cheeks. "All we do is fight. Do you think we are capable of a ceasefire?"

"I think we have to try to get along better. It's likely we'll be stuck here all night and-"

"I beg your pardon?" The tension that usually held her rigid returned as she arched her neck and looked down her nose at him.

"No one will even know there is something wrong until morning. Even then, they might assume we were delayed and decided to stay in Sheffield for the night. Dominic knows what to do if we don't return on time."

Misty knew her way back to the tavern and the warm barn. If she arrived without the cart strapped to her back, a search party would be organized, but they wouldn't be able to set out until morning. The dangers were too high to blindly grope about in the dark. Especially on a road that hadn't seen a repair in years. Damn Blakiston's laziness.

"We'll have to build a fire against the cold and a shelter in case it rains."

"We can't…" she stuttered. "I can't stay here all night." She whirled around and started to walk. "If we go now, we'll make it in a few hours."

"Sophie," he called after her. "It'll be at least three hours until you reach Blakiston on foot and full night in less than one. There are dangers in traipsing about the countryside in the dark." He didn't want to add to her anxiety, but nor could he walk back to the inn in his current state.

She stopped, turned back to glare her haughty glare. "You will protect me. Now come along."

He shook his head, ignored her imperious command. "I'm not walking anywhere. I hurt, I've lost too much blood and I know 'tis pure folly. I'm going to find wood for a fire. You may do as you wish." As he turned his back, he knew she debated ignoring him and forging on, but he guessed it would have been a very long time since she'd been alone in the wilds of England. By day the pastures and fields may look innocent enough, but by night foxes prowled for their dinner, wild dogs, bats and more he didn't even want to think about, foraged. At least with a fire and the protection of the cart, they stood half a chance.

He stepped over the ditch at the side of the road but lost his balance and fell to his knees with a strangled cry of pain.

In the time it took for the agony to subside and his vision to clear, Sophie was instantly at his side, her small hands around his shoulders. He was more hurt than he had planned to let on.

"You shouldn't have moved so quickly," she admonished, her gaze snapping this way and that, presumably searching for a suitable place to push him back on his arse.

"I'm fine." But the way he hissed the words through his teeth once again belied any conviction.

"You most certainly are not fine. You will sit and I will collect wood for a fire."

"What?"

"I do know how to find sticks to start a fire, Blake. I have not forgotten everything from my childhood."

You could have fooled me. He bit his tongue on the smart retort. He knew she would worry less if she was kept busy, so he inclined his head and let her lead him to the back of the cart. He was then forced to watch as she stepped off the road, scouring the ground as she went.

In no time, she found kindling to get started and then went back for larger pieces. By the time she returned again, Blake had dug three blankets from beneath the softer fruit —cushioned so as not to spoil and bruise with every bump in the road—and draped one over Monster's back. One he wrapped about his own shoulders and the other he placed in his lap to warm for Sophie. They would have to spend the night leaning against the dead horse but what remained of his warmth would keep their teeth from rattling when the cold set in.

When finally she sat next to him, the fire a warm glow against her pale skin, Blake knew she must be exhausted and freezing. He placed the blanket on her shoulders, felt the stiffness of her back as he smoothed it over her arms and tucked it around the edges of her skirts. "Now is not an ideal time for maidenly sensibilities, Sophie."

She relaxed a fraction, her hands outstretched over the small flames and let him come closer. They would have to rely on each other this night to stay comfortable. Though the way she bit on her bottom lip in consternation worried him. He didn't break the silence. Let her be the one to vent what was on her mind. For sure as he drew breath, she had something to say.

"Do you really think we can have that truce?" she asked into the darkness, her head turned away so he couldn't accurately read her eyes.

"Only if we can agree to be civil."

"Agreed," she said as she turned her face back to the fire.

Awkward silence descended once again until Blake felt compelled to take advantage of their unexpected isolation. Perhaps this was the time he needed to discover who she had become. The faces she let everyone see were not hers. They were all masks and he desperately wanted to pull them away so he could see *her*.

"Tell me more about your infirmary," he prompted.

She shrugged her shoulders in a gesture that was so much more Little Sophie and a lot less Sophia than he'd seen from her in the last three days. "I was very ill not long after I arrived in London and I had no money for a doctor. My friends took me to the infirmary where I was nursed back to health. As I got better, I helped where I could and now I give back to those who helped me."

"But you aren't a doctor or a nurse."

"No, but I can bandage, stitch wounds, play with children who are sick and in need of more than their parents or guardians can offer. You have no idea what it's like in London. People lie down on the side of the road and never get back up again in the poor quarters. No one should ever have to be *that* alone."

"I'm shocked." And that was an understatement. He could picture her in a white apron bent over a child with a skinned knee crooning words of comfort more easily than he could picture her in a ball gown laughing with a lord.

Was this the her he wanted to find out about or was it yet another front to make her decisions easier to live with?

Sophia smiled for the first time in hours. She was glad to shock him. Every time she tried to convince him there was more to her than her courtesan status, he mocked or huffed or openly disbelieved. He didn't know the half of it. She wouldn't label herself a philanthropist, but she did help as much as she was able. What more could she do? Sit back and watch as children died because the most basic aid couldn't be found? Mothers lost babies because they didn't know the difference between a fever and a disease. Men lost their lives because they were too stubborn or poor to seek help. The infirmary had saved so many. They had saved her when the pregnancy she had tried so desperately to hide in those early days had gone terribly wrong and nearly killed her. The memories of her first miscarriage, the fever that followed and the fear that even after everything she had already gone through, she was going to die anyway, would stay with her forever.

Her first months in London had been terrifying but she had done it, with the assistance of her four friends. Molly, Addison, Caroline and Amy were the closest to sisters she could ever lay claim to. They had supported her through some very, very tough times and she them. But the five of them could be no more different than sisters could. Amy worked in a gaming hell at night as the woman who distracted men so they lost more money to the tables. Addison was a milliner's daughter, her father owned a shop on Bond street and was far too busy to notice his daughter's habit of disappearing for days on end.

Molly worked in a brothel, second in charge to the madam who ran the establishment. Molly had been Sophia's second friend in the world after Caroline. The brothel was actually a lovely building close to Mayfair. From the outside, it was a shop front boasting a fine tailor. Upstairs was an entirely different matter.

Caroline was possibly the most presentable and respectable of them. When they had first met by the pond, Caro crying her eyes out over a boy, she had been a scullery maid. Now she was companion to a gentlewoman, who gave them the majority of their funding. Mrs. Pendleton's husband had died, leaving her a very wealthy widow. But he had also left her a shell of the lady she had once been.

Sadness had taken over her life and turned her into a hermit. Caro was her only window to the outside world.

"How often do you work there?" Blake's question pulled her from thoughts of her life and her far away friends .

"About three days a week when Daemon is out of town." Damn. She hadn't meant to mention her former lover or indeed anything to do with her occupation.

"Daemon is your duke?" he asked without scorn, without insult. Perhaps they had reached a truce.

Sophia didn't correct him. Daemon was a duke but never hers. "He is the Duke of Clifton."

"St. Ives?" Blake asked.

Sophia nodded again. "Do you know him?"

"He was close to the old duke."

Sophia's heart skipped first one beat and then another. "No, he wasn't."

"He didn't tell you?"

"You must have your dukes mixed up."

"I can assure you he was close to Blakiston."

"They were not friends." Why had Daemon never mentioned the connection?

Perhaps because you never told him where you came from.

Not even with her first protector, Noah, had she shared all the details of her life before London. The more years that went by, the more she had stuck by her decision, tried to forget. She knew deep down that if ever she was in need of a safe place, the town of Blakiston would be there, undiscovered, undisturbed. But while the old duke and her father lived, she would not have stepped foot anywhere near the town or her borders.

In fact, since she had fled, she hadn't visited outside of the city at all. Until now. And look how it turned out.

Silence once again engulfed them. They were mere inches away from each other and yet worlds apart. She was a courtesan, and he was a countrified tavern owner.

Never mind that as children they'd seen each other without clothes, that they had lain on the banks of a river and quenched their thirst. They had endured so much, had each known everything about the other, yet the years had borne a gap too wide to breach. Sophia missed the camaraderie they once shared more than she would ever admit aloud. Blake had been a brother to her just as much as Matthew had. But that was over now. They were no longer children, no longer friends. But there were things she wanted to know.

"How long ago did your uncle die?" It was blunt but she didn't think he would mind much. There had never had been love or affection between Blake and John.

"Six years. Best thing that ever happened to me."

"Did Blakiston ever try to claim you as his son?" she asked, snapping a twig between her fingers and feeding it to the hungry flames of the fire.

Blake shook his head. "Never. The bastard tried to destroy me but it didn't work. Eventually he gave up trying and let me be but by then it was obvious to all with eyes that he was my sire."

"What did he do? To try to ruin you?"

"First there was the poison."

Sophia gasped.

"Not intended for me," he assured her. "Took down every last cow and chicken I had, nearly got the horses as well, but they were fed a different grain then."

"What did you do?"

He shook his head. "Not me. We. The town rallied around me, ate vegetable pies for a month, gave me a cow for milk, a few chickens for eggs to make the basic biscuits, bread and cake. I was able to start again."

"Did you confront him?"

"I went to the estate," he said but offered no more.

"He actually let you in?"

They hadn't had a choice when he'd kicked the front door down and strode in as if he did indeed own the mansion. If the old duke had been nicer to his mother instead of making her appear his mistress, if his mother had demanded respect from the man who married her and then denied it and had had the evidence destroyed, he would have owned the place.

Unfortunately for the folk of Blakiston, there appeared no legitimate son to take the mantel, to carry on a name dragged through the mud and back for generations. It fell to Charles Falston, not even a real man, more a sniveling brat, who now had power and the hunger to wield it, to fill the shoes of the depraved duke.

Charles could have it. Blake didn't want any part of a title or the responsibility. He'd been raised a bastard. Nothing would change that. He and St. Ives had made sure of it.

"You don't have to talk about it anymore."

Her voice pierced his internal rage, gave him something to hold onto, to pull himself out of the pit of anger and despair that tried to drown him. "Or do you not want to hear it?"

This is why he didn't talk about it. He tried not to think of his mother, the woman who'd birthed him and then abandoned him. So many people in his life had betrayed him. Sophie would always sit at the top of the list. "You and my mother are the same, you know."

"We are not," came her indignant reply.

"You both just threw away my love like it never mattered a damn."

The awful silence, the one that held the demons of their pasts, settled around them again. How did she manage to draw his emotions from him like a bucket dipped into a well? It was none of her business and deep down, Blake knew she didn't care. She had her grand life in London and in a matter of weeks, this trip would be but a distant memory, more fodder for the gossip that filled drawing rooms and salons. Salons she would sit in with St. Ives and live her shallow life.

He couldn't sit still anymore. He was a fool and a hypocrite. He wanted her to open up to him, yet he hadn't done the same with her. Hadn't told her of his friendship with her protector or that he and St. Ives were related.

For the first time ever, he was actually jealous of his only two friends. Matthew had Violet and the baby. St. Ives had Sophie and her trust. He had nothing. Nothing at all.

As he got up and stamped away into the cold night, wishing she would call him back, wishing he had the courage to stay, he realized he was the biggest fool of them all.

Despite what she was, whoever she was now, he still loved her and that made him angrier than anything else had in the last fourteen years.

"Damn you Blake! Damn you and your fool notions. I am nothing like your mother!" A temper difficult to leash pushed her to her feet and drove Sophia to follow the stubborn man into the dark. She stumbled, nearly fell, righted herself only to stumble again.

Out of nowhere, his body loomed until he stood face to face with her, his eyes and mouth twisted into a fury so great Sophia trembled but stood her ground. There wasn't anything he could do to her that hadn't already been done.

"You are the fool," he roared. "You could have had it all, a family, a husband, a good life, but you were a coward. You should have stayed and fought your father but you ran away and hid from it."

If it was a fight he wanted, it was a fight he would get. "I'm the coward? You hide behind your so called farming accomplishments so you won't have to step out on a limb and make something of yourself. You could have had it all too, Blake. You could have been so much more, but you were too frightened to make your father see you. Too busy hiding from responsibility and respectability."

"Is what you think? That I should have been a duke? Would you have had me then, Sophia? If I came to you in

London and told you I loved you, would you have given it all up to come back here with me? To rot in the countryside with thousands of pounds and an estate? Because that's what you want isn't it? That's why you never wrote me, never thought of me. I'm just a peasant and you want a title."

"What are you talking about? I don't want a title."

"That's what you say, but it's all a lie. You sleep with St. Ives in the hopes that he will one day offer you the life you ran away for. How did you first get the notion? Did you read it in a book? Did you meet him when he came to visit the estate? Did your London friends help you think up the lie of your father selling you to Blakiston to win Daemon's heart?"

"They aren't lies. It's the truth."

"No, Sophia. I think the truth is that you wished for a better life long before you had the notion to flee. I think that is why you never said goodbye. You wouldn't have been able to hide your enthusiasm, your eagerness to start your new life."

Sophia's heart stopped its rapid thump-thump against her ribs. Stopped beating altogether. "Is that truly what you think? How you see me?"

"How many men did you sleep with before worming your way into the bed of a duke?"

Sophia shook her head until her hair came loose from the chignon she'd tied it in. He was wrong. Oh, how wrong he was and there wasn't a thing she could say or do to sway him.

Suddenly, warm hands gripped her arms hard just above the elbows. "How many men, Sophia?" With each syllable, he shook her, shook her until her teeth rattled and her neck hurt.

Wrenching free of his brutal grip, Sophia pulled her hand back and swung hard. The resounding crack echoed in the night air, fog from their heavy and harsh breaths drifted into the sky above them. Sophia's palm stung but she wanted to hit him again. She wanted to lash out and hurt him just as much. How could he be so wrong? He saw her with only disgust and pity and it gnawed her soul that his opinion had fallen so low.

Well, if he wanted the truth, she would give it to him, but in return she would know the same of him. "I will tell you how many men, but you must tell me how many women." How she wished she had the eyes of a night owl. She would have given it all to see what he felt in that moment. His anger and condemnation she could feel but there was something else there. Some other kind of anguish that tore him up. That probably had nothing to with her and her occupation so much as his own hurt pride.

"I don't have to tell you that and you shouldn't ask."

"Very well, then." Whipping around so fast her dirty, ripped skirts snapped about her legs, Sophia headed back to the warmth of the fire. He would follow or he would not. For all she cared, he could perish in the dark on his own.

Shaking the blanket free of anything that might have taken a mind to crawl in, Sophia wrapped it around her shoulders and dropped back down in the space between the dead horse and the hot coals. A chill pervaded her body, but she doubted the night had anything to do with it.

The minutes stretched, the only sound came from the crackle of the fire and the occasional call of night birds. Just when she was about to give up and close her eyes, Blake's heavy tread approached.

"How many?" he asked.

She sighed. "Why does it matter? What concern is it of yours?"

"It does matter. It matters to me for the stupidest reasons of all, but it matters."

Finally she nodded and gave him the number. "Seven."

"I'm not an idiot. Tell me the real number."

Must he continue to heap insult upon injury? "That is the number. You asked and I told you. Now it is your turn."

"I won't tell you until you stop with the lies."

Sophia jumped back to her feet. "What do you want me to tell you? Do you want to know everything? Do you want to know that I was saved from a fate worse than death when I arrived in London? That I was polished, preened and beautified until I shone and then sold to save my life? The reason I landed in a duke's bed is because lies and gossip travel faster than the truth. By the time St. Ives found me, I had a notorious reputation for dazzling men in their bedrooms--all lies but lies that helped me stay alive."

All was quiet for a time, Sophia's chest rose with each breath she heaved in and then whooshed out. Why did he do this to her? Slumping to the ground, she rubbed a hand over her face and stared into the fire. "Believe what you will. I have nothing to lose by telling the truth." Well, some of the truth. There was more to it but she would never reveal it. Ever. What would he do to her if he knew that when she arrived in London, she carried his father's baby, his own half brother? He would never speak to her again. Even in anger.

"Do you ever feel regret?"

She did. All the time. Regret that she hadn't run sooner. Regret that she hadn't been able to truly trust Blake and Matthew to save her. Regret ate away her defenses each time she peered into the face of a baby knowing she would never have one of her own. Nothing in her life had so far gone to plan, but she had been happy, or at least some version of it. "Regret is a luxury I cannot afford," came her eventual reply.

"Some would call that denial."

"I define it as the intelligent option. And denial has her uses."

"One day you will have to face it all, Sophie. What will you do then?"

She didn't hesitate. "I'll face it when it comes. But that won't be this day or any other day soon."

"How do you know? You can't keep it at bay forever."

Staring into the mesmerizing flames, she muttered. "Oh, yes I can."

Eight

The distant sounds of horse's hooves drifted through Blake's mind, threatening to bring him more fully awake, to take him from a place where he was content. Beneath floating apple flowers, his hands molded her curves as his mouth brushed her jaw, her ear lobe, her cheek, consigning her taste to the deepest parts of his memories. In this place, in his dreams, Sophie was his wife and life was perfect.

He didn't want to wake up, but the drumming of hooves meant a customer. His delirious dreams could wait.

He flexed his fingers and stretched but the woman of his nighttime invention didn't move. She didn't disappear when he opened his eyes, her apple scent continued to tickle his nose. Her warmth still filled his arms as he held her tightly to his side, heat radiating from both their bodies.

His sleepy gaze shifted as he remembered where they were. Who she was. Right about the same time she did.

A sudden stiffness infused Sophie's body. Her head rose and her back straightened.

Shit.

Pulling his hands away from her, Blake cried out when pain exploded in so many parts of his body at once he thought he might die. The dream must have been God's idea of a nasty joke.

The skin on his arm pulled, pain from ribs that were surely broken took his breath away, and a thousand other little hurts made themselves known. He couldn't feel his sleeping lower limbs at all.

Before Sophie could berate him for his actions, before he could explain that he'd dreamed of happiness while holding her tight, she was on her feet and in the middle of the road.

"Sophie," he called out to her.

"Don't you dare say a word!" The finger she held out to him, the accusation in her eyes as she pointed in his direction, flustered and embarrassed him and made him click his mouth shut with a snap.

In the cold light of the morning, he was right. He wasn't a duke and she wasn't interested.

As crude as the truth was, Sophie sold her body to the lord with the deepest coffers. The very idea of sleeping with her head on his shoulder had to be causing no end of inner turmoil for her.

The silence between them intensified, the thumping in his ears testified to his weakened state, his aroused state.

He'd lost enough blood yesterday to fell the mightiest of men and anything remaining had flooded south at the mostly innocent sharing of body heat.

He stared at Sophie, standing in the middle of the road, hands on hips, one foot tapping the gravel beneath her toe. What was she doing? Would she stand there until someone came along? He'd need help getting to his feet and was about to ask her when he realized the thumping in his head was actually the sound of horses, the sound that had woken him.

From where he sat, his back still against Monster's, he couldn't see down the road, but he could hear the driver's order to the horses pulling the carriage to slow and then stop.

Doing his best to ignore the pain that wracked his body, Blake rolled to his side, the side on which his ribs were unharmed, and willed blood back into his legs. The carriage could hold any manner of filth.

"Good morning to you, sir," Sophie said, her voice clear and loud and sweetly feminine. "As you can see, we have met with some trouble and require assistance."

"Who is it, Gaspar?" a voice asked from the inside of the carriage. Whoever it was sounded frustrated.

"A...lady, Your Grace." The hesitation in the driver's words made Blake want to punch the man in the face. He wasn't at all sure if Sophie was a lady due to the richness of her clothes or just another woman standing in the middle of the road, but his hesitation implied he would as soon as run her down than render assistance.

"Please, sir, it has been a harrowing night already, I would be most appreciative."

Why hadn't she ever used that tone of voice with him? She sure knew how to stroke a man's conscience.

He groaned, the pain in his legs taking his mind off the thought of Sophie stroking anything.

He heard the door of the conveyance open, boots hit the earth and the traces jangle as the horses shifted.

"And who might you be?" Frustration seemed to be replaced by curiosity.

Blake rose to his feet, worried about the black spots swimming before his eyes. Taking the few steps toward Sophie, Blake saw who stopped to offer them aid and swore.

Sophia itched to march over to the bone-head and kick him. What kind of man welcomed their rescuer with a string of vile, offensive curses? Did he think she wanted to stay on the side of the road with him?

Not likely!

Dropping a deep curtsey, Sophia tried her best to appear every inch the lady. If this man knew her status by birth, he would probably beat her out of the way with the ivory handled walking stick he held. "My name is Sophia Martin, Your Grace." She hadn't missed the title the driver had so carelessly thrown about.

"And what kind of trouble have you come across?" The question was asked as the duke assessed first Blake, then their broken cart and then her. His gaze started at her toes and traveled slowly, insolently up, pausing at her chest, and then finally meeting her eyes.

Sophia remembered when Blake made much the same perusal. She narrowed her gaze in his direction before turning back to the duke. "I'm afraid one of the horses went lame and the other ran off. After spending the night on the road, I find myself eager for a warm bath and a glass of wine." Sophia knew what she was did perfectly well. The inflection she put on the word *bath*, implied she wished for company. She played with the devil not knowing whom she addressed, but faced with two evils, she would choose a stranger over Blake's nearness any day.

"Oh, dear lady, of course I will offer you the sanctuary of my carriage. I expect the ambience will be improved with your presence."

Sophia tittered. "Your Grace, you are too kind."

"Ah, but you must call me Blakiston if we are to be traveling companions."

Her heart skipped a beat. It couldn't be. Resisting the urge to let her jaw fall open in shock, or to look to Blake to seek confirmation, she merely inclined her head. The presence at her back told her Blake had finally pulled himself from the ground.

"You needn't risk the mud to your leather, Blakiston. Sophie will be quite fine here with me until the search party arrives."

Ooh. Her foot itched again, only this time she would do more than kick his shins.

Blakiston didn't give her the chance. "I'm sure the lady would rather join me than stay here in the cold with you." His tone challenged, condescended.

"And I'm sure our searchers will be along any moment now, so you needn't bother yourself. Why don't you get back in your carriage and be on your way."

The duke's face turned a rather unbecoming shade of red, his lips tightened to a thin line and Sophia swore she heard his teeth grind together in his mouth. But then he closed the distance, his hand held out to her. "I believe the choice is yours, milady. Stay here in the cold with a barkeep or join me in my warm carriage for a glass of

French brandy. I will have you back to your lodgings and in that hot bath before the lunch gong sounds."

Oh, she played with fire. The way Blakiston's charm oozed from his handsome mouth worried her, but she would surely kill Blake if she had the chance to have him alone right now.

"I would be eternally grateful, Your Grace."

As she stepped toward the duke with the feeling akin to entering a snake pit, Blake's hand shot out and gripped her arm hard. "Sophie, you can't go with him."

"And why not?" she asked through teeth gritted against a frustrated shriek.

"He is nothing more than a slimy worm. You are better than this."

Sophia's cheeks heated and before she knew what she was about, her free arm swung, her palm flat and for the second time, Sophia slapped Blake's face with all the anger he made her feel. Did he think she would perform sexual acts with a duke in his carriage for the pleasure of a comfortable seat back to the tavern? His tone implied that was exactly it.

Wrenching her arm from his hold, she turned to Blakiston, placed her fingers in his hand as if nothing had happened and let him lead her to his carriage and the promise of spirits. She could certainly use something to calm her nerves and her fury.

Nine

Sophia fumed. If she'd been elsewhere, she would have paced, she would have thrown her arms in the air and ranted like a lunatic. But she was here. Instead she had to keep the smile on her lips and charm the current Duke of Blakiston all the way back to the inn.

She clasped her hands around her bare arms in an effort to get warm and shake the melancholy that threatened.

"Are you cold, m'dear?" Blakiston asked, his voice charming, his manner not in the least bit threatening.

So why did she feel such a deep sense of impending doom?

"A little, Your Grace." She watched as he stood, stooped and lifted the top of the bench seat he sat upon. He pulled out a blanket of rich maroon wool large enough to warm her entire body if she wrapped it around herself.

"Here you go." The duke placed the blanket on her lap and tucked the edges beneath her legs. He was so close she could smell his cologne—an off-putting scent filled with enough sandalwood to make her nose itch—and his touch evoked yet more shivers, but this time of revulsion. Even though Charles was a very distant relative to the previous duke, the same blood flowed through his veins. Through all men of the Blakiston line.

Blake included.

"Thank you, Your Grace. I only hope my gown doesn't soil the fine wool." The mud had dried from her ruined dress, but sand and dirt still fell with only the slightest of movement. She didn't like to think of the picture she made, blood and mud and dirt combined.

"Nonsense," he replied with a wave of his bejeweled hand. "Can't have you freeze to death just to save my linen."

The intent cat-like gaze he turned on her after he sat made Sophia squirm and pull the warm blanket to her chin.

"Would you like to tell me what you were doing there with that oaf?" he asked.

Sophia thought about her reply for a moment before deciding a lie would be far better than the truth. "I had heard of a milliner in Sheffield that I thought to visit, so Blake accompanied me. It wouldn't do to travel about alone."

"What of your carriage?"

Yes, why hadn't she thought of that? "Blake had to collect supplies and they wouldn't have fit in my small conveyance."

"Pardon my ignorance, but are you are good friends with the innkeeper?"

Sophia laughed out loud. "Friends, Your Grace? I would hardly count Blake a friend. I am staying at his inn for a short time is all."

"So you hail from this part of the country then?"

"I grew up close to here if that is your question, Your Grace."

"You don't have to Your Grace me, Sophia. You can call me Blakiston."

She would rather not, but under the circumstances it was better than him offering his Christian name, so she inclined her head.

"What lures you from the comforts of London? I imagine the delights there are far more interesting than any you will find hereabouts."

"Daemon is out of the city on business and my brother invited me to attend the birth of his child."

"Your brother?"

"Matthew Martin." She gave the name, but then wished she hadn't.

"You're that Sophia Martin?"

She swallowed hard. "I am."

Blakiston reclined further into his seat unknowing of the damage she had just caused. The village of Blakiston was the only place in the world she could hide herself from the eyes of London, but no more.

"Does St. Ives know you are visiting?" Blakiston asked, a small smile on his pale lips. She would have believed he merely passed the time and made conversation except for the smugness about him.

"He is not my keeper in all aspects, Your Grace. I do not have to inform him of my every movement."

"If you were mine, I would want to know your whereabouts at all times."

"Oh?" The sick feeling multiplied in the pit of her stomach.

Blakiston reached across the carriage and put his hand on her knee. She suddenly had the urge to kick a second man.

"I would want to know if I had to challenge any man who tried to steal you away."

Sophia let out a strangled laugh, the lump in her throat made it hard to draw breath. "Daemon knows I can't be stolen easily, Your Grace."

He shrugged, removed his hand and reclined once again. "Perhaps there are those out there who don't fight fair, who enjoy the thrill of a challenge?"

"Then there will be those out there who will be disappointed," she replied, hoping that would be the end of it.

He shrugged again. "You are in love with St. Ives then?"

Hers was an easy answer. She may no longer share his bed, but St. Ives was her friend no matter their relationship status or station difference and she owed him everything she had left. "I would give my life to him if he so chose it."

"Such loyalty," he muttered with a shake of his head. Then he closed his eyes and leaned back against the squabs.

Sophia quietly exhaled the breath she hadn't known she'd held and relaxed a fraction. So many lies told in such a small amount of time. She often wondered what the devil would do to her for her thousands of untruths when her time came to answer for her sins. But it was part of her existence.

It had been four long months since she had enjoyed a man's touch, since she had enjoyed Daemon's protection. Now she was on her own. With a little bit of luck Violet would soon have her baby and give Sophia a reason to back out of their ridiculous bargain. Then she could begin to consider the rest of her life. Contrary to what the ton believed, it had been she who had separated from him. Discovering that she was pregnant had quickly put an end to their affair and given her the hope of a new beginning. He'd handed her a very large sum of money and extracted a promise to be kept up to date with the child's progress.

But then the worst came about and she was forced to creep back into his life. Offering him his money back days after losing the baby had nearly destroyed her mind. It probably would have had he been a lesser man and reclaimed the money. Instead, he had folded her into his arms and held her as she'd cried, promising her that things could be different for her now. She was wealthy enough to be independent. To never have to rely on her charms to put food on the table or a roof over her head.

She had never before been in that situation and had had no idea where to start. It was why she had sought the comfort of her old home, of her brother, while she sorted out her mind.

As she peeked at her companion beneath her lashes, she was mightily glad of St. Ives. If men like Blakiston were to be options, she would have become a chambermaid long ago. Luckily she was adept at handling unwanted advances. It helped that her reputation had been upheld by St. Ives. According to the papers, she managed to land the Earl of Whitcombe on his back with only one hand after he pawed her. The real truth was that St. Ives hit him, but unless Whitcombe wanted to be hit again, he would leave the truth alone and let the lies do their work. Her career was based on lies, her friends having put it out that she had more experience than most practiced courtesans. It was a large gamble and her first protector, Noah, had seen through the fabrication at their first 'meeting'. But after she risked all and poured her story out to him, he took her in and showed her what it was like to truly be touched, to feel passion, to try to let go of some of the scars and move on.

It didn't happen often to women like her, but she had been cared for. After Noah, she'd had her pick of fine but lonely gentlemen, if she treated them right, they treated her to houses to live in, money and gifts of jewels and trinkets. She couldn't say it was an ideal life but she had lived. Survived to fight another day.

No thanks to Blake's ancient horses and a road not fit to walk on, let alone drive a carriage or cart. She could have broken her neck in the accident. They both could have.

The man's insults did nothing to blunt the desire she felt when close to him, when watching the dance of his muscles, the mischievousness in his grin, the tilt of his jaw.

But Blake had more erratic mood swings than a fishwife.

Sophia shook her head and bit down on the end of the tongue. Why did her mind always come back to him? Why couldn't she see him for the bitter man he was, take his insults for what they were and flee back to London?

Because Matthew needs you.

She barely contained a snort. No one needed her. Violet certainly didn't need her help. Matthew wanted her there, but he didn't need her. Daemon didn't need her. Blake didn't want her. That much was blatantly obvious in the way he looked at her, as if disgusted by her even sleeping in his inn. She was yet another problem to be dealt with. She wasn't sure if it was a man thing or a Blake thing.

There she went again. Thinking of Blake.

She knew all his faculties weren't straight this morning when they'd woken. The startled look in his eyes and his jerky movements showed he hadn't meant his actions even though they caused him pain. She really hadn't even been angry with him, she'd been furious with herself for reacting to his touch. A touch that made her burn. But it had felt so good. He had felt so good.

Even the roughness of his hands provoked sensations she hadn't experienced. Each and every callous on his fingers and palm had scratched at her skin, sending pleasure shooting right to her sex.

Damn him! Damn him for making her enjoy his touch, for making her want him to touch her again. For if the truth were told, she wanted him to kiss her. She wanted to feel the texture of his unshaven face against her cheek, across her stomach, the inside of her thigh.

"You're looking a little flushed, m'dear." Blakiston's voice startled her out of her reverie.

"I'm afraid I'm not feeling quite the thing right now, Your Grace."

"Not surprising. It must have been rather cold and lonely out there last night."

The implication in his tone sent a shiver up her spine. "Indeed, Your Grace."

She was saved from any further conversation when the driver slowed the horses and announced they had arrived at the inn. Sophia looked out at the mud-covered ground and sighed. Her gown and shoes were already ruined. But Blakiston had his own agenda.

"Allow me, Sophia." He climbed down from the carriage with surprising speed, bowed and then held his arms out for her and all before his driver had even jumped down.

"Your Grace, I can't... You can't. I'm filthy."

"Nonsense." He stepped closer. "And I asked you to call me Blakiston."

Had his voice risen a notch? Perhaps it was her imagination or simply fatigue that made her see more in his gallant action than was actually there.

"Thank you." She let the man pick her up as though she weighed no more than a picnic hamper. Each slow step he took through the drying mud made his arms tighten around her until she was positively crushed to his chest.

The door to the tavern burst open and Matthew's brooding face appeared in the early morning light. Sophia couldn't have been happier to see him or his anger at that moment.

Blakiston stepped over the threshold and released her legs, causing her body to slide against his on purpose. Involuntarily her arms tightened about his neck to keep her balance. As soon as her feet touched the ground, she stepped away and mumbled her thanks, eyes downcast.

"Any time you are in need of assistance, Sophia, you know where to find me."

"Thank you, Your Grace, I shall keep that in mind."

From the corner of her eye she noted Matthew watching the exchange. His expression went from brooding to furious at the use of her Christian name and the almost pleasant way she responded. Sophia barely held her groan in check. There was going to be a lot of explaining to do.

"I'm very grateful for your assistance, but now I think it is time I retired." She turned from the knowing grin on the duke's lips to her brother's obvious concern. "Matthew, Blake is still out on the road with the broken cart, he needs a rescue party of his own."

"The wagon's hitched and ready to go. I believe thanks are required, Your Grace, but I'll take care of my sister now."

Blakiston raised his thin brows, flourished yet another of his overdone bows and retreated to his carriage.

Sophia sagged and fell heavily into the nearest chair. Suddenly her head ached abominably and her stomach felt hollow and sick.

"Are you going to tell me what the hell happened? Why were you with Blakiston at this time of the morning and what happened to Blake? Where were you last night?"

"One question at a time, Matthew, I have the most horrendous headache."

Once the words passed her lips, the events of the night and morning caught up with her and her bottom lip trembled. Hot tears pricked her eyes but she willed them back. She was made of sterner stuff than to cry when she was whole and healthy and safe.

"One of the horses went lame and we had to shoot him. The other horse ran off, so we were stranded."

"Why didn't you walk back?" Matthew asked, suspicion still front and center in his eyes.

"I think Blake may have broken his ribs and he lost a lot of blood."

"Christ! Are you all right?" Matthew finally took in her ragged appearance, the nasty gash on her head, how pale she must appear.

She nodded. Nothing a bath, a sleep and new coat of dignity wouldn't repair.

"How could you leave Blake out there?" There was no question of why he hadn't come back with her and Blakiston. There was no way Blake would get in that man's carriage even if his life depended on it. Rot him anyway, she thought. It would do his ego good to think about his situation and his treatment of her. Never mind that being alone would also give his temper time to heighten and burn out.

"His injuries are not life threatening and someone needed to get word to you."

Matthew raked a hand through his hair and then pulled her into his arms and hugged her tight." I was worried about you."

For a moment, she stiffened and wanted to push him away, and then in a moment of pure exhaustion and vulnerability, she melted into him and hugged him back. "You needn't worry over me," she whispered. But never had the words sounded so hollow in her life. For once, just once, she was glad someone worried for her. Maybe there was a person in the world who loved her still.

Blake scowled when he saw Matthew's wagon approach. It was obvious he hadn't hurried out to find him. Damn Sophia and her tears. She probably got back and spun a fine story about how he pawed her and shouted and drove her to get in a carriage with that slimy weasel. Her lips would have trembled and a fine show would have been witnessed by all.

His scowl was accompanied by a growl.

"You took your sweet time," he called when the wagon neared. Two old nags trailed behind, Matthew and the bar hand, Dominic, rode up front.

"I can go back and leave you here if you want." came Matthew's laughing reply.

Laughing? Why wasn't he facing him down with a pistol in his hands over his sister's honor? "Damned if I want to spend another night like this." His ribs were on fire and the multiple cuts and scrapes pulled at his skin to remind him how much of a sorry state he was in.

"You should have come back with Blakiston."

"Is Sophia all right?" Blake asked despite knowing he shouldn't care what went on between her and the Duke of Slime.

"Sophia it is now? I thought you were only going to call her Sophie?"

He shrugged. "Slip of the tongue. Is she all right?"

Matthew nodded and set to work untying one the nags from the lead ropes. Dominic was already at work on the other. There wasn't much he could say when the boy was there too. He would not give yet more fodder to the gossips by talking about Sophie behind her back.

It took a good half an hour for Matthew and Dominic to move Monster's body far from the road. They shouldn't just leave him there, but dragging the once majestic horse back to the inn would be of no use to anyone. Blake was forced to watch as they pulled on ropes tied to his body and the harness he still wore. Once he was far enough from the roadway, Blake said his final goodbyes to the old boy, then went back to his wagon.

Dominic sat on the driver's bench with the two horses already crudely hooked up and ready to be gone. Blake checked that the makeshift preparations would hold and then went to climb up beside him.

"You ride with me," Matthew called.

"I'll ride with the boy," Blake called in return as he gritted his teeth against the pain that would come once he grabbed a hold of the cart.

A warm, firm hand came down on his shoulder, stopped him from jumping up.

"You can't seriously mean to be jostled around on that seat all the way back?"

Blake turned to Matthew and knew by the look in the other man's eyes that this was a battle he'd already lost. He didn't have the energy to protest. All he really wanted to do was lie back down on the ground and sleep for a day or more.

"I suppose not." He let Matthew help him into the back of the wagon, where a makeshift bed had been thrown down on the timber boards. He would have put up a fight at being treated like an invalid, but it felt so good to finally relax. How had he thought sitting on a driver's seat a good idea?

Matthew chuckled again and climbed up. He took the reins and rolled on slowly as the pair set their own speed.

"You never answered my question," Blake reminded him after a few minutes.

"She's fine. Blakiston made quite a show of carrying her into the inn, which should set tongues wagging for a while to come. Apart from the dirt and that scrape on her head, she says she's fine."

Blake tensed. He wanted to meet Matthew's eyes, but couldn't quite raise himself to his elbow. "Blakiston's not there with her now, is he?"

"So what if he is? The two of them obviously know one another."

"They do not."

"He called her Sophia and she called him Blakiston."

"I knew I should have stopped her."

"Yes, you should have," Matthew said as the first hints of anger crept into his voice.

"And how would you have stopped her?"

"Any way I could have. Blakiston is a toad-"

"Worse than a toad," Blake interrupted.

"Worse than a toad. He is going to come back to see her."

"Did he say that?"

"He didn't have to. The look in his eye as he stared at her, he'll be back. I'd bet my baby on it."

"You don't have to go that far," Blake laughed in spite of his anger. Some of the finely wrought tension left his body but the motion stung his side so he had to pause before drawing his next breath to continue. "Sophie can look after herself."

"I wouldn't be so sure," Matthew said, the line of back sitting up straighter.

Blake remembered the way her palm had cracked his cheek, the shock wave it had sent through his body. The little minx would be fine even in a fight to the death. "She has slapped me a few times since her arrival." If she kept it up, he'd have a permanent imprint.

Matthew laughed loud and long, slapping a hand to his thigh. "Did you deserve it?"

Blake smiled and closed his eyes, remembering the fury that fired those slaps. "Of course I did."

"Sophia isn't as tough or as strong as she makes out," Matthew said, sobering in an instant.

He knew that too.

He just wished she did.

Ten

"I'm coming!" Matthew's voice yelled from beyond the kitchen.

The sudden sound made Sophia jump and she only just managed to suppress a shriek as she stood at the bottom of the stairs leading to the tap. When he came into view, Sophia cleared her throat to let him know she was there since he walked with his head down, eyes on the floor.

"Ah, there you are."

"Here I am." She didn't know what else to say. Had Blake told his side of the story yet? She knew the longer she hid, the worse the situation would become, but she was a coward and it had taken a nap and a bath before she had the courage to show her face. Seems she needn't have bothered. There wasn't a soul around. Where were the patrons? Where was Blake?

Bang, bang, bang, bang came from the closed door leading into the tavern. She hadn't heard the thumps when coming down the stairs but Matthew must have.

"Where is everyone?"

"Blake is in his office with the doctor. Could you please go and try to talk some sense into him while I tell the village dinner will not be served."

"Why?"

"Blake refuses to see just how injured he is and wants to go about business."

Sophia stepped forward. "No, I meant why will dinner not be served?"

"Sophia, he may have broken ribs and he certainly has a head injury that affects his balance. Blake couldn't walk a straight line, let alone prepare a meal."

"I'll do it," she said.

"What?"

Bang, bang, followed by, "Open the door!"

"I will cook the meal."

"Don't be silly, Sophia. You can't do it."

"And why not?" She tried to hold her foot still but her traitorous toes tapped and gave away her frustration.

"Don't give me that look. I know what you think you can do, but it was a long night for you too. You need to rest and so does Blake."

She touched her fingertips gingerly to her hairline. "You have no idea what happened out there." Otherwise he wouldn't stand and argue.

"We can talk about this later. Wait there and I'll tell these men to go home and eat their wives' cooking for a change."

She didn't wait to hear what Matthew said, didn't wait to hear the reply, angry or sympathetic, over Blake's convalescence. This perception they all clutched to so tightly that she was useless grated on her nerves and made her furious in more ways than Blake's insults alone.

Bursting into his office, she was about to tell him exactly that but then she stopped dead, the breath stalled in her lungs.

"It's not as bad as it looks," the doctor assured her in a rough Scottish accent.

"Don't tell her that," Blake said with a frown.

A multitude of black, blue and purple bruises covered his side, back and shoulders and what Sophia had at first assumed a graze must have been deep enough to be stitched, the thread almost camouflaged by discolored skin on all sides. The fact he sat with only a blanket over his lap, hairy legs swinging from the edge of the desk, barely registered as she took another step into the room. She couldn't take her eyes off his torso, not because of the injury or his nakedness but because she didn't want to meet his eyes.

"See, you've scared her." Blake's tone teased, but his usual mischief was strangely absent. No. His voice held something like worry. She still couldn't lift her gaze.

"I'm so sorry," Sophia whispered, the hot prick of tears back and threatening.

"This isn't your fault," Blake reminded her.

The doctor slipped from the room, but still she stared at his chest, at the mess and ruin.

"Sophie?"

In that moment she felt more like the frightened and helpless Sophie than in all the years she'd spent away as Sophia.

"Look at me."

She shook her head, squeezed her eyes shut.

"You didn't do this."

"I could have… We should have… Oh God."

"We did everything right," he said with that uncanny ability to guess her thoughts. "*You* did everything right."

A warm hand closed around her elbow and with only the slightest of pressure, Sophia was hugged for the second time that day. Despite how much pain he must have felt, his arms wrapped around her strong and tight, pulled her close until she had no choice but to rest her head against his shoulder. She didn't dare return the embrace for fear she would hurt him.

"I do. It could have turned out a lot worse and you know it."

She did, but wouldn't think about it. She had to hold those thoughts at bay until she was alone. Sophia concentrated instead on the words as he spoke them.

"So, the pie is already made, all I have to do is bake the biscuits and something sweet to top it off."

"No," Sophia said.

"All right, they don't need sweets anyway. Pie and biscuits it is."

He tried to lighten the mood and distract her but she wouldn't let him. "No. You will not bake anything." She stepped out of his embrace and towards the door of the office. "You will not step one foot into that kitchen."

"You sound like Matthew," he huffed. His genial mood disappeared with a whoosh of breath. "The inn has to open. I cannot afford to miss even one meal."

"And you won't. But you can't make it."

Understanding dawned but was quickly followed by a familiar glower. "Whatever idea you have in that head of yours, you can think again. This is my inn and I make the decisions."

"It is your inn, but unless the doctor says you can turn cartwheels in the yard outside, you are going to bed to rest."

He spluttered. He choked. Then he coughed.

"No cartwheels then?" Sophia glowered back even though Blake's eyes were now filled with more pain than anger. "I didn't think so."

The door opened and Matthew entered, followed closely by the doctor. She ignored her brother for the moment and narrowed her eyes at the other man. "How long must Blake stay in bed?"

The red-headed physician looked from her to Blake and then back to her. He clearly knew when he'd already lost an argument. "One week."

"Be damned!" Blake surged to his feet.

Sophia stepped back as the blanket fell from his lap and averted her eyes even though he wore smalls. "I'll get started in the kitchen," she said and slipped from the room. As hard as she tried, she could not completely ignore the pained cry from Blake, the curses from Matthew or the laughter from the good doctor.

Her own brief smile fading, Sophia entered the kitchen. Could she really do this? Sure she'd helped a little, so she knew the layout of the kitchen and where everything was, but could she really serve a dinner at an inn? And should she? If word were to get out, her reputation would be... What? It certainly couldn't hurt her as a courtesan.

So why didn't she move? Her legs were heavy as though weighted down by rocks and her fingertips tingled as her breaths became shorter, faster.

One, two, three.

Would the townsfolk eat a meal prepared entirely by her own hands?

She nodded her head, rolled her sleeves to her elbows and stepped toward the stove where the fire had gone cold. She would do it because Blake would become her friend again. She would do it because she was a resourceful, independent woman who needed acceptance from no one. And she would do it to prove to herself that she could. That she had come far from the frightened, battered and scarred fourteen year old who'd left this place and not glanced back. If the villagers didn't like it, they would go hungry or go home.

Eleven

F or the moment the rain had stopped and birds sang happily from the bare branches of the trees at the back of the tavern but Sophia didn't take any of it in. She stood staring at her hands, her dirty nails and cracked skin, a splinter in the third finger on her left hand. She may have come far from the terrified fourteen-year-old, but in that minute, after putting bread in the oven and before collecting more firewood, she felt much, much further from a courtesan.

Is this what she missed out on by running? Is this what Blake meant when he'd said she could have had it all? She didn't have time for deep contemplation but Sophie couldn't seem to shake her melancholy thoughts. She had a meal to prepare and then she had to get back to the tap to help Matthew and Dominic with serving. She wanted to curl into a little ball and cry, not run a tavern. Emotion overwhelmed her and her fists clenched.

"'Ere now, it can't all be that bad." The voice shook her from her daydream and she whirled to find a man watching her. He wasn't very close, but he wasn't as far away as she would have liked either.

"I...I got a splinter. It hurt a little is all." She longed to curse for good measure.

"Did you want me to take a look at it fer ya?" He stepped forward, his hand out toward her.

Sophia shook her head a little harder than she probably needed too and her heart thumped loudly against her ribs. He didn't look terribly frightening, but it was the quiet ones she had to watch out for. "I will be fine, thank you. It isn't the first and it won't be the last."

"Yer that Martin girl, aren't ya?"

She nodded, her eyes narrowed as she tried to figure out if she had once known this man. He looked vaguely familiar, but then so did most of the men thereabouts who wore farmer's clothing. "Do I know you?"

This time it was the stranger who shook his head. "Not yet, lass."

When he smiled, Sophia cringed. What was left of the man's teeth were blackened and his lips were stained yellow.

"Well, I really must be getting back to the kitchen. If the bread burns, I will be in mighty trouble with Blake."

The stranger made a sound of dismissal and shook his head again. He also took another step toward her.

"Good day, sir." She couldn't turn her back and flee, but neither could she return to the kitchen without the timber. Before she had a chance to make a decision, another man rounded the corner of the inn. Her stomach flip flopped. Now she was outnumbered and the new man stood between her and the kitchen door. Between her and safety.

"Roger," the new stranger inclined his head slowly, taking stock of the scene they must make.

Sophia's clammy hands clenched in her skirts now. If she had to flee, she would lift them high and run like the devil was after her.

"McFarlane," Roger replied but said nothing more.

McFarlane. She remembered that name. He was holding the dance on Friday night at his home. She wouldn't go so far as to say she was relieved, but the fact that Blake had mentioned his name more than once told her he was the lesser of the evils before her.

"Miss Martin, I wonder if you could use some help with that firewood?" Mr. McFarlane asked with an easy smile in her direction.

She nodded and stepped away from both men. She was moving further away from the kitchen, but she had to do something. In London, she was virtually untouchable since Daemon was her protector, or had been, but here, here everything was different and she would be foolish indeed to forget that.

"I was about to offer the lass assistance," Roger told him defensively.

"Is that what you were doing?" Mr. McFarlane replied, putting himself between Sophia and Roger. "What about your back?"

Roger scowled. "That's none of your damned business."

"It is now. I don't think Blake would take kindly to you being out here with the one woman who has come forward to help him."

"I was only going to talk to her."

Relief made it hard for Sophie to know what to do. Did she stay and argue? Did she leave and let Mr. McFarlane have it out with Roger?

"Sophia?" Dominic crashed through the kitchen door but then stopped short.

Thank God. She didn't bid the gentleman a good day. She didn't thank Mr. McFarlane for coming to her aid or rebuke Roger for his being there to frighten her. She just picked up her skirts and walked as fast as she could without it looking as though she was terrified and running away. Why was it that the story of her life could almost be summed up with those few words? She was terrified, so she ran.

When she finally made it into the warm, safe confines of the kitchen, she leaned against the bench and took several deep breaths.

Dominic entered the kitchen with Mr. McFarlane not far behind him. "Are you all right?" he asked.

"I am. Thank you."

Mr. McFarlane sighed and dropped the load of wood he held. "He didn't... Well, he didn't *do* anything did he?"

"Roger? No. I really am grateful that you came along. Thank you."

"You should not be outside on your own."

She smiled at the kind man. "I will remember that."

"Sophia?" Dominic was tense as he also dropped firewood into the box by the hearth. "His Grace just arrived. He says he won't leave until he sees for himself that you are 'unharmed from your nightmarish ordeal'. But if you aren't up to it, I'll tell him to leave off."

Sophia groaned. Dominic laughed.

Only five hours had passed since she had rolled her sleeves up and dived into flour and herbs, but it felt like ten or even twenty. The hair on the back of her neck was plastered to the skin there and itched abominably. She longed to lay her aching head down on a pillow and sleep.

What was the duke of Blakiston doing back again anyway? She needed to rest. At least that's what she told

Dominic to tell His Grace if he asked after her, because they both knew he wasn't there to quench his thirst with bitter ale.

"I can't let him see me like this."

"Why not," Dominic asked with a shrug. "Perhaps if he sees you with flour on your face and suds on your dress, he'll be disgusted and leave you alone."

If only it were that easy.

"He's in the dining room and has ordered supper and a glass of brandy." The way he turned his nose up as he said brandy made Sophia chuckle.

They had reached an easy camaraderie, she and Dominic. He'd warned her when the men heard she was in charge for the night, none had left. In fact more had arrived and she doubted it was her skill with bread that kept them so late. Her first meeting with the men the day of her arrival had gone badly enough for her to not wish to repeat it and the incident just now told her she should probably stay in the tap.

She almost wished Blake was there now to send the duke away. But then she was being silly. She didn't want his kind of protection. The kind that would see her stay in her room and never venture out.

Blakiston was still under the assumption that St. Ives was the one doing the protecting and while he was, she would be relatively safe. Only she had a feeling he was going to ruin her night completely. If she didn't talk to him, he might deign to come looking for her and if one man did, what would stop any other from the notion? Roger had obviously thought it all right to seek her out.

Her stomach chose that moment to growl. She did have to eat and she owed the duke her thanks for bringing her home that morning. She went to the bench where her flat bread lay and cut two thick slices from it, making far more mess with the flour than was necessary until the front her once burgundy gown was almost white.

Memories of another time a messy appearance had saved her came to mind. She had only been accosted on the streets of London a handful of times and had actually been thankful that she had been at the infirmary tending a head wound earlier in the evening.

When the much bigger man had approached her on the street, he suddenly dragged her into an alley and threw her on the ground. All the kicking and screaming in the world hadn't helped her. Fear held her immobile as he'd torn the front of her coat open, buttons popping and fabric tearing. Here was another man who wanted to take what she hadn't freely given. When he reached her bloody gown he'd paused, his own hands now tinged pink. It was long enough for her to retain her wits as he stared. Long enough for her to grope around until she found a solid lump next to her hip. She still wasn't sure what she hit her attacker with as she ran away as fast as her legs could carry her. But whatever it was had at least temporarily laid him low. From that day, she spent the coin on hacks and didn't wander the streets. Perhaps she would arm herself with a heavy object next time she had to collect firewood?

Or perhaps she could hit the duke in the head with a plate if his behavior stepped over any lines.

Satisfied with her appearance, and that Blakiston would be suitably horrified that she looked more like a scullery maid than a courtesan, she left the safety of the kitchen and approached the dining room.

"Sophie?" Blake's voice stopped her when she walked past his office. He was supposed to be resting in his bed. God, she hoped Dominic hadn't already told him about Roger. He was like a mother hen when he thought any man got too close.

She considered pretending she hadn't heard Blake speak, but their truce was still fragile. "Yes?" she replied as she stopped in the doorway but made no move to enter.

"How are things in the kitchen?"

"Things are just fine, you needn't worry."

He began to chuckle, but then hissed in a breath through clenched teeth, and muttered something that sounded like a curse.

"Can I bring you something?"

"New ribs?"

Now it was her turn to chuckle. "I'm afraid that is not on the list of my talents."

His gaze narrowed but not with anger or suspicion, more curiosity. "I have to admit your list of talents is growing." So Dominic hadn't told him anything? She breathed a sigh of relief.

"No, it isn't. When I told you I could do it, I wasn't talking with my ego. I truly thought I could."

"And you have."

"A few days hardly counts."

"All the same, I owe you my thanks."

Her cheeks warmed as she broke eye contact and stared down at the tray in her hands. What could she say to that? His praise wasn't unfounded, she had done a good job tonight, but all the same, it was unexpected and he shocked her with his open honesty.

"Is that my supper?" he pointed to the tray.

"Blakiston is here to check on my welfare."

All was silent for a long moment forcing Sophia to look into Blake's stormy grey eyes. She didn't like what she saw.

"He will see I am fine, I shall do my duty and share a meal with him and then he'll leave."

"And then he'll come back again and again."

"No he won't. I'll make it clear that he can't."

Blake snorted. "You can try but I'll wager this inn he won't listen."

"Careful, Blake, you seem to be in danger of paying me another compliment."

"A fool would have to be blind to miss your beauty, Sophie, and the duke may be an ass, but he is no fool."

When her cheeks warmed this time it had nothing to do with the compliment, more to do with embarrassment that they would speak so openly. "What will it take for you to believe that I can look after myself when it comes to men?" She hoped she sounded more confident than she felt.

His lips pressed together in a thin line, but he didn't answer.

"If that is all, I'll take his grace his dinner and then get back to the kitchen to tidy up."

"Be careful."

"I always am," she replied before turning from the threshold. What she should have said was that she always would be from then on.

"Sophie?"

She stopped. "Yes?"

"I know you can look after yourself, but if you do need assistance, scream."

"I will."

She didn't have to look back to know he would be happy with her answer, but she had no intention of screaming for help. She'd done that before, for three long days until her voice was hoarse. It hadn't helped her then.

Outside the dining room, Sophia paused and shook her head free of thoughts of the past. It took some effort to lift the edges of her lips into a smile, but she did so before knocking softly and entering.

"Sophia." He rose from his chair. "You look... well, you look..."

"Filthy, Your Grace? I am sorry to have to greet you thus, but I didn't have time to freshen up." Only half a lie but the duke was still fixated her floury gown.

"What on earth have you been doing?"

"Preparing the evening meal." She almost smiled when his lip curled with distaste.

He sputtered for a moment before asking, "Why?"

"Blake is on bed rest for the remainder of the week and couldn't do it himself."

"That doesn't mean you have to."

"Someone must and he is my friend."

"I thought you said you weren't close." His expression was full of suspicion, of disgust.

Hmm, she had said exactly that. "It is my fault that we were on the road yesterday and my conscience was rather loud about making some recompense."

"But making supper?"

Sophia shrugged and placed both plates on the table. "The pie only needed heating and the bread didn't turn out, so what I did do, I did poorly."

"You shouldn't have been forced to do it in the first place. I shall send one of my cooks over so you don't have to do it again. A woman with your delicate nature shouldn't be reduced to kitchen work."

To delay her next words, to choose those words carefully, Sophia sat and made a show of organizing her floury skirts about her tired ankles. "You are very kind, Your Grace, but you needn't bother yourself or your cook. We will get along, I'm sure."

"That blackguard is probably just fine. He uses you to do his work."

"His injuries speak clearly enough and I am happy to do it. After all, I was born in this village, I suppose that makes me a villager." What she really wanted to do was take his snide attitude and choke him with it, but for the moment she would have to settle for reminding His High and

Mightiness that she was a commoner. Even though she also hated to remind him of her ties to the town, perhaps that would be enough to keep him from returning to plague her with his presence.

The duke's responding words told her she fought a losing battle. "Don't be silly, you could never be compared to the likes of peasants."

Biting her tongue on a sharp retort, she inclined her head and lifted a forkful of pie to her mouth. She needed to eat and then leave.

The duke had other plans. "How long ago did you leave this godforsaken place?"

"I have been away fourteen years."

"So you knew my uncle then?"

Sophia almost choked. Knew him? God, how she wish she didn't. How differently her life would have turned out. "Only in passing, Your Grace."

"I asked you to call me Blakiston."

"Of course." Sophia couldn't eat fast enough. She had to get out of there. Blakiston had barely touched his dinner. Instead he leaned back in his chair and regarded her with an interest that made her skin crawl.

"What made you leave?"

A change of subject was required. Yet swallowing was almost impossible as terror seized her limbs and heart.

"Would *you* live in this tiny village? Anyway, it's a long and boring story and I would rather hear more about you. When did you take the title?"

A sigh of relief escaped her as he launched into a monologue about his life before inheriting and how mean his uncle had been before his death, but Sophia barely heard any of it. Her heart raced and her fingers grew so clammy, she nearly couldn't hold her fork up any longer. It was bound to come up again, but the real story was only known by two other people and they were both dead.

And the truth would never come from her mouth.

Within hours of Blake's forced convalescence, he was bored out of his mind. Within twenty four hours, he was more than ready to end his own life rather than be still for one more minute. Forced to endure the sight of Sophia doing his chores from the corner of the kitchen where he sat. Forced to watch her carry water for the dishes and firewood to heat the water. It made his arms ache to relieve her burden. Sure, she protested that she was up to the task, but when her brow creased and she had to bite her lip from exertion, he would stand to help and she would stop him in his tracks with one raised-brow glare.

There was a difference between being stubborn and being stupid, and she didn't seem to know where the line was drawn. He couldn't even get away from her by spending time outdoors, since a thunderstorm raged around them.

"Damn pot," she mumbled beneath her breath while scrubbing vigorously, delicate sleeves pulled past her tiny elbows as lightening lit the room through the open back door.

He'd had much time to study her over the course of the day. He'd never before noticed just how fragile she appeared. Her fingers and hands were dainty and elegant to the point where he was surprised she didn't break bones doing the most menial chores. She may adamantly insist upon being up to the responsibility and in her mind she probably was, but physically, there were jobs she would have trouble doing.

"Did you muck out the pig pen today, Sophia?"

She must have forgotten he was there, her head snapped up and she pinned him with a glare. "Of course I did."

"And the chicken coop?"

"Yes, Blake." She puffed a lock of hair from in front of her eyes. "I did everything on the list."

He smiled. There was no way she could have done everything. "What about greasing the wagon wheel? Did the rain make the job harder?" It was partly her fault that he couldn't get about since she had sided with the doctor and he planned to make her squirm.

"All done. The rain was no hindrance. It did stop for a spell today." She turned back to the large pot and continued to scrub.

Blake rose from his chair in the corner of the kitchen and hobbled over to her. "How did you do it?"

Her hands stilled for a moment, but then the scrubbing became more furious. "I had help."

"Oh?" The flush on her cheeks betrayed that there was more to the story. "Who helped you?"

"Ah... Mr. McFarlane, Matthew, some lads from the village and Dominic. It was easier than I thought with so many hands."

Blake gritted his teeth. "What were all of those men doing hanging around?"

"You underestimate the strength of your friendship with the villagers. I don't think there's one person who hasn't raised their hand to help you. It's one of the aspects of village life I'd forgotten."

When she'd finished scrubbing almost clear through the bottom of the pot, she placed it upside down to drain and then reached for the next one, but Blake caught her hand mid-air. "And the firewood you chopped in record time?"

He pulled her closer and turned her wet hand palm up to inspect her skin. "With nary a callus or blister or splinter?"

She went pink again and snatched her hand from his grip.

"What about the vegetables you pulled for the meal? Your hands or someone else's?"

"Someone else's."

"I don't want them hanging around you."

She hung her head for a moment and sighed. "I thought we established that I can take care of myself, though you flatter me if you think they only stay for my presence."

"You haven't seen the way they look at you."

She dropped the pot in the suds and turned on him, "You think I am blind? Deaf? Stupid? I know that the deWinter wife came here last night looking for her husband. I know she spat in the portion of pie he hadn't yet finished and dragged him from the room by his ear. I know how the men look at me. I also know how the wives see me. Words do not hurt me anymore, Blake. If they did, I would be a bedlamite."

He didn't have a response for that. Words did hurt her. Or at least his had.

She must have taken his silence for anger as she forged on. "You have to understand that I just didn't have time to do this without help. I did the pig pen first, gathered the eggs and fed the animals and then it was almost noon. I had to start the meals. Without their help, you would be starving as well as ornery."

He shook his head and chuckled. "I am not ornery, but I am thankful not to be starving. I don't blame you for asking for help." He did blame the ones doing the helping.

She sighed and reached for the last pot, but Blake stopped her again. "Leave that one to soak. You're tired and you need to rest."

"I'm fine, really." But her stomach chose that moment to growl loudly in the quiet space.

Blake's brows rose as he stared at her. "Did you eat?"

She shook her head. "I didn't have time."

"I don't believe that. You could have sat for a moment. I would have."

When she turned from him and crossed the expanse of the kitchen to replace a ladle on its hook on the wall, Blake worried. Why hadn't she risen to his jibe? He'd deliberately put it out there to test the strength of her bite, but all she did was walk away?

"What is it? If you've had enough, we can end this. I won't hold it against you."

"It's not that. I wasn't even thinking of your silly challenge."

"What were you thinking about?" He wanted to ask what had suddenly put the sadness in her eyes and made her shoulders droop, yet he didn't think she'd appreciate him voicing his concerns aloud. Even if his concern was for her.

"Blakiston."

Anger rose pure and swift at the mention of his enemy. "You seemed quite taken with him last night after dinner."

"Did I? Appearances don't always tell the full story. You should know that."

"Are you saying you didn't enjoy his company? He is a powerful and wealthy duke."

"Wealth does not buy you manners," she snapped.

"Did he say something bad? Sophie, did the duke do something to upset you?" He waited to the tune of his own thumping heart while his hands curled into fists. He'd always known the current duke was a blackguard. Thunder shook the walls as though it agreed with his thoughts.

"It's nothing he did."

He calmed a fraction but even with his ribs still hurting like the devil, he wouldn't hesitate showing Charles what he really thought of him. He schooled his face to a gentler emotion and followed Sophie from the kitchen back into the now empty common room.

He watched as she fidgeted with chairs and cleaned imaginary crumbs from the tops of already clean tables before he spoke again. "What is really worrying you?"

"I told you, it's nothing."

"Another thing I won't understand?" he said the words softly but couldn't keep the hurt from them. "There was a time when we could tell each other anything."

"Those days are long past."

"They don't have to be." He stepped to her side, caught her wrist in his hand when she made to walk away. "I hate this distance between us, Sophie. You can tell me what's on your mind. I promise I won't judge."

She shook her head, her gaze on the floor.

Blake crowded her against the wall until she was forced to look up at him. Her blue eyes sparkled with tears and she bit her lip until the normally pink bow turned pale.

"What is it?"

"Yesterday…"

God, she was trembling. He let go of her wrist so he could pull her close and wrap his arms around her. The shock from their accident must only just be settling in and because of his injury and his convalescence, she hadn't had even a moment to herself all day. "I'm sorry. You're working so hard and caring about everyone else, but no one is caring for you."

"It's not that," she sobbed.

He tightened his embrace and tried to swallow past the unfamiliar lump in his throat. Did he push her too hard? Let her do too much? In the back of his mind he knew he still punished her for leaving. He would never say it out loud, but he wouldn't let her continue to do his work if she was going to fall apart. He wouldn't be held responsible for that.

She pushed against his chest and met his eyes with her own. "You could have died."

Thump-thump went his heart against his ribs again. *What*?

"You could have died and the last words we shared were nasty and hateful and I would never have had the chance to take them back." By the time the words were out, she cried in earnest.

"Died? It was just a little accident, Sophie."

"It was not," she cried.

"Sshhh. I'm right here." He gathered her back into his arms.

"I know." She sniffed against his collarbone. "But what if you weren't?"

"You don't even like me."

She leaned back again, shock written all over her beautiful face. "I never *said* I didn't like you."

He could understand that. "Could we start again? Could you forget that I'm a pigheaded oaf and just be my friend again?"

"Can you forget who I am?"

It was on the tip of his tongue to ask her once again who she really was, but it wasn't the time. "I'll never forget who you are." When she made as if to wrench herself from his grip, he softened his tone, pulled her closer again so they were nose to nose. "You're the woman who saved my life, who gathered firewood and kept me warm. You fixed me when you should have kicked me and left me on the road to die. I know who you are and I'll never forget that. Neither should you."

This time when she pulled free, she didn't turn and stomp away. She didn't slap him or shout abuse. She raised her hands and placed them on his cheeks and whispered, "Thank you for being so nice to me."

"You're welcome," he whispered back.

And then the damndest thing happened. He didn't move. He didn't breathe or blink or have time to react before Sophie pressed her lips to his. If it was comfort she sought, he would ensure she received it.

When she melted against him, smooth, liquid honey in his hands, Blake put his arms back around her and pressed his body to hers. When she angled her head, he deepened the kiss, and coaxed her lips apart so he could truly taste her. With the gentlest of pressure, he walked her back a step until the dining room wall brushed his forearms. She threaded her hands into his hair and moved against him until all he could think of was her. He could smell her, taste her, feel her and he wanted more. So much more.

His lids were only half closed when the darkened room around them lit with the power of lightning and thunder shook the walls a scant second after. The booming sound of it made Sophia jump with a gasp, stealing the air from his lungs, her blue eyes wide, her breathing heavy.

He looked from those sparkling eyes to her swollen lips and back again, his hands running the lengths of arms from her fingers to her shoulders as though he could calm her sudden skittishness.

She stared at him for half a second longer and then with a muttered, "Oh my God," stepped from his embrace and turned her back.

"Sophia?"

"That shouldn't have happened. I'm sorry."

Of course it should have happened. "Why not?"

"I... I'm so sorry, I can't do this."

Blake didn't say a word. He let her run up the stairs, her door slamming just before thunder once again shook the inn.

He shook his head and looked heavenward. What had he done?

Twelve

All night Sophia castigated and tossed and turned and called herself ten different kinds of fool. Why had she kissed him? Why did he have to be nice to her right when all she wanted to do was fight? At least if they were fighting, she wouldn't think of his strength and safety. His half-naked chest, his comfort when she'd needed it the most, his cheeky grin and smug shrugs.

Damn her traitorous body! It really wasn't her fault that she craved human contact once in a while. It had been months since she'd been held intimately. When Blake had wrapped her in his arms, the feeling was so much like coming home. Then the events of the last few days had caught up to her and she couldn't stem the flow of emotion. What had started as her needing comfort had ended with her hands in his hair and her back against the wall.

In the early hours of the morning, when she beat the stuffing around in her pillow in an attempt to get comfortable, she blamed her vulnerability on him. It was all Blake's fault that he made her *feel*. Why couldn't he tease and taunt and fire her fury? It was a better alternative to this!

Sophia had learned very early in her career as a courtesan that feelings were simply not the done thing in London. If she was happy she had to look nonchalant. If she was sad or angry or homesick, she had to appear nonchalant, bored even. Overeagerness would lessen her value and seeming not eager enough would cast her as coy. Even here, a place she should be able to express her emotions, she could not. She wondered if perhaps all the years of switching them off had somehow broken them. Perhaps that was why she couldn't decipher her own mind?

By breakfast her eyes were scratchy and swollen. She'd slept barely a wink. She'd given up and risen early to see to the animals in the barn, gather the eggs and cut enough bacon for the morning meal and the pie she had to prepare for lunch.

After returning the rest of the bacon to the icebox, she chopped wood for twenty minutes until her muscles burned and her breath came in short pants. But even looking over her shoulder constantly, even with the distraction of waiting for someone like Roger to amble along, she still couldn't get the taste of Blake from her mouth. She couldn't forget how he'd filled her senses and scrambled her thoughts. How could she face him over coffee? How would she work when he sat there in the corner of the kitchen watching her every move? It was impossibly complicated. She thought about hiding. A headache or some other feminine malady would help her avoid the whole damned situation. But she had meals to make and at some stage over the day, she would have to get close enough to check his wounds and change his dressings since the doctor had been called away.

With a deep sigh, she dropped the axe, picked up the poorly hacked timber and carried it to the kitchen through the washroom door.

Surprise filled her when she finally gathered the courage to look toward the chair perched in the corner. It was empty. All day yesterday, Blake had sat in that chair and stared at her. His gaze had drilled into her shoulder blades until she'd wanted to scream and send him to bed.

Her cheeks warmed at the vision of Blake in bed.

Sophia pinched the skin on the inside of her wrist to snap herself out of the sudden breathlessness that claimed her. To blame it on anxiety would be lying to herself.

Taking the wood through to the tap room, she stopped and nearly dropped the load at the sight that greeted her. If she hadn't been so lost in thought, she might have heard the sounds of twenty or so women milling about in the common room. Some were seated, some stood and while she stared, the main door opened to admit another two, huge baskets hanging from their elbows.

It took less than five thumps of her heart against her ribs for the room to fall completely silent. Less than four more for them all to look in her direction.

"I beg your pardon," she said, recovering quickly, but not quite quickly enough. "I didn't know anyone was in here." She sounded as if she lied, her voice wavered so.

The crowd parted at her words and Violet stepped forward. "Good morning, Sophia." Her gaze took in Sophia's filthy dress, the wood she still held in her arms and eventually returned to her face. "How is Blake fairing this morning?"

"Blake?" she repeated dumbly.

"Matthew told me he had been injured, is he all right?"

She nodded. What were all of these women doing here? Surely they weren't there to check on Blake's welfare. Perhaps they were going to help her run the inn? She almost snorted.

Violet took another step forward. "Are you all right?"

Sophia nodded again.

"She doesn't look all right," a shrill voice spoke from the back of the room.

The almost sneering way it was said snapped her back to the present, back to the splinters pushing deeper into her skin and the ache in her muscles. "I am perfectly fine, startled perhaps, but fine nonetheless. Would someone kindly tell me what you are all doing here?"

"That's none of your business," an elderly lady said, stepping forward until she stood by Violet's side.

"Annie, don't be so unkind," another lady admonished before pointing to Sophia. "You might want to put all of that down before you drop it on your feet."

Sophia bobbed her head in the lady's direction and tried to appear nonchalant as she walked down the middle of the assembled gaggle. She felt rather like Moses parting the red sea. She did feel as though the edges would fall in on her at any moment.

Silently she unloaded her burden by the hearth, dusted the front of her gown of dirt and bark, pushed her damp hair from her forehead and turned to face everyone. "Will you be staying for long?" She truly didn't mean the question to emerge the way it did, but her nerves once again threatened to destroy her. What were they all doing there?

The one called Annie puffed her chest out. "We'll stay for as long as we do every month, maybe longer."

Every month? Why hadn't Blake warned her? From the corner of her eye Sophia noticed Violet shake her head, her flushed face downcast, wringing her hands in front of her large belly.

"What do you do here every month?"

"None of your business," Annie told her.

"We sew," a fair haired woman offered from the back of the room.

She didn't bother asking any more questions after that. "I will leave you to it, then."

"Best you do," came Annie's acid reply.

Violet sighed and a number of women shook their heads, but not one stopped her from leaving the room.

Hot tears pricked her eyes as she strode down the corridor past Blake's office, through the kitchen and out into the yard where the rain still fell in sheets of freezing droplets. She heaved huge breaths of frigid air until her lungs burned but nothing stopped the tears.

This is what came from emotions. It's what happened when she was made to feel. Then all the thoughts she had pushed away for so many years were able to creep over the wall she had erected. Women hated her. What more could she expect from gently bred females taught to despise what she was.

"Sophia?" The very last thing she expected was for Blake to choose that moment to appear.

She didn't turn. Her latest humiliation didn't require yet another witness. "What do you want?"

"Are you all right?"

"I am fine. Perfectly fine." Maybe if she repeated the words enough times she may start to believe them.

"I'm sorry, I forgot to tell you they were coming."

"Forgot?" She knew what she implied with the question. Did he leave out the information to hurt her?

"The ladies use the tap on this one morning a month to make quilts and talk nonsense. With the accident and all…"

Should she believe him?

Then the realization dawned. "You heard all of that, didn't you?"

"I heard enough. I'm sorry, Sophie."

"You've nothing to be sorry for and neither do they. Everyone has an opinion and I predicted that theirs would be like this. It's one of the reasons I wasn't going to come at all. In London my lifestyle is accepted in some circles, but here…" She sighed. "Here I may as well have leprosy for all anyone will give me a chance."

"I gave you a chance."

She finally turned to look him in the eye. Is that what he thought this was? This was her chance? "You gave me a chance to prove my mettle only after losing your temper."

"That might be so, but it's a chance nonetheless."

"Why, how magnanimous of you to bestow this great honor upon me."

"Don't twist my words. You are doing a fine job here, Sophie. Not a one would argue that."

"That entire room full of women would beg to differ."

"This is where you show them what you have shown me. Show them that you are a woman and not a leper. Since when did their opinions become so important anyway?"

He was right. She did not need the approval of her sex. She did not need their disapproval to make her regret her life either. She wasn't proud to be a courtesan though she did take pride in her handling of the situation. She had arrived in London with barely more than the clothes on her back and a child of rape growing in her womb and now she had means. She was really quite wealthy, and until she had returned to Blakiston, she had been content if not happy.

How could a few remarks from an old biddy reduce her to tears? She was Sophia Martin. She straightened and lifted her chin.

"There you are," Blake murmured.

"Here I am," was her reply.

Sophia and Dominic's sister, Maria, had only met the day before and already Sophia liked the girl. At thirteen she was young enough to have not been informed about the inner workings of London's demimonde and old enough to form her own opinions. It gave Sophia hope, having just one ally. Two if she counted the fact that Maria's mother knew Sophia worked at the inn and still let her only daughter go to work.

After waiting for Maria to arrive and take over the lunch preparation, Sophia went back in to the tap to try to make peace and show the women for that day, she was in charge.

"Ladies, can I have your attention please?"

It wasn't entirely necessary for her to raise her voice, since they had all fallen silent again within moments of her arrival, but it made her feel better. As though she had rediscovered control in a situation that needed it.

"I'm afraid Blake is indisposed at the moment. Would you like refreshments? Morning tea?"

When Sophia met Annie's eyes, the woman paled. "Annie, would you care for tea?"

"I am Mrs. Simpkins to you, gel."

"Since we weren't properly introduced, I wasn't sure. Tea then?"

Sophia didn't wait for a reply as her gaze moved from one woman to the next.

"I would like tea," Violet spoke up.

The poor women was likely famished. It must have taken a great deal of courage (or discomfort) to ask. "Something to eat as well?" While she was pushing her luck, she may as well see how far she could go.

"Yes, please."

She could have hugged her sister-in-law in that moment, but had to settle for a smile in her direction. She wasn't sure why Violet was treating her less like she was diseased than she had at their dinner on her first night, but she didn't care. It was progress. "Excellent. I will only be offering once, Ladies. I have many things to do and Blake is quite ill, so I don't have time to spare."

"Ill?" came a voice from her right.

"You said he was all right," came another.

"He has some injuries, but nothing rest won't cure. For the moment he is unable to run the inn."

"So you're doing it?" This question came from a young girl. Sophia would guess her to be around twenty-one.

"I am."

A murmur rippled through the women and Sophia had to bite her lip to stop her smile. This was how to win over a room full of Blakiston women. She couldn't hope to impress them all, but perhaps showing her strengths and that she wasn't there to steal husbands would do for a beginning.

Once the tea was served and the general atmosphere less hostile, she retrieved her basket of medical supplies and went in search of Blake. Regardless of how she felt about being close to him, his health had to take precedence over her embarrassment. Perhaps after their moment in the yard, he would have forgotten the previous night's lack of self control on her part.

Raised voices from his office indicated he wasn't alone.

"You have to do something about that bridge," a male voice complained.

Sophia paused in the corridor, eager to hear what Blake's reply would be.

"There's nothing I can do about the bridge and you know it. We had this conversation last summer and the autumn before that and still the bridge stands."

"It's different this time. The creek turns into a river with every passing hour and the footings are under pressure from debris from further up stream. If something happens, half the town would be cut off."

"Only four properties line that side of the river and I'm sure they're all more than prepared for a few weeks without access to the village. The ground's higher over there than it is here, Fred. We should be more worried about the river bursting the banks and taking out our crops and us with it."

"The duke will be furious if we can't provide him with his vegetables."

"Fuck the duke," came Blake's reply. "He should have had that bridge rebuilt. If we lose, then so should he."

"A couple of the men have been talking about digging a few extra trenches for runoff in case, you know..."

Blake's sigh reached her ears. Whoever the man was, he wouldn't leave without knowing what Blake thought their next move should be.

"If the rain keeps falling, we'd all be better off moving valuables to higher ground. If that river goes, nothing will stop it, not trenches, not anything."

While the days had been relatively clear since Sophia's arrival, every evening the steady tattoo against the tavern's roof sounded well into the night.

Thank the lord the night they'd spent by the side of the road had been only freezing and not miserably wet as well.

To save Blake another question, Sophia thumped her feet against the floor boards to feign arrival and pushed the door wide.

"Oh." She stopped short and forced surprise to her face. "I didn't realize you were with someone."

"Sophie, this is Fred Thurgood. Fred, this is Sophie Martin."

Sophia summoned her brightest smile and shook the hand Fred held out for her. "A pleasure to meet you, Fred." She didn't bother correcting Blake or telling Fred that her name was Sophia.

"And you. I've heard a lot about you and your skills in the kitchen, little lady. Reckon I might stay on for lunch."

The next smile she gave Fred she didn't have to force at all. "Then stay and eat. But you must tell me what you think of the pie. I tried something new."

Blake's attention snapped to her. "New?"

She nodded and dropped her basket on his desk, her confidence returned. "You'll see."

"I don't like surprises, Sophie."

"You don't like anything, Blake."

Fred laughed and left the office with no more questions of compromised bridges or rain, but that left Sophia and Blake alone. Alone in a space that suddenly seemed far too small to hold both of their temperaments.

"You don't need to check my ribs anymore. I'm feeling much better."

"You are not a good liar," she told him as she laid out a fresh bandage and the salve the doctor had given her for his cuts and grazes. The fact it stung until Blake hissed through his teeth gave her a small measure of satisfaction.

He harrumphed, but took his shirt off when she gestured. Her breath caught and for a few moments, she forgot to breathe again.

"Does it still look so bad?" Blake asked, trying to twist his body so he could see halfway around his own back.

Sophia shook her head. It certainly wasn't his healing ribs that made heat pool in her middle when she touched his warm skin. The man was built for hard labor and it showed in every inch of his muscular frame, tight skin and tanned arms.

She was in trouble.

"Is it safe to ask what you're thinking?" Blake said quietly.

Her arms wrapped around his waist, passing the bandage from one hand to the other. The deep breath she inhaled was full of Blake's scent and it didn't give her the space she needed to come up with a good lie. "Uh, the bridge."

"The bridge?"

"I was wondering why Fred comes to you about the bridge and not the duke."

"Don't get any ideas, Sophie. He comes to me because I've lived here forever."

"He values your opinion more than that of a fellow villager."

"He, much the same as the others, couldn't make a decision if the answers were written in stone before their very eyes."

"Hmm," she murmured, unconvinced.

"What do you mean by that?"

"You need to work on your lying skills."

"Not a trait I would like to become known for," he commented. "Do you lie very often?"

"It's almost a prerequisite for living in the city. And yes, I know when to fabricate, when to reveal and when to bluff."

"You sound like the perfect card player."

"Life in London is a gamble."

"I thought it was oh-so-glamorous."

"Those were your words, not mine."

"You truly do enjoy it, don't you?"

"It?" Her hands stilled, the beat of her heart was the only sound to fill her ears.

"Living in the city."

She exhaled in a whoosh accompanied by a shaky laugh.

"What did you think I was asking you about?" Blake said, a wounded hint to his tone.

Sophia lifted her eyes to his and half shrugged.

It took a moment, but then full realization filled his eyes and he edged out of her reach. "Oh, good God, no. That I do not want to know about. Daemon is my, uh, friend of sorts. You are my... Please don't say any more words."

You are my... What? What was she? Their awkward truce and close proximity meant that their friendship might be back on track, but full friends? The way they used to be? Sophia wasn't even sure that was possible. The fact that she wanted to jump into his lap each time he took his shirt off was bad news. Add to that, the fact that his smell and taste still lingered in all her senses.

She had to think of something else. Perhaps provoke him into another fight, go back to the way things were before the accident. She certainly had to see less of his naked body and find a way to keep her hands to herself. She should have told him about Daemon then and there, but it was neither the time nor the place nor any of his business.

"I thought you said you barely knew the Duke of St. Ives?" At least that's how she remembered that conversation. She had just hit her head and had the fright of her life when the subject had been broached.

"He has stayed at the inn a time or two."

"Why?" In the few years they'd been intimate, Daemon had never mentioned traveling to Blakiston or business with either duke, current or previous.

"I'm sure I wouldn't know what goes on between one duke or another."

"You could at least try to be convincing," she chuckled. She doubted a thing happened within ten miles that Blake didn't hear of eventually. She would have to ask Daemon about his connection to the area. He didn't have to tell her everything, but she didn't like surprises and coincidences ranked even lower.

"If we're done here, I have the books to go over."

With her head in the clouds, she'd almost forgotten he sat without his shirt. She had to stop doing it to herself. Had to stop the feast for her visual senses. Perhaps keeping busy, finding something else to do with her hands, would help.

If only there was an easy way to turn off her thoughts.

By day seven of their agreement, Sophia had the kitchen running smoother than ever with the help of Dominic's sister, Maria. Despite what the townsfolk had previously thought of a courtesan cooking their dinner, her confrontation with the women seemed to have significantly thawed most attitudes. Offers for help flowed from all quarters of the village.

If only they didn't flow from the Duke of Blakiston. He was an ever-present thorn in her side. Every day he'd come and every day she'd taken tea with him, chatted, exchanged niceties until her cheeks hurt from the effort of forcing smiles. She should have tried harder to discourage him, to make it plain she didn't wish for his company, or his sly questions and barely concealed innuendo. In the back of her mind she knew she only did it because Blake hated his attention her. The moment Blakiston stepped into the tavern, Blake turned surly, childish, angry, and for some reason, Sophia enjoyed baiting him.

She did not enjoy Blakiston. He was relatively nice, on the outside, but on the inside, there was something not quite right. She had hoped talking about Daemon and the chores constantly that he would give up on her and leave, but that never happened. She could not risk making a most powerful enemy by turning him bluntly away.

And so she found herself pouring tea, talking of the weather and wishing her gown rose all the way to her neck rather than just above her décolletage. It didn't matter what she wore, the duke always looked at her as though she were naked.

"What have you planned for this evening?" he asked with his customary lecherous grin on Friday morning.

"Oh, this and that. You know how it is when you are running a business." Every chance she had, she reminded him that she worked. Whether it was the tavern or her life as a courtesan, she worked. Hard.

"Why are you running this business still? Surely with your...capabilities?" He paused, drew out the moment until Sophia wanted to grab it in her hand and shove it down his throat, and then finally he continued. "This is so beneath you."

Sophia shook her head. "It doesn't matter what station you are born to, Your Grace, when a friend is in dire need, you offer your hand and help."

"But this? What would St. Ives say?"

She nearly bit the end of her tongue off to stop the reply she longed to slap him with. She was her own woman. St. Ives had never owned her. "He would roll up his sleeves and lend a hand, I'm sure." Another lie.

"Hmm," he mumbled, picking his tea cup up and sipping loudly. He had the table manners of a pig.

"What are your plans, Your Grace?"

"There is a barn dance this evening that I thought to attend, but if you won't be there, I mightn't bother."

"Do you usually attend such events?" she asked as though it should have been beneath him. She would bet her favorite bonnet barn dances were not his thing.

"Every now and then the people must see me as a person. They have to think me their friend otherwise their loyalties will start to slide."

"Slide where?"

"It doesn't matter where. An estate is not productive if the inhabitants do not have the proper respect and fear of their leader."

She almost choked on her tea. Fear yes. Respect? Never. She'd heard the 'inhabitants' of the village talk about their duke and none of it was nice.

"You don't agree?" he asked.

"Of course, Your Grace, what would I know about the internal mechanics of village life?"

"Well, you did used to reside here, did you not?"

"That was a long time ago. I am much more accustomed to city life now."

"So you're not back to stay?"

"Only one more week, hopefully." Which was a lie but she didn't want to give Blakiston an accounting of her movements. The baby could come tomorrow or it could come in three weeks. But then what? For the moment Matthew wanted her there, but what about after the birth? It's not as if Matthew or Violet would need her. Blake, however, did. He still couldn't lift a pot or chop fire wood or make beds. But even her usefulness at the inn would come to end when he was healed.

"St. Ives will be thrilled to have you back, I'm sure."

The statement held more questions than any other Blakiston had uttered so far and she wondered whether to answer or feign innocence.

"I'm sorry, I don't mean to pry or be impertinent."

She almost snorted.

"You have to understand I'm curious to know what he thinks of his lady love rusticating in the country while he stalks around the city on his own."

"I hardly think one such as St. Ives stalks, Your Grace. As to our understanding, that's none of your business or anyone else's." Even though most of the ton thought it theirs. Her name had been mentioned so many times in the gossip pages, she'd given up writing angry letters to the editor. She was very happy the columnists hadn't yet heard the news that she and St. Ives had parted ways. She had a feeling Blakiston would have been so much more dogged in his pursuit of her if he had been armed with the knowledge.

"I understand. I'm sorry to pry. Please say you'll accompany me to the dance."

"Too late, Blakiston. Sophie has agreed to accompany me to the dance."

Blake stepped into the room without knocking on the closed door first. "I have?" she asked.

"Provided you finish the chores. We can't have you enjoying yourself too much."

Her jaw dropped and she just stared. Was he serious or was he baiting the duke to rise to her aid?

The duke didn't bother standing, just looked Blake up and down and twisted his lips. "You don't look injured at all."

"And you don't look like a barn dancer."

Blakiston shrugged. "A man can change his habits, especially when there is a beautiful woman involved."

"Perhaps," Blake mused.

He looked as if he would speak again, but Sophia beat him to it. "I'm afraid you'll have to excuse me, gentlemen. There are chores to be done if I'm to dance this evening."

Over her dead body. She would drag out the chores until the rooster crowed on Sunday if she had to.

Barn dances and public engagements with women and children were not places she wanted to be. Blake and Blakiston fighting over her as though she were a trophy to be had and men staring at her would only add to her discomfort. She would probably trip over her own feet and break her neck. There would be no dancing for her. Not with a tavern owner or a duke.

Thirteen

"I think I left something on the stove, we had better turn around and check." Words Sophia had never thought to utter under usual circumstances. Her knees almost knocked together beneath her dull grey gown, she was so frightened.

"You did not leave anything on the stove. You didn't leave the axe anywhere near the path where someone could fall over it in the dark and for the last time, the piglets will not starve if you are not there."

Sophia grimaced. She was out of excuses but so far none of them had worked anyway.

In the end, she'd dressed in her plainest gown, tied her hair back in a simple knot, squared her shoulders and stepped from her room.

When she considered how terrified she was on the carriage ride to Blakiston, how she feared a pitchfork-bearing, stone-throwing crowd, this was worse. Far worse. Even though Blake had only just handed her down from the cart, Sophia already felt the eyes of the judgmental, the frowns of the disapproving and the sharp sting of rejection.

She inhaled until she felt it all the way to her stomach and then exhaled slowly.

"You will be fine. You are Sophie Martin. If you remember that, you will be more than fine." Blake squeezed her hand and towed her toward a barn where music, laughter and light spilled out into the wet night. As much as she didn't want to go inside, they couldn't stand there waiting for it to rain. Even the elements worked against her.

"I can't do this, Blake."

"Can't go into a room full of people enjoying themselves? Or can't be Sophie Martin?"

She bit her bottom lip. She wasn't Sophie Martin anymore and they both knew it. She was, however, no longer Sophia Martin either. She hovered somewhere in the middle of an e and an a.

Of one fact she was most certain. She wasn't a frightened mouse. She was a woman who had fled her domineering, greedy father to start her life anew still bleeding and battered from the ordeal. She was a woman who stood on her own two feet and didn't let anyone or anything concern her. Least of all a silly little barn dance.

Her heart skipped a beat.

It didn't matter how many times she told herself, she couldn't quite believe the words.

As Blake pulled her through the wide doorway, Sophie tried to pull back, tried to come up with a plan, another excuse, anything, but by then it was too late.

It seemed every face in the room turned toward her, her breath hitched, her mouth dried and she actually flinched, hiding her face behind Blake's shoulder. She couldn't even think of the number she was up to.

Before she had a chance to process what happened, why no stone bit her skin, why no nasty whispers reached her ears, she was folded into the embrace of more women than she could count. Men kissed her cheeks, ladies squeezed her hand and a whole village thanked her for being there for Blake when he needed help. Some thanked her for keeping Blake out of the kitchen, some thanked her for cooking delicious meals and others thanked her for a friendly smile over a soup bowl. Even Annie smiled in her direction.

Finally, after being passed around the room, she ended up next to her brother.

"Did you do this?" Sophie asked.

"I had nothing to do with any of it."

"It must have been Blake then?"

"You still can't see it can you?"

"See what?" She turned to him, to search his face for that which he hadn't said, but then Blake brought a very heavily pregnant Violet to join their conversation.

She had to change the subject before she blushed. "Violet, Matthew let you come?"

Matthew groaned, "Not you too."

"We reached a compromise," Violet said. "This is the last time I will be allowed to leave the house. For anything."

"Just until the child is born and then you can go anywhere you want. I just can't have you out of my sight in case anything happens." Matthew's eyes held so much love, so much concern, Sophie had to look away.

Violet spoiled for an argument. "Women have borne children in fields in the open since the dawn of time. Mary lay down in a dirty barn. In other countries babies are born in filthy huts on the floor, on the decks of ships and worse. I will be fine and so will our child."

"I don't think you will win this fight, Matty." Blake clapped his friend on the shoulder hard enough to warn him to drop it and Sophie coughed to cover her laughter. "The women have the upper hand."

"Shall we dance?" Blake's eyes told her he wanted to, but she wasn't sure if he asked because he didn't want her to stand with her back to the wall all night. There wasn't a man here whose wife would let him dance with her, good wishes notwithstanding.

"Let me ask again. Sophie, I want to dance with you."

"That wasn't a question," she murmured as the blush she feared warmed her cheeks.

"Then I don't need you to say yes." With that, he took her hand and dragged her to the middle of the straw covered floor, her hem twisting about her ankles.

"You shouldn't do this," she told him.

"Why not?"

"You are supposed to be injured, for one."

He shrugged. "I feel much better already."

The music began and in all the places, of all the songs, it was a waltz. In a barn. In the country.

As the first lilting strains filled the timber barn, Blake stepped toward her, took her hand in his and with his other, pulled her toward him, closer and then closer again. "You're safe here. Have fun."

Right now, right there, everything was perfect. Or perhaps that was the ale talking. She'd lost count of those too. As Blake swung her from one end of the crowd to the other, the courtesan extraordinaire actually laughed with real pleasure. She didn't have to force merriment on this night. The simple knot that tethered her curls to her nape loosened until her black hair shook free and swished around her shoulders and still she laughed.

She was gorgeous. Blake couldn't tell her in words just how much she had helped him over the last week but he could make sure she had a night of fun. Everywhere he looked he saw his friends delighted at the way she had rushed to his aid. More than cooking and running his inn, she'd kept everyone happy until he was better and could return to doing what he enjoyed. He owed her this night.

His problem now was, he loved having her there. He enjoyed watching Sophie work. He wasn't taking a perverse satisfaction out of seeing her break her back; Dominic was doing all the heavy lifting, but it was nice to see the pleasure in her smile when a recipe came together or when she'd helped a sow deliver her piglets.

Blake tamped down that line of thought. He'd fallen in love with her once before and it was not going to happen again. It couldn't. He'd only just survived when she'd left by putting one foot in front of the other, taking more beatings for his 'soft' heart and sullenness. Until he'd grown bigger than his uncle. By then he was beyond being upset. Blake long ago had hardened his heart to love, to family and to women. They were nothing but trouble.

Beautiful trouble, he thought as he watched the curve of Sophie's throat as she laughed, felt the whisper of her silky hair over his hand when he turned her.

"May I cut in?"

Blake stopped so suddenly, he had to tighten his grip on his dance partner to stop her from falling to the floor. "Don't you have someone else to annoy, Blakiston?"

"It doesn't appear so, no."

Blake dropped Sophie's hand, his own fist clenched, ready to set the duke on his arse for interrupting possibly the best moment of his life. When Blakiston's mouth stretched into a vile grin, Blake wanted to wipe it from his face with the back of his hand. Or perhaps a pistol. At dawn.

"Blake," Sophie warned. "Be nice."

"Yes, Blake, be nice."

A gentle squeeze by Sophie and he stepped away. To hit a duke in front of so many witnesses would leave his inn without an owner for a lot longer than bruised ribs had. "As long as the lady approves." The words left a sour taste in his mouth.

"Of course, Your Grace."

The stiffness in her spine when Blakiston took her fingers in his almost made Blake feel better but the emptiness in his hands, in the circle of his arms, made him seek the ale cask and a very big cup. Leave it to Blakiston to ruin a perfectly good evening with his very presence.

"You know you could have given him one. No one here would have complained or borne witness."

Blake turned to Matthew and raised his now full cup. "Thank you, but I wouldn't give him the satisfaction. Anyway, Sophie can dance with whomever she pleases."

"You and I both know he doesn't please her in the least."

"I don't care either way." As the lie left his lips, try as he might, he could not bring himself to look away from the couple they made. Her life in London depended on suitors like him, on the income and the trinkets they could provide.

Every time he began to see her as simply a woman, something or someone had to remind him that she was more than that.

What really bothered him was that he needed the reminder at all.

To enjoy oneself at a London ball or ton event meant gluing a smile to one's lips and if one made it through the night of warm champagne and stale food without someone making a snide remark, then it was also deemed a success. Sophie had smiled so much on this one night that her face felt as though it might crack. The only time she had to force the action was in the arms of that disgusting toad, Blakiston. The sooner his attention was caught by some fleeting chit or more interesting gossip, the better!

As soon as her dance with him, where he squashed her toes not once, not twice but three times, was over, Sophie rushed back to the table where Blake and Matthew sat and squirmed her way in between the two large men. She suddenly felt the need to be protected. One look in Blakiston's direction and the calculating way he watched her told all present that he had more than an interest in her dancing.

She reached forward, took Blake's mug from his fingers and gulped the remaining contents.

"Thirsty?" he asked, his tone heavy with sarcasm.

"Why does he pay so much attention to me?"

Blake and Matthew shot her identical knowing frowns.

"Apart from that," she muttered. "I have done all I can short of outright asking him to leave and still he pursues." She tapped the cup on the table and stared at Blake until he refilled it from a jug.

"Why don't you say the words then? Even a man as thick as Charles would get the message if you made it clear."

She looked at her brother and returned his frown before gulping more of the sweet ale. "I can't be so rude to a duke, Matthew."

"I would," Blake said. "Did you want me to tell him to leave off?"

"I hardly think he would take well to that. No. I will be gone soon and the duke's affections will be taken with something or someone else. I'm sure he has horseflesh or a young maid to salivate over."

"I hear he's selling the old duke's horses in the next few days."

"To whom?"

Blake and Matthew shrugged, but Sophie thought she detected a hint of uneasiness in the two. "Then why? Surely he doesn't need the money?"

"Don't know that either," Matthew admitted. "We aren't involved in the inner workings of the estate and anyone who is won't speak of the business. They're terrified they'll lose their positions."

"Perhaps it *is* about the money then? Not much else would have the staff as scared as they are. Especially not him." Blake pointed to where the duke had missed his mouth with his cup and spilled the contents down the front of his jacket.

The men burst into laughter and once again, Sophie relaxed. Finally, even though the divide between them was wide, she began to feel as though she was home.

As the duke flicked ale from his coat, he cast them a foul look before disappearing into the rainy night. Piercing her bubble of contentment was the reminder that theirs were precarious positions and upsetting a duke wasn't going to help anyone.

Fourteen

S ophie had never felt as small or delicate or fragile as she did tonight. Even in her life as Sophia, she couldn't recall a time when she'd felt likely to shatter at the first fumble. Each time she danced with Blake, he held her as though one wrong move would upset the newfound balance they'd achieved. Perhaps it was the ale talking rather than her own mind, but she almost wished he would upset the balance.

There was only a small part of her that occasionally yearned for another's touch, for the closeness only a lover could provide, and it was howling tonight for Blake to forget manners, his position and hers, and take her in his arms.

With every mouthful of the coarse ale, Sophie remembered what it was like that morning on the cold road in the middle of nowhere.

Blake's hands had lit a spark in her belly and if she had to delve deep, right into her inner woman, she would admit that some of the anger she'd felt before climbing into Blakiston's carriage was that she'd liked it.

It had taken her years to accept a man's touch without feeling as though he was going to beat her or not take no for an answer. Years more of pretending that she felt pleasure when all she was really capable of feeling was revulsion and pain. Noah had been so patient and gentle, instructing her how to use her control as a woman to ensure her safety. It was in that time that she had discovered how powerful she was as a desirable woman. There were still times she acted braver than she felt, but those times were few now. Well, they had been before she'd returned.

You could trust Blake not to hurt you.

He would never hurt her in the physical sense, of that she was sure, but Blake abhorred her. She wondered what it would take for him to forget all that and forgive her, to move on. She would like to know that he was her friend again and that her decisions were her own to make.

You are accepted here, that tiny voice in her mind whispered. Yes, but only because she had come to Blake's aid. There was a real difference between being accepted and being wanted. She frowned. A big difference indeed.

"What are you thinking about?" Blake asked, his voice making her jump.

"Only how much fun this was tonight." And in that admission there were no lies. To dance, to laugh, to chat with women about recipes and meals and gowns, to find the stone throwers replaced by friendly faces almost made her teary.

Blake must have truly learned to read minds when he said, "You've made friends tonight, Sophie."

She shook her head. "I wouldn't go that far."

He didn't comment further, only took her hand in his and placed a light kiss on the back. "Are you ready to head back?"

Sophie stared at her hand, her small pale fingers entwined with his as heat shot up her arm. All she could do was nod. She felt like a sparrow being led by a hawk, not to her demise but to safety. They said their goodbyes even though Matthew and Violet had left hours before and in a few minutes were perched on the bench seat of the cart making their way back to the inn.

"You looked as if you were having fun," Blake said once the mare found her footing and rhythm.

"I was, I mean I did. It was nice." Why did she have to feel nervous now? She'd been alone with him so many times, but with the ale flowing in her veins and lust warming her middle, she was in trouble.

She was saved from any further conversation right then when the heavens opened with a deafening crack of thunder and let its full fury rain down in fat, cold droplets.

The journey back usually only took about twenty minutes, but it was hard to see and soon the horse who wasn't really familiar with pulling a small load, slipped and slid in the mud so they had to slow their pace even more.

Sophie shivered and wrapped her arms about herself. She should have insisted they take her carriage, but there wasn't anyone to drive it. Her own driver had left on the mail coach to await word from her as to when she wanted to return to London.

"Come closer," Blake yelled over the onslaught, and when she didn't respond, put his arm around her and pulled her close so she wasn't quite sheltered from the rain but could at least share in some of his heat.

She was forced to lean against him for the rest of the slow, silent journey back. She breathed a sigh of relief (at least she thought it was relief) when the lantern light outside the barn came into view.

"I'm going to rub the horse down and put her in a pen. Can you go to the bar and get the bottle of brandy?"

"Brandy?" she shivered as he leaned away from her. He wanted more alcohol?

"I'm frozen, Sophie, the brandy will warm us."

The last thing either of them needed was to spend a week in bed with a fever, so she nodded, but she couldn't seem to move. Her fingers were numb and her legs had stiffened.

The warmth of the barn enveloped them as soon as they entered and Blake jumped down to close the doors. He came to her side of the carriage and put his arms out for her. "I know it's cold, but you need to move. You need to get out of those wet clothes."

That did it and the arrogant man knew it. The way he slowed his words and then winked made her face warm. Shuffling to end of the seat, she held her arms out and he caught her and lowered her to the floor slowly. When she had her balance, he let her go and went to see to the horse, leaving her feeling strangely bereft. She had thought that was the moment when he would kiss her. He had her in his hands, she was pliant, willing, eager even, and then he'd turned away without so much as a blink.

"Sophie," he called over his shoulder, "the brandy!"

She blinked once, twice, then moved. Brandy. From the bar. One foot in front of the other. Concentrate. But there was only enough room in her brain tonight for what she wanted and when could she have it. As she fumbled with the door to the kitchens and then with a flint to light a candle, her fingers shaking, her heavy gown dripping, she damned her libido to the deepest—warmest—pits of hell.

Not everyone was cut out to be a courtesan and it certainly wasn't the occupation she would have chosen under normal circumstances, but with the right protector and the right to choose a protector, she could enjoy herself, let her guard down and be cared for. So long as she kept the terrible memories locked tight behind the wall, she could find her pleasure as Noah had shown her.

"I quite like pleasure," she said under her breath as she reached for the brandy bottle and two glasses.

"What are you muttering about?"

She whirled to find Blake close, oh so close, and snapped her mouth shut. Her thoughts were slow to respond and frantically she looked around for an answer. She held the glass up in her hands and tipped the contents down her throat. "Brandy. I happen to like brandy very much and be damned who knows it." Damn her feeble, sex-deprived mind.

"Can't stand it myself, but there's nothing better for firing your blood and warming you from the inside out." He gulped down the first glass, her glass, his mouth touching where hers had.

She licked her lips, tasted the brandy there and wanted... Something. Companionship? A friend? More? Her brain was too sluggish to completely comprehend anything.

"What?" he asked as he poured more from the bottle. "Do I look like a drowned rat?"

She couldn't get her mouth to move, she couldn't get anything to move. But then she shivered again and fat water droplets landed at her feet with an audible splash.

"Damn it, why are we standing here? I laid the fire in your room before we left."

Her room? She wasn't sure that was a good idea at all, but before she could protest, Blake took her hand again in one of his, the bottle and a glass in the other and towed her up the stairs. He didn't wait on the landing, didn't wait for her to go inside to bid her a goodnight. He let go of her hand long enough to throw the door open and then pulled her through into the warmth.

He pushed her to stand in front of the fire, poured another brandy and passed the glass to her. "Drink."

She was beyond saying no. She was beyond any thought as the glow from the fire showed where his fine shirt had become transparent in the wet, outlining every corded muscle, every dip and hollow of his chest and abdomen. She remembered the warmth of his skin as she'd checked him over for injuries after the accident. He was always so warm. She licked her lips again and lifted the glass, draining the contents in two swallows.

"Take your clothes off."

Her gaze finally snapped from his stomach to his eyes. Had he really just said...?

"Sophie, you are going to catch your death, now take your clothes off." He went to the armoire and took out two robes. One was the rich red she had curled in up a few times because it was so large and warm and the other was hers. A white, almost transparent flimsy material that was hardly worthy of the label robe.

"Sophie, move."

Her actions were shaky, erratic and rough, but she soon had every button undone down the front and slowly the feeling came back to her fingers with the movement. She leaned down to take the hem in her hands, pulled, dragged the heavy material up, but then as she stood with her arms over her head, the wet bodice stuck to her body, the hem in her hands, she found herself stuck.

By the time the fire roared and heat blasted from the hearth, Blake had stripped all of his clothes off and pulled on the red robe he'd accidentally left in his room. This room. The one where she now slept.

The tinkle of Sophie's giggle reached his ears and he turned to see what she laughed at. In his fuzzy, ale-filled mind, he'd almost forgotten her presence. Almost. Except lately he couldn't forget she was there. Everywhere. In his kitchen, in his dining room, in his bed—since he'd given her his room—and in his life. Her laugh, her smile, her scent--she was everywhere. Right now, she stood before the fire, her dress in the air, and she laughed. Not the practiced, sophisticated laugh of a courtesan. She laughed like Sophie. Like she hadn't a care in the world.

"Are you stuck or trying to tempt me with your petticoats?"

Sophie's giggles became muffled as she tried again to lift the wet skirts over her head with another tug.

"Would you like me to help you?" he asked, his fingers itching to undress her.

"Please."

She stopped struggling and just stood there. He stepped closed, willed his hands to remember he only helped. They were friends and that was it.

Friends.

He did not want to ruin anything between them by letting his prick do the thinking.

But think it did. So much of his blood traveled south that he almost felt lightheaded.

Once he'd removed the heavy gown, she stood in a shift, no corset, and her petticoats. The shift was made of the palest, most translucent fabric he'd ever seen. He didn't even have a word for it beyond delicate. Perhaps fragile. Just like her.

He turned away as she peeked from beneath long dark lashes. If she saw the longing in his eyes he would frighten her. He should leave her be, but hers was the only fire already lit. His small temporary room would take some time to warm up and with the twinge in his ribs and the ache in his leg, he couldn't take the cold. At least that's the story he told himself. He hadn't been in a weakened state for at least two days. But she didn't know that. He enjoyed the way she fussed when she thought he did too much. He couldn't remember a time in his life when someone had fussed over him. Not even his mother had shown him much love before throwing him into the arms of a drunkard.

Sophie needed to fuss as much as he needed to see her do it. It kept her mind off darker matters. She could deny her worries until it snowed in hell, but she had her fair share and when she thought no one looked, she brooded. So he made her think he was still too injured to work.

He stepped wrong with his aching leg while hanging her dress on a peg on the back of the door and nearly faltered. He must have drunk more than he thought. Before he'd completed the thought, Sophie was under his shoulder, her small body supporting his large one and damn him if he didn't smile like an idiot.

"I'm all right," he assured her.

"You are not. Why did you not tell me your leg pains you also?"

Blame the ale, blame the lack of blood to his brain or the cold, but before he knew what happened, his mouth opened and he said, "It's not my leg that pains me." But it wasn't only the words he'd stupidly said, it was the way he said them that made Sophie pause, one hand at his back and the other on his chest, only the red robe's lapel between his skin and hers.

"Oh?" she hesitated, her gaze on the floor. "Is it your ribs?"

The very stupidest thing he could do was to admit the real reason for his current state. And if she didn't get her hands off his person in the next five seconds, words wouldn't be needed at all. "Yes."

"Well, you need to sit down and get warm. Shivering will hardly do you any good."

He let her lead him to the chair in front of the fire, his conscience not nearly as heavy as his growing erection.

"Close your eyes," she said, her hands on the ties of her petticoats.

Gladly, he thought as he dipped his head and closed his eyes. It would be the end of his straining control if he were to see any more skin than she already showed. He heard the rustle and slap of fabric and bit down on his bottom lip. Hard.

"Damnation," she swore.

Damnation indeed. Blake sighed. "Are you all right?"

"Yes. No. Damn these cold fingers."

"Do you need help?" He should have bitten his tongue off.

"I don't think that's a good idea."

He gave her a moment and when her litany of curses continued, he opened his eyes and lifted his head. Big mistake. Huge mistake.

Sophie stood before the fire, her back to the warming flames, her fingers at the tiny buttons that ran from the valley of her breasts almost to where he imagined her navel. It would have been marginally bearable but for the fact that the wet fabric was so sheer that he could see the tiny mole to the left of one dusky nipple.

She must have felt his stare. When she looked up, her blue eyes deepened and her hands moved to cover her chest. This just presented more problems. Only one of a good many. Now she cupped her breasts—her cheeks flushed, her eyes sparkled, her skin glistened. She looked every part the siren.

"I think you do require assistance."

As she shook her head, wet hair slid over her bare shoulders and left tiny droplets on her pale skin. "I don't. You need to sit...and...and...close your eyes."

If there had been any strength behind the command he would have sat back down and tore his gaze from her form. But there wasn't. Thank God.

He stepped toward her, waited for her to say no, to put a stop to what they both knew was the inevitable next step. Because he laid some claim to manners still, he gave her one more chance. "Will you let me help you?"

"It's not a good idea," she whispered.

"Please?" He took another step. Here he could breathe her in. Fresh rain and the soap she used to wash her hair heightened his awareness. Not that it needed it. It was almost as if the world outside this room ceased to exist the moment he'd closed the door. "Sophie?"

Slowly, so slowly that he nearly swallowed his tongue, her hands dropped to her sides, her chin rose and she nodded.

"You have to be sure," he said as he took that final step.

"I'm sure."

Fifteen

Truth be told, Sophie shivered less from the cold than the anticipation. It ran from her neck, down her spine, into her legs, so she felt it clear to her feet. She had to resist the urge to curl her toes against the smooth timber boards.

Right here, right now, she wanted Blake and no other man would do. She'd had to endure his close proximity for a week, touch his skin to check his wounds, tolerate his eyes on her every move. The flex and shift of his muscles fascinated her and she wanted to know how his body would react when he leaned over her, pressed her into the mattress and drove her to oblivion.

It was a bad idea. He didn't even like her. But none of that mattered when he placed both of his huge warm hands against her flushed cheeks, tipped her head back and touched his lips to hers. At first his kiss was gentle, protective, caring; he didn't crowd or push her.

She sighed again and leaned into him. He treated her with such reverence and she wanted to let him, but when she touched her tongue to his, the fire grew in her belly to a raging inferno and she did something no courtesan should ever do. She lost control.

Wrapping her arms around his neck and threading her fingers into his hair she pressed her body to his, the material of his robe the only blockade.

Blake tasted of brandy and rain and all things good, but kissing wasn't enough. She'd dreamed of being in his arms ever since the morning they'd woken on the road. As much as she'd been shocked and then angry, she couldn't help but think how far it could have gone if their angry words hadn't ruined everything. The possibilities had kept her up night after night until she'd had to pace in the cold to dampen her desires.

"Do you know how many times I've thought about this?" she finally admitted.

His hands paused on the curve of her lower back. "How many?"

She let go of him and stepped back a half pace. She took the ends of the robe's tie in her fingers and gave it a pull until the knot unraveled. "I lost count."

"That many?" Blake's eyes glazed over and his intent stare shifted from her mouth to her hands. The vagueness in his question said she had his full attention.

"Hmm. Have you thought about it?" She slid the material over an inch, teasing, taunting, tempting.

"That and more."

"How did it go in your dreams?"

"I think even you are a little too innocent to hear about my dreams, Sophie."

She laughed. "Why, Blake, I do believe that's the nicest thing you've ever said to me."

He pushed her hands aside. "And I do believe the time for speaking has come and gone."

Before Sophie could fill the space with more nervous chatter, Blake pressed his mouth to hers and she forgot every moment that had come before the perfectness of this one. It was almost as if he poured his very heart into the kiss.

Together they stepped back, little tiny steps so as not to break contact. Her hands were everywhere as she traced the contours of his shoulders, his back, his neck. His hands moved over her hips, over her buttocks to tighten on her thighs, to lift her so she straddled his sex where they stood. God, he was strong. "Wait," she managed between drugging kisses. "I want to see..."

"You've seen it all before," he groaned.

Sophie pushed against his chest until she was back on her feet. "Humor me."

With fast jerky movements, Blake ripped the robe from his shoulders and dropped it to the floor. "There, happy now?" he teased, his tone impatient.

"Not yet." She stepped forward again, her gaze low as her hands skimmed the muscles of his stomach until they reached their goal. As lightly as she could with her fingers still numb with cold, she stroked and then cupped him. Her other hand, she wrapped around his length and tightened her grip.

"Wait," he murmured, his voice tight with tension. "It's not fair for me to be naked and not you."

"I would never want to be accused of unfair play."

Blake chuckled as he reached for her hem, the last barrier between them and certain pleasure. It was also the last barrier between friends and lovers. Sophie wanted it gone. She lifted her arms.

Her chemise landed on the floor by the door with a slap, but they both ignored it. Blake's hands rose to mold her curves from her hips up to her breasts and back to her bottom. His callused palms did scratch, but they only served to heighten the moment, to increase the urgency, her response was instantaneous. She wrapped her arms around his neck again and pulled him until their lips crashed at the same time their bodies did. Furious need drove her as she all but climbed his body until she once again straddled him, his hands on her bottom to hold her up as he walked the last few steps toward the closest wall. Her back slammed into the cold timber and she laughed.

"God, I'm sorry. I don't want to hurt you."

Blake went to pull back, but Sophie tightened her legs, linked her ankles and nipped his bottom lip. "I'm not going to break. I can handle anything you throw at me."

His mouth curved into a smile of challenge. "Anything?"

"Give it your best, I promise I can keep up."

With a flex of his fingers, he parted her, pulled back and eased in until she felt so filled with him, so complete it was almost scary.

A moan crept from her lips and her head fell back.

"Are you still with me?" he asked, fingers tightening, kneading, stoking the fire, the lust between them.

"Mmm-hmm. I think so." She gave a wriggle and took him even deeper. "Good God."

He chuckled, but when she finally met his gaze, the strain was evident. He was holding back, holding still, protecting her.

"Too late to retreat," she whispered.

"I wouldn't dream of it." Blake shook his head and withdrew a fraction. "But I think we would both be more comfortable on the bed."

Before she could argue, he swung her around and, as one, they dropped to the warm quilted top. As he leaned on his hands over her, the fire light glistening over his body, Sophie felt her first hint of panic. He was so big, he blocked out the rest of the room as his muscles corded and bunched beneath her hands as she ran them up and down, from shoulder to wrist and back again. Much the same as he did to her.

When her gaze lifted to his, he watched her, intent, unnerving. He didn't move at all, not even a twitch. "What is it?"

"Nothing, I..." She shook her head to dispel the awful memories trying to push through the lust.

"I would never hurt you Sophie, if you want to stop, you have only to say the word."

She linked her ankles tighter. "I don't want you to stop, it's just...I..."

"Spit it out, woman."

She glared up at him. "I am always on top."

His brows rose in question, but she shook her head. "But I actually quite like it here."

"Only like?" came his reply. "Perhaps I need to try harder?" He withdrew almost all the way and then eased back in.

Once again he stopped her answering words with his mouth and this time she let him. Slowly, so slowly it almost hurt, he withdrew and then slid back in, the friction causing a slow burn inside her as he repeated the action over and over.

In her hazy mind, she realized he was making love to her. This was no furious coupling such that her body wanted. He was going to take his time and drive her crazy. Tears burned her eyes so she closed them, moved with him, against him. After a few minutes of the sweet torture, her body screamed for release and she needed to take control. Tensing her legs and arms, she pushed until he rolled, taking her with him.

"My methods don't please you?" he asked with a naughty twinkle in his eye.

She leaned down and kissed him, nipped his jaw, licked the side of his neck, all the while pushing down and grinding her pelvis against his. "You might like things my way."

She lifted, her inner muscles tensed, and then she sank down. If he could tease her by taking it slow, she could do the same.

He sat up, wrapped his arms around her and took a hardened nipple deep into his mouth, flicking the peak with his tongue until she was sorry she didn't beg him to finish. Unless that's what he waited for? She wasn't ashamed. "Please, Blake."

"You wanted control, minx."

"Take it back. Take me." For once, she didn't want to be the one in control. When had he wrested that kind of trust from her?

With a growl, his arms locked behind her back and he flipped so he was once again on top, in control, the look of determination on his face sent a thrill through her. This is what she waited for.

"God, but you're sweet," he whispered, placing feather-light kisses along her shoulder as he withdrew and then slammed back home.

There was no time to answer, no time to argue about her sweetness, about who had control, no time for thoughts of trust or anything else as pleasure built and built inside her. It was hard enough to breathe let alone form words.

Words were unnecessary anyway. Especially between them.

Sophie's head pounded. Her tongue lay heavy in her dry mouth. She swallowed slowly and worked to move the lump in her throat. Liquor and she had never mixed well and it seemed last night was no different. A groan from the bed next to her made her freeze to the spot, her eyes still closed. So it hadn't been a dream? She was terrified to open her eyelids not just because she knew the light would be blinding, but what would she say to Blake?

What could she say? The only thing she knew was that she ached in places that had never ached before. Ever.

Her cheeks warmed at the memories, but even as her body tingled, her mind rebelled. What did this mean for their future?

She shook her head. They didn't have a future. Both had been drunk and naked. Neither would have been able to walk away from that. She felt a little better knowing it wasn't her fault even though she had been the one to instigate it. Sort of.

"I know you're awake." Despite the gravity of what they'd done, his husky morning voice sent shivers through her body.

"No I'm not," she replied, her eyes still closed and her own voice pitched lower than she'd intended. Maybe if she ignored him, he'd go away. Her dignity needed it in that moment.

"You'll have to face me eventually, Sophie. I'm not going anywhere."

That's what she was afraid of. She sighed and opened her eyes, squinting for a moment against the harshness of the bright sunshine streaming in through the open curtains. "Good morning." It seemed the only appropriate response.

He seemed to assess her, but for what she had no idea. And when had he dressed? She was normally such a light sleeper. It was scary that she hadn't woken. Scarier still that she could almost imagine the last fourteen years had been a nightmare and she'd finally woken to the life she was meant to lead. With him.

"Are you all right?" Blake asked, his gaze full of concern as he leaned over her, his hair falling over his brow. She longed to reach up and run her fingers through it.

"I'm quite fine, thank you. And you? Your ribs seem to be recovering well." She injected just a touch of wry accusation into her tone when she remembered how miraculously he'd healed last night. They'd left for the dance with him limping a little and favoring his right arm still, but when he'd thrust into her body, held himself poised above her, held her tight, it was evident his injuries weren't as bad as he'd made them seem. "Why didn't you tell me you were better?"

He shrugged. "I didn't want to do too much too soon."

He lied, but she let him. That grin that was so ingrained in him stretched his lips and she wanted him to lean down and press his mouth to hers. But that was a bad idea. A terrible idea. "What do we do now?"

"Now?"

She pulled the bed coverings tighter over her chest and sat up forcing him to do the same. "Where do we go from here?"

"I'm going to the kitchen to get started on breakfast. I'm due at a town meeting about the bridge at midday."

"We aren't going to discuss what happened here?"

"I think we both know what happened here."

Sophie wasn't sure if he was being deliberately obtuse or stubbornly pigheaded. Maybe both. "And I think we need to talk about it. About last night as well."

"Are they two different events?"

Sophie would have slammed her hands down on her hips if she hadn't held the sheets in a death grip. His flippancy fuelled her anger as she recalled more and more of the night before. "You know what I'm talking about. The villagers are miserable under Blakiston's poor excuse for a rule."

"Oh that." His gaze dropped and he stood, giving her his broad back.

"Yes that. What are you doing about the high taxes and levies?"

"What can I do? If you think he'll listen to me, then you have rocks in your head."

"So you'll stand by and let your people be bullied?" She climbed from the bed and stood, only a blanket and sheet to hide behind.

He spun to face her, fury glittered in his eyes. "They aren't my people, Sophie."

"You may not be the legal duke, but they look to you. They respect your opinion and treasure your advice. You could go to Blakiston, you could get him to act."

"You are too romantic in your observations. They ask me because I know this area better than most. They ask me because they fear my temper, not because they see me as a bastard duke."

"You could have been a real duke."

"I am a bastard, not a duke. Is that what this is about? Do you wish me a duke, Sophie? Do you feel as though you lowered yourself by sleeping with a commoner and a farmer at that? Should I pay you or was that one free?"

Deep inside her chest, Sophie's heart gave one thump and then an eternity later, another, and then split in two. "That's not fair. Not fair to me or to you."

"Then why did you do it?"

"I slept with you because I wanted to. Because I stupidly believed that the man you are would be enough for me. But you've just proved you haven't changed one bit. All the work I've done, all the mornings, all the... It seems *you're* the one who feels he has sunk low, not me."

"I didn't mean it like that. Jesus, Sophie, you bring out the worst in me every time I'm near you."

Her eyes pricked and burned and it was hard to push the words out. "I want you to go."

"I will but before I do, will you tell me what is so special about your duke?"

"You won't understand. You don't understand anything I try to tell you."

"So now I'm ignorant, too?" He stalked toward her.

She stepped back but not far enough, she couldn't get away from his fury, the pain in his eyes and the rigidity of his body. They'd had this conversation already. She doubted he would listen any better now than he had then.

"Will any title do or does it have to be a duke? Is a deep purse enough? A hunting lodge and mansion on Mayfair too? What is it that makes your callers so much better than me?"

"That's the part you'll never understand." Sophie tried to remain calm, tried to leash her temper and not enter yet another fray with him. But it was too late. It was inevitable. "It has nothing to do with titles, purses, hounds or horseflesh. Daemon treats me like a lady even though I'm as far from it as any woman can get. When he looks at me, he sees only me. He doesn't see my occupation, he doesn't see the men who have gone before him, he doesn't even care about the dress I wear or the house I live in. He cares about me. Sophia Martin. Not the courtesan, but the woman. That is the part you will never understand.

You've been so caught up on the ways in which I have changed that you haven't actually seen the changes. This is who I am, Blake Vale. This is the woman I have become and this is the woman I want to be. St. Ives accepted that and never tried to change me. He never made me feel filthy. That is the difference between a duke and a tavern owner, between Daemon and you. He is a gentleman down to his very soul. You are a bastard through and though."

Her chest heaved with the effort to breathe. Her hands clenched until her nails bit into the palms of her hands leaving crescent moons in their wake. She should take back her words. She should never have spoken them to start with, yet there they were, out in the open, like a ravenous wolf who wants only to eat the hearts of the pained and lonely for his breakfast. Tears burned her eyes, but she wouldn't give him the satisfaction of seeing them fall.

"I understand."

Sophie slowly calmed, as if his answering words had popped the bubble of her anger. Blake's shoulders slumped and for a moment she had to bite her lip against an apology. What had started out as a pleasant evening of companionship and passion had ended in pistols at dawn after all. She wondered who had won.

"If it means anything to you, I am sorry."

God, why did he have to punish her so? And why did she have to believe he meant what he said? "You should go." Before he specified if he was sorry for the hurtful words, or sorry that he'd crawled into her bed.

But before Blake could take one step, there was a frantic knocking at the bedroom door. She met his gaze with a little shake of her head, willed him not to answer, not to make a move or a sound.

"Who is it?" she called, panic filling the pit of desolation.

"It's Dominic, miss. There's a problem downstairs and I can't seem to find Blake."

Sophie shuffled to the door, careful to keep the blanket around her still naked body. "What's the problem, Dominic?"

"The Duke of St. Ives has just arrived and there's no breakfast and no one in the dining room to tend him. I have to take care of His Grace's flesh and I can't do it all by myself."

"I'll be down in a moment. Keep looking for Blake."

"Thank you, miss. Thank you."

Sophie held her breath until long after his thumping footsteps had receded. She turned, her head fell forward until her chin almost rested on her chest, a single tear fell down her cheek. "What have I done?"

"There's no need to tell him." Blake actually sounded concerned but when she looked up and met his gaze once again, she saw only fury.

"I wasn't going to tell him," she said. "Nothing happened. Nothing more than a bad mistake."

"So that's what it was? A mistake?"

"What else could it have been? You said it yourself, you are no duke and I'm nothing but a gold-chasing whore."

"Sophie-"

She held up one hand. "No. I asked you to leave and I meant it. Get out."

"I can't go out there now. What if St. Ives is standing in the hall?"

"I don't care. I'll tell him you were fixing a chair or stoking the fire or something."

"While you are undressed?"

Her cheeks burned. He made her feel hot and cold at the same time despite treating her worse than a free tumble at the docks. She should have slapped him then and there. She certainly shouldn't have opened her heart or her body to him. Why had she ever thought that he'd changed? That he was different? That in his mind there might be some small place that didn't think her useless or dirty or tainted. Mistake was an understatement.

He may not be his father, but like his sire, he used her, hurt her, made sure she had no idea which way was up and which was down. At least this time the damage was on the inside—invisible but no less intense—rather than bruises and broken bones.

She had to watch while Blake pulled his shoes on, the same clothes he'd worn the night before when they'd danced and laughed and enjoyed each other's company. When he opened the window and stretched a leg over the sill with all the grace of a panther, all signs of his previous injury gone, she turned to face the wall. She couldn't bear to watch him leave like this. She wished she could go back and wake up with a smile, not bring up the subject of his heritage, just ask for breakfast. If only.

When she turned back again, words on the edge of her tongue that would take the sting out of the morning's insults, he was gone.

Sixteen

Everywhere Blake turned, he saw red. Was he angry with her or himself? Both if he had to be honest. He'd wanted to sleep with her. Hell, he'd wanted anything she would offer like a pup waiting for a crumb, anything the duchess would throw his way and then when he had her, he had to go and ruin it all. The story of his life lately.

Why couldn't he wake her up with his hands, his lips, his mouth? Why hadn't he stayed in her bed, her curves all snuggled into his side and done the right thing? Instead he'd woken, realized he'd taken advantage of a drunken friend and then dressed hoping to slink out and not say a word about the night. Pretend it never happened so he wouldn't be tempted to do it again.

But then she sighed and shuffled as she rose from a deep sleep to awareness and he'd wanted to look into her eyes. He'd wanted to hear what her first words for the morning would be, see her tousled hair on his pillows in the bed that was his before he'd given it up for her. He craved that kind of domestic bliss with her, but then he'd opened his mouth and ruined it all. Again. Damn her! Damn him!

When his feet hit the ground after climbing down the side of the wall outside the kitchens, he didn't stop. He stomped right to the barn and threw the doors open. What did make him pause was the realization that he couldn't saddle his barrel of a horse and ride out his frustration in the cool country air.

Frantically he searched for something else, something else that could take the weight of his anger but there was nothing here. He would have to chop wood. Lots of wood. When he turned to leave, a shadow fell over the ground before him.

"Matthew? What are you doing here?"

"I told Sophie I would chop the firewood for the day. What is going on?"

"You shouldn't be here right now. I'm not…myself at all."

"What happened? Did you fight with Sophie again? Please tell me you didn't."

"It's none of your business. What happened is between Sophie and me and that is how it will stay."

"Fine, I will go and ask her what happened."

"Don't go anywhere near her."

Matthew stepped toward him, his face grim. Blake stepped back.

"What happened?"

"Nothing. A mistake." He used her words and it cut him to the bone. A mistake was when you added salt to your custard instead of sugar. Or when you didn't saddle your horse right and fell off because of it. Sleeping with her hadn't been a mistake. He'd wanted to. Hell he still wanted to. He groaned.

"Is she all right?" her brother asked, his fists clenched.

Blake wanted to tell him the truth. Then Matthew could swing the first punch and Blake could let his frustrations go, but his friend didn't deserve that. As much as Blake wanted to hit someone or something, it would not be Matthew Martin.

He turned away from his old friend, unable to look him in the eye and say nothing happened, that Sophie was fine, that everything was fine. The red hot fury faded to a kind of numb desolation. Damn.

"I'm serious, Blake, if you don't tell me what happened, I'll ask her and she'll tell me and then I'll come back and…" He didn't finish the sentence. He didn't have to.

"I slept with her." He still had his back to Matthew; he couldn't bear it.

"Did she consent?"

He didn't have to look around. He heard Matthew's teeth grind while he waited for an answer. "She started it."

"Are you blaming her?" Another shuffling step.

Blake finally faced his friend, the man who knew him better than any other. "We were drunk and our clothing wet. I would have walked away, I swear, but she... she was very persuasive. I couldn't say no."

"That's my sister you're talking about, Blake. Be very, very careful."

"I'm so sorry, Matthew."

"Do you think I'm the one you should apologize to? From the look on your face when I came in, you should be saying sorry to Sophie for whatever it was you did."

"You don't understand." He borrowed her words again, the meaning finally beginning to sink in to his thick head. "I really began to admire her."

"You say that as if it's a bad thing. She's an admirable woman."

Blake shook his head. "If only I'd seen that sooner."

"Are you going to tell me what's got you looking as if you lost your best friend?"

"I think I just did lose my best friend." He slumped down the side of a stall to the dusty ground and put his head on his knees. He hoped it wasn't true. God, he hoped he hadn't ruined everything. He'd loved once; he still did in a way.

"Why don't you go and tell her that? Why don't you go and throw yourself at her feet and beg for her mercy? She's not the woman you thought her to be when she first arrived. She will forgive you."

Blake was saved any reply when Dominic walked a majestic black horse into his barn. It was possibly one of the finest horses he'd ever seen, other than Blakiston's own steeds. "Is that St. Ives's?" he asked the young man.

"It is. He came up for Blakiston's auction. He asked to see you when you're free."

"So it's true?" Matthew breathed once the lad had gone into another stall.

"It must be. But surely Blakiston doesn't need the money? He's bleeding us all dry already. What could he possibly need more for? Unless he's thinking about adding to that damned house out there." Blakiston Manor was huge and imposing and didn't need to be upgraded. Well, not since Blake had last seen it as a teen. Sophie's terrible story came back to him. What would he do about it?

"I had better see what St. Ives wants."

"Are you going to talk to Sophie?" Matthew asked, brushing dirt and hay from his dark trousers.

"If she will let me anywhere near her. If St. Ives will let me anywhere near her. If he finds out what happened, it may be the end of us both."

"Don't let him find out."

As they walked through the double barn doors and into the yard, Blake looked up to her window, the same window he'd fled only hours earlier. The couple he saw silhouetted stopped him in his tracks. "That'd be easier said than done," Blake muttered with a curse and a gesture towards the inn's second floor.

Sophie sighed into St. Ives' familiar warmth and breathed his scent. He was spicy and sweet while remaining masculine and forbidding. How she loved to hug the man. With her emotions crumbling around her she needed to hug him, to know he was there for her.

Over his shoulder, she saw Blake enter the yard with Matthew. Even with the distance, it was impossible to mistake the hard lines of his face, the tension in his shoulders and the disapproval in his eyes. He must certainly now think her lower than a whore. Not that she cared. He'd done nothing but belittle her since she arrived. To think that their truce could have survived intimacy had been a mistake on her part. One of many to add to the still growing list. She wondered if he would have acted differently had he known she'd cut her ties with St. Ives before traveling to Blakiston.

She pulled out of the duke's embrace to put some air between them.

"Sophie, it's great to see you, but what are you doing here? I thought you were off to the seaside with your friends. You are supposed to be resting."

That's the story she'd told him. She'd thought the small white lie acceptable. The truth hadn't been. "I lied. I'm sorry."

"Why?"

He didn't seem angry and for that, the guilt deepened. "I didn't want you to know where I was really going. What I was really doing."

St. Ives sat in the worn chair before the fire—the same chair Blake had sat in last night—an expectant look on his handsome face. "What are you really doing?"

She nodded, braced herself, "I was running."

"From me?"

"From everything. After I lost the baby, I just couldn't face any of it. I've done it before and it's a living nightmare."

"Done it before? You're not making any sense. Are you sure you're all right?"

She nodded again. She could trust him with her story and should have before now. She told him about being held against her will, but not about the rape. She left out the early years in London and the last twenty or so hours as well. But the rest she told him. About leaving her family in the dead of the night, about the babies she had lost over the years she had sold her body.

She should have known relief at the unburdening, but she was still a common liar. Even with sympathy etched all over Daemon's face, Sophie still couldn't tell him the whole truth.

"Why didn't you tell me?" he asked when she was finally done with the sordid tale.

"I didn't want anyone to know about my family, about my past. There had to be somewhere safe I could return to when the time came."

"Is that what you are doing? Are you going to stay in Blakiston?"

She shook her head and moved to the corner of the room where the cradle was still hidden under a blanket. She ran a finger along its crimson edge, but made no move to unveil it. "My brother is to have a baby. He asked me to be here for the birth, to be her godmother if I choose. After that, I haven't yet decided."

"A blessed event for your brother and his wife, to have you here."

"Do you know my brother?"

"Of course I know him. I've been coming out here for more years than I care to recall."

There was a thoughtful look on his face that made Sophie fearful she'd missed something. "Why do you come out here? Are you friends with Blakiston? Why are you here now?" She had a thousand questions and as each one bounced into her mind like a child's toy, her anxiety grew.

"I would rather lick a chamber pot than be in the same room as the current duke of Blakiston, but he has something I want."

"What is it?" Her interest was piqued. Daemon only ever got that particular look of determination when he planned to win. Nothing would stop him now, whatever it was.

"It's a long story and not mine to tell." He stood and moved toward the connecting door leading to the room he would stay in for his brief visit. "I'll see you at luncheon? Shall we dine in the private parlor?"

"There's something else I haven't told you."

St. Ives stopped and turned back to face her. He wasn't a man who looked capable of violence, but he also wasn't a man to be crossed. She still was not ready to tell him everything that had transpired since her arrival, but there was one very important detail he would find out soon enough if she didn't tell him first.

"We may have to dine a little late."

"Why is that? Do you have an engagement? I can eat by myself."

"The thing is… I have to make the meal."

St. Ives stared at her for a full two minutes before he threw his head back and laughed like a man who'd lost his senses.

"Why do you laugh at me?"

"You're having a joke. Why would you make the meal?"

"It's a very long story. Let's just say I fell into a trap made of my own stubborn pride."

He began to laugh again. Not the reaction she expected.

"When I arrived, I asked to speak to the man in charge and the boy downstairs looked at me rather strangely. He asked if I wouldn't rather speak to the woman in charge, since the man was injured and not able to run the inn. I thought he meant Blake's wife. Are you telling me *you're* the woman in charge?"

"Sort of. Blake was injured and I stepped in to help him, but it was my own fault and I forgot the kind of boy he was and… It's another rather long story." She babbled. She never babbled. Too many half-truths were going to make it very hard to keep her stories straight.

"Does he know how stubborn you get?"

"He does now."

St. Ives shook his head before turning back towards his own room. His chuckles carried back to her along with the words, "Poor Blake."

Seventeen

P oor Blake was already at a loose end by the time St. Ives made it to his office. Had she told him? Should he brace for a fight or welcome an old friend and offer him a glass of something able to stand on its own two feet? He needed two glasses before he could summon the courage to open his office door. Things could not have gotten farther out of hand.

What no one, not even Sophie or Matthew knew, was that Daemon and Blake were half brothers. It was the reason they hadn't been in the same room for years for fear that someone would recognize the similarities between the both of them and the previous duke.

When Daemon had discovered who his real father was, he'd come to confront the man. Courageous for a twenty-one year old trying not to reveal his mother's secrets. He'd also paid a visit to the tavern to meet his half brother. The sibling he hadn't known about until their sire let the information slip. On purpose? They still weren't sure. There was probably an ulterior motive for the revelation but by then the old duke's mind had cracked. Daemon had only sought Blake out so he could know if Blakiston lied or not. Though they had different color hair, the other resemblances were too strong to deny the truth.

Blake eyed Daemon warily, tried to gauge the other man's mood as he picked his way through the crowded tap room. The morning rain that had just started to fall was proving to be good for business, and lunch would be see the place packed to the rafters as men sought refuge from the cold.

As Daemon came to stand in the doorway, Blake stepped back like the coward he was, he didn't say a word. Just waited. Never had he felt more like a younger brother than in that moment.

Daemon looked him up and down from his boots to his head and back again, but Blake couldn't detect any anger, no fury set to be loosed.

"They told me you'd been injured, but you look hale and hearty to me," Daemon said with a half smile.

Blake released his breath on a relieved sigh. "As do you. Obviously inheriting a dukedom agrees with you."

"I'm happy if that's what you are asking."

"I'm glad to hear it." There was an awkward pause where Blake simply didn't know what to say. They hadn't seen each other in six years. Not even a letter had been exchanged in the three since the old duke's death. What could he possibly have to say now to the man sleeping with the woman he loved?

"I met your cook earlier," Daemon said with a chuckle as he settled into the chair opposite Blake's desk, seemingly oblivious to the roiling tension in the room.

"My cook? I don't have one."

"Sophia said she has to cook the meal before she can sit down to eat it."

Blake scowled. Of course she revealed that part of their story. "It was her fault. She is still as stubborn now as she was at ten years old."

"You've known her a long time then?" Daemon asked. The question seemed an innocent one, but Blake knew better than to fall into that trap.

Daemon was a lot like a cobra. He lulled you, dazzled you and made you feel comfortable just before he moved in for the fatal bite you never saw coming.

"I've known Sophie since she was born."

"Sophia?" Her betrayal had run so deep he hadn't even told his brother about her. For most of the fourteen years she had been absent, he had refused to even say her name.

"Her name isn't Sophia. It's Sophie Martin."

"I know that, but she prefers to be called Sophia."

Not lately. "Yes, she does now."

"How did it come about? That she is working in your kitchen??"

"You don't want to hear about that," Blake groaned.

"I do want to hear about it. The tale sounds humorous."

It wasn't. There was nothing funny about what had transpired. "She said that my work was easy and that she could do it without an ounce of effort."

Daemon laughed. "She did not."

"Aye, she did."

"And you couldn't let it stand? Let me guess, she stood with her hands on her hips, her eyes shooting fire and told you she was better than you?"

"She already told you about this, didn't she?"

"No. But I know Sophia and she is not one to back down from a fight or a challenge. Therein lies your first mistake."

"And not the last, let me tell you."

The two men spent the next hour renewing their friendship and apprising the other of what they'd missed over the years. Each time Daemon mentioned Sophie, Blake would maneuver the conversation back to neutral ground. He truly liked Daemon and didn't want to hear about his relationship with Sophie even if he was blissfully happy. Especially if he was blissfully happy.

"Tell me about Blakiston's auction," Blake said once all the other mundane conversations were out of the way.

"Since he inherited, he's done everything possible to bankrupt the estate. The man wants to gamble with the finest, but can't hold his liquor or his tongue. Five years of neglect and debt finally prompted the King to take an interest."

"He's been sniffing about Sophie in the last few days," Blake told him.

"Damn," Daemon swore. "I should have questioned her more about where she was going. Does he know about her connection to me?"

Blake nodded.

Daemon breathed deep. "Does he know about ours?"

Blake shook his head. "Even Sophie doesn't know about that and I don't want her to. You aren't to tell her anything."

"I won't. Yet."

"You had better not. Ever. Just make sure it doesn't come up in the bedroom or anywhere else you may find yourself in a weakened state."

Daemon laughed again, though this time the action was strained. "Weakened state? I don't know who you've been consorting with, brother, but no woman has ever led me to that state in the bedroom."

Blake swallowed. It would be the perfect time to reveal his betrayal. But then there was never a perfect time to tell your half brother that you'd slept with his paramour.

"Don't worry. I won't tell her."

The look on Blake's face must have been a serious one for Daemon to suddenly get serious in return. Blake nodded his thanks, but didn't speak.

"I won't be telling her any secrets from now on anyway."

The way Daemon spoke, Blake would have to be deaf not to apprehend something wasn't right. "You won't?"

"We parted ways some months ago."

Blake's mouth fell open.

"She didn't tell you?"

He shook his head and snapped his mouth shut. Why hadn't she? He had been torturing himself for nothing? Maybe not nothing, but she should have let him know.

"I met someone," Daemon said.

"You did?" he replied but he was still reeling. Sophie was available? Nothing tied her to London or any man? What was it that held her back? He could offer her a life in Blakiston, yet she hadn't shown the slightest interest. She spoke of returning to the city at every opportunity she could.

"You don't have to be so dramatic. It had to happen one day. I have to marry eventually and take care of the business of succession."

"What about Sophie?"

He misunderstood the question. "I can't marry Sophie and we all know that. Anyway, she wouldn't marry me even if I begged."

"How do you know that?" Blake's head swam with the possibilities and his conscience let go a half of a fraction.

"Because I already asked her."

"What?" He felt as though the floor had just disappeared under his chair.

"I asked her to be my wife shortly after we first met. I thought I could save her and I wanted to upset both dukes in the process, my birth father and my cuckolded one. Could you imagine the fallout?"

"And she said no?" The woman was so damned confusing.

"Don't worry about a thing, Sophie isn't the type of woman to make a scene. We can peacefully exist in the same space. We parted as the best of friends, so your inn will stand come morning."

Blake nodded but there were no words. God, how he wished there were. The mess just got thicker, deeper and messier. He recalled the words he had said to her that very morning about wanting to be a duchess and wished the floor had swallowed him whole.

"What the inn might not withstand is the other reason I came to see you."

Blake's mind was slow catching up, but the intent in Daemon's eyes caused him more worry than the enigma that was Sophie.

"The other reason? I thought you were here for Blakiston?"

"I am. I'm here for the real Duke of Blakiston to finally come out of hiding and take his rightful place."

"Why would you say that? What if someone were to overhear you?"

"I wish someone *would* overhear me, then they could talk some sense into you."

"You can't prove anything. We burned the evidence a long time ago. Do you think anyone would listen?"

"There are some privileges to being a duke. One of them is that when you speak, others listen and take notice. It is quite rude to call a duke a liar. Not many would dare."

"I would."

Daemon leaned forward in his chair and placed his glass on the smooth surface of the desk. The turbulence of the liquid drew Blake's eye and held it while his brother spoke.

"Would you denounce the truth if it became public knowledge?"

Blake continued to stare at the glass as he answered, "To my last breath."

"What if I told you there was still evidence?"

"I would call you a liar right now. We watched them burn. You lit the spark that dissolved my birthright."

"I didn't want to."

"But you went along with my wishes. Where is this going, St. Ives?"

His half brother didn't miss his use of his title and not his name. "I sent my man on a wild goose chase to keep him busy earlier last year and he uncovered dozens of sets of documents."

"Impossible." Blake shook his head as his hand slashed through the air. "We burned those records to ash. Why would the clergyman make a second set?"

"Apparently the vicar had problems sleeping and spent his time monastically copying papers. He replicated the most important documents and kept them at a different location."

"What location?"

"I won't tell you that."

Blake rose from his seat, put his hands on the desk and leaned in close so his brother wouldn't miss the sincerity of his next words. "I'll kill you before I let you release those papers. I don't want to be a Duke. I'll never enter that house for as long as I live."

Daemon watched him for a moment before nodding and indicating for Blake to sit back down.

Blake sat, but his heart wouldn't stop racing and his nerves wouldn't sit still. The repercussions of the two of them even having this discussion were so far reaching it actually terrified him.

"I went to see the old man before he died," Daemon said.

"You did?" Blake didn't care. He didn't want to think of that sorry excuse for a man. He didn't want to think of his brother having a relationship with a man who should have had a sword run through him the first time he took advantage of an innocent. He shook free of murderous thoughts. A man couldn't die twice.

"He thought I was the vicar come to offer absolution. The things he told me, the things he was sorry for, they made my stomach hurt."

Blake didn't want to know if his mother was one of those he sought forgiveness for. It no longer mattered. It was all too easy for contemptible men to beg leniency when about to meet their maker.

"Did you forgive him?" Blake asked, despite not wanting or needing to know the answer.

"I said the words he wanted to hear," Daemon said with a shrug.

"That was not my question. Did you forgive him?"

"I forgave him a long time before that."

"Then why don't you be the duke? One word from your mother or one more set of documents would solve everyone's problems."

"I made a promise to my mother that I would never to reveal the truth in any form, that she had an affair with Blakiston. It would kill her and what would become of the dukedom I already claim? What would become of the villagers depending on me if they knew my father is not actually my father? I've worked hard for them and they for me. I don't want or need more titles even if it were possible."

Blake sighed. Some of the tension left his body in sheer defeat. Daemon laughed.

"What could you find so hilarious about this situation?"

"In the eyes of God I am the true bastard here, not you. You are the only one of us who has a legitimate claim to any title since you are the only one of us born in wedlock to your rightful parents. If my parentage were to emerge, my dukedom would be contested and I would probably lose everything. This one is yours and yours only and you have to step up to it."

"I don't want it," Blake said for a second time. Or maybe it was the third? He'd say it a hundred times if he had to.

"I don't think you have a choice anymore."

He surged from his seat again. "The hell I don't! We all have choices, I made mine and I won't go back. Not you or any other man will force my hand in this."

"That's where you have it wrong. Do you think Sophia had a choice?"

"This has nothing to do with her."

Daemon ignored his words and went on regardless. "One of the gruesome truths our father shared with me is a story about Sophia. Do you want me to tell it to you?"

"I don't need to. She already told me."

Finally Daemon showed some emotion in the shocked look on his normally nonchalant mask. "I don't think she would have told you the full story."

Had she? Or did she only share the parts she thought he needed to hear? He wasn't going to share any of her secrets with this man, but one of the pieces of the puzzle fell into place. "That's why *you* have her." It was a simple statement, no need for questions.

"I already had her. I just didn't know exactly who I had until then."

"She sold her body to you, and you expect me to believe you didn't know where she came from?"

"She *gave* her body to me. And no. I didn't know. She kept her secrets very closely guarded."

"Yet once you did know, you didn't bring her out of her degradation. You didn't save her, you just kept her in the same state you found her, only more comfortable."

"What Sophia and I had is none of your business. I offered to marry her and she refused me. She still has no idea who I am. Her reputation and her beauty and her unavailability are what led me to pursue her. It seemed a betrayal of who she had become to tell her everything, to dredge up the nightmare and cause her to once again look over her shoulder every day. You've seen the light in her eyes, the vibrancy of her soul, I couldn't remind her of her past and dull that light."

"It's not right. She should know who you are."

"She should know who you are."

"I am a tavern owner, and in her eyes, a pig. She wouldn't believe your lies any more than Charles or the magistrate would." For more than a few minutes, Blake's treacherous mind stumbled over the truth and all its possibilities. She had said no to a duke. Here was an honorable man offering her a way out, offering a life devoid of labor and filled with comfort and coin, and Sophie had said no. There were so many questions and a less than zero chance for the answers.

"So you won't even think about it?" Daemon's softly spoken words interrupted Blake's thoughts as they chased each other from one side of his mind to the other, from one side of the argument to the other.

He had thought of it. He'd thought of little else since Charles had taken the Blakiston name and dragged it into the mud. When the Branson child died because Charles refused the loan of his carriage to fetch her to the doctor, he'd thought how differently he would have handled the situation. When the taxes continued to rise, but the roads remained in their sad state of disrepair, the bridge to the south almost crumbling into the creek it sat over, he'd thought of nothing else. There were so many things he would have done differently had he been duke, but it wasn't that simple. It could never be that simple. And he'd made a promise to his mother all those years ago. Even though she'd left him and never looked back, he would honor the promise and stay true to himself.

Great wealth warped the minds of those who held it. It made strong men weak and great women greedy and conniving. It made those in high positions think whatever they wanted was theirs for the buying. The untitled may not be rich, but they were happy. He was happy. Or at least he had been before Sophie had re-entered his life and thrown it into chaos.

Blake shook his head. He didn't need a dukedom. He didn't need wealth or an estate atop a hill. He simply needed to remember who he was and who he wanted to be. Sophie was right when she spouted off about choices and decisions. His wasn't even a hard one to make.

"No."

"No, you won't think about it, or no, you won't do it?"

He sighed and looked directly into Daemon's unwavering sea-green gaze. "I will never be a duke. Not ever. Burn the remaining documents and forget what you know. Forget that I should have been Duke of Blakiston and wait for Charles to go to hell so you can find a new successor. If you can't do that, forge some new documentation and thrust it on another man, because I don't want it."

"Do you understand what you're giving up? You could have it all. A wife with an entrée into society, children, a fortune."

"I do understand. I don't want any of that. I have never wanted that kind of power or responsibility."

This time it was Daemon who shook his head as he stood to leave. "You're making a mistake here, brother."

"A mistake is something you grow to regret," Blake muttered. This was one decision regret would never sink its claws into.

A duke? Blake was the rightful Duke of Blakiston? Sophie couldn't have heard right. She couldn't have. But that wasn't even the worst revelation of her eavesdropping. Daemon and Blake were half brothers? Why hadn't she ever known that? Daemon had asked her questions only hours earlier and hadn't let on one little bit that the two were related.

She turned from Blake's office door with a hand pressed to her suddenly fluttery stomach. No wonder Blake never wanted to talk about his sire. No wonder he'd gotten so angry when she'd asked him why he didn't want to be a duke. But he'd told her bastards don't inherit. He'd said it over and over. She thought for a moment that she would cast up her accounts right there on the floor. Everyone had their secrets, but this? This was a flat out lie. A betrayal of everyone whose life depended on work from the estate, on the duke, on the word of a man who had apparently been born on the right side of the blanket after all.

This was it. This was the moment she could either confess to what she'd heard and confront the two men who claimed to care something for her. Or she could take the new information away and think on what she could and would do with it. She felt her head would explode from the pressure.

She fisted one hand in the skirts of her gown, and with the other, pushed the door to Blake's office open. Daemon saw her first and began to rise, but Sophie stopped him with a curt gesture. Blake was slower to her presence and didn't make to stand, didn't make a move at all.

"Sophia." Daemon addressed her warily. "Is it luncheon already?"

She drew breath, opened her mouth, and asked, "Blake would you fetch more wood for the fire in the common room? That rain is still falling and it's bringing a chill with it."

Both men stared at her for a moment too long, and she wondered if one would call her on her hesitation or her flimsy lie. Blake rose without a word and Daemon picked his glass up and drained the amber contents in one swallow before addressing her.

"You heard all of that, didn't you?"

She gave a shake of her head, another curl breaking loose from the knot she tried to tame them into. "Heard what?"

Daemon smiled then. It was a lifting of lips that for as long as Sophie had known Daemon, he reserved just for her. Only today there was something else there—a weariness he didn't normally let show.

She did have so many questions. How did they find out they were siblings? How long had they known? Was the old duke aware of Daemon as his son? So many questions but if she blurted them all out now and Daemon told her to mind her own business, how would she respond? She had to work it all out in her own mind and choose carefully what she wanted to know. Daemon was a private man and only released the details of his life that he wanted to be made public. The rest were cards he held very close to his chest.

"Are you ready to eat?" she asked, shifting all her jumbled thoughts to the back of her mind for later. For now, all she wanted was to eat a meal with a man who didn't insult her at every turn. Or make her head hurt with the effort to decipher him.

Eighteen

L ater that day, Sophie stood by a makeshift corral as yet another fine thoroughbred went under the hammer and more of Daemon's money spilled into the pocket of a ducal toad. She wasn't quite sure what was happening, but Daemon had purchased a total of fifteen horses much to the disgust of the other men who'd traveled for the auction. She wanted to ask him what he would do with them all, but all she could do was stand and smile prettily as her brain whirled with questions. The barns at his estate were tiny and he wasn't a horse man at all. And then there were the dozen more questions about his relationship with Blake she longed to have answered. Why hadn't he ever mentioned even travelling to Blakiston? She also wondered how often the half-brothers saw each other. Too many scenarios skated in her mind and it was giving her a headache.

"Are you all right, m'dear?" Daemon asked, looking pointedly at where her hand was supposed to rest lightly on his arm. Instead her grip was tight, his coat bunched beneath her gloved fingers.

Sophie relaxed her hand and smiled. When she peered at the others around her to make sure no one else had noticed her agitation, she met the gaze of Blake who scowled in her direction as if she was the one bidding on all of the flesh.

"I'm perfectly fine, thank you." If she could have a guinea for every time she had said those particular words in the last week...

"You don't look fine. Perhaps you need to sit for a moment?"

"No, thank you." She leaned closer so no one would hear her. "What are you doing?"

"What do you mean? I'm trying to see to your obvious lack of comfort."

"Why are you buying all of them? That one over there looks as though she is about to fall over. Her ribs are poking out."

The stiffness under her hand was not imagined and when she looked to his face, Daemon was now the one wearing a scowl. "He has not fed them properly in a month. Wait till you see the foaling mares. He's lucky this mob haven't taken matters into their own hands and hung him from his own barn."

She didn't want to see the foaling mares. Not if they appeared as pitiful as the last two. She didn't want to be there at all, but the whole village had turned out and she didn't want to be left behind at the tavern on her own. And she still had to find a way to confront Blake with what she knew. And soon.

Four pathetic beasts later and finally, a spirited grey gelding was led into the corral. This one was skinny like the others, but intelligence and defiance shone in his stormy eyes. When he whinnied and reared onto his back legs, the shadow he cast over those standing closest shuffle back in fear.

"Ten pounds," Blake called as he stepped from the shadow of the barn.

A laugh was the only answer from her left as Blakiston also stepped into the light. "You'll need to do better than that, Vale."

"Only if there is another bidder," Blake said, looking around at his fellow villagers and friends. There was just enough firmness in his tone to let everyone know this beast was marked as his.

Sophie waited for Daemon to buy this one as well, but his mouth remained closed, his lips drawn in a tight line. Fascinating.

"Thirty pounds," came from a stranger in a dusty bowler hat and black coat.

"Fifty," came Blake's reply.

Her heart sped up a little in anticipation.

"Sixty pounds," Bowler Hat countered.

"Eighty."

This went on for several tense minutes until the amount reached a staggering one hundred and sixty pounds. From the corner of her eye, Sophie noticed the man in the bowler hat look to Blakiston. If she wasn't standing so close, she wouldn't have noticed Blakiston's small nod, which prompted bowler hat to place another bid. The duke was cheating to push the price higher. She wondered if Blakiston had more men in the crowd bidding on his own flesh.

Once the sum hit two hundred pounds, Blake had to be almost at his limit, and yet bowler hat kept countering with ten more pounds to his every bid. He was about to pay far too much for the horse and everyone present knew it. Sophie let go of Daemon's hand and began to drift through the crowd toward Blake, but before she moved more than three steps, Matthew appeared at her side.

"Where are you going?" he asked as he blocked her path with his body.

"Blake is being swindled. I have to warn him."

"Blake knows what he's doing, Sophie. He's a big boy."

"And Blakiston is cheating him out of more money than that horse is worth."

"He knows that."

What? "He does?" What hadn't they told her?

Matthew led her away from the auction and crowd. "Of course he does. Why do you think St. Ives has purchased every horse so far? They have a plan."

"Do you know what it is?" Sophie wondered if they'd told Matthew of Blake's claim to the title or their real relationship.

He shook his head, but the expression he wore said he knew more than he let on. She kept walking until they were both a safe distance from prying ears. "Do you know about Blake?" she demanded. If she didn't talk to someone and soon, she would explode.

Matthew became instantly wary. "What about Blake?"

He was her brother, so surely she could share with him a secret that wasn't her own. It was Blake's fault he hadn't told her the truth when he'd had the chance. She'd answered his questions honestly when he'd asked, but all he'd given her were lies and subterfuge. She owed him nothing. "Did you know that Blake is indeed the true heir to the Blakiston title?"

"He is a bastard. He cannot inherit."

"He is no more illegitimate than you or I."

"That's impossible. Why didn't he say anything to me? Why would he tell you?"

"He didn't tell me. I overheard him telling his brother to burn the documents proving his claim."

"He has no siblings. We are the closest he has to family. Are you sure you were listening in on the right conversation?"

"Of course I'm sure. Daemon and Blake are half brothers. Daemon tried to talk Blake into ousting Charles and taking the title himself."

Matthew paced away, one hand rubbing his forehead as he processed the information. "What? How? I don't understand."

"I don't know the entire tale, but needless to say, Blake would do a much better job than Charles does now. He doesn't care about the village or its people. He only cares about gambling and women. We have to do something."

"No."

"No?"

"We do nothing. Leave it be."

"We can't just stand by and wait for Blakiston to destroy our home."

"This is not your home. Why are you so worried for us now?"

His sudden hostility caught her off guard and she didn't know how to respond. He was right. She didn't belong here and what happened after she left would have no effect on her further than what it meant for Matthew, Violet and her niece or nephew.

Sometime over the course of a week, Sophie had begun to think of Blakiston as home. She'd barely thought of London, the clinic, her friends. In the parts of her mind where hope still shone, she'd even thought of how it would be to live out her life in the tavern alongside a man like Blake. Down the road from the estate where her life had ended and Sophia's had begun.

But who was she kidding? She'd blamed her errant thoughts on nearly losing him. She'd blamed them on the fact that her world had been turned upside down when he'd kissed her. So many feelings she'd long buried had risen to the surface. As a child, she'd idolized her older brother's best friend. As a young woman, she'd watched him grow, watched him fight and run and laugh but it had been a hopeless child's crush. When she'd overheard her father's plans to sell her to the old duke, all thoughts of a happy life, being courted and wooed, spending her summer days with Blake and Matthew, all had flown from her mind. Even up to the day her father marched her up the steps to the estate and handed her over, she hadn't thought he would go through with it. Surely his only daughter was more important to him that a piece of land.

Evidently not.

It made her skin crawl and her stomach to heave to recall the many times she'd wished the old duke would kill her rather than touch her again.

He almost did kill her, several times over. If it hadn't been for the drink, she would have died. Instead, he'd drunk to such an excess, he forgot to turn the lock on the door all the way. After spending what seemed an eternity before daring to try the door, Sophie hadn't even known if it would be night or day when she finally emerged from the lowest levels of the house. When Blake had told her how they'd searched for her, the hours her father had spent looking for her...she had been there all along.

Nothing had been more important that night than putting distance between herself and the man who traded her innocence for a farm. Sure, she could have woken her brother and let him see the bruises, but then they would have both had to run. She should never have written to let them know she was alive. She should have let her brother and her friend think her dead, but her sadness had weighed too heavily so she'd put pen to paper. She could have told them so much more, but the rest she kept to herself. Only the old duke knew the whole story and he was dead.

Blake would never understand that a courtesan's life was preferable to no life at all.

She'd seen an opportunity to escape and she'd taken it. When she looked back on her flight that night, she was very lucky to have made it to London at all. She could have fallen into a ditch in the dark. She could have been attacked by animals or chanced upon a stranger on the road. It was no small miracle that she'd survived to reach the capital. She'd lived every day since as if it could be her last. She developed street sense with the help of her friends and she'd made decisions that were right at the time, not right for the future. The situation she now found herself in was no different. She had to make a decision about the information she now held and she needed to make it now, not for her future or Blake's, not for their pasts or the possible outcomes, but for the future of her niece or nephew and the life he or she would lead.

Charles may not be exactly the same as the old duke, but he already showed he was not the man to take care of these villagers. To take care of her family.

Whether Sophie accepted the village as her home or not, she had to ensure her family would be happy, taken care of, protected. She would accept nothing less and, like it or not, Blake was the only one who could make sure that happened.

With each swing of the heavy axe, Blake split huge logs into smaller pieces for the kitchen fire and the tavern pit. His side hurt a little with the exertion but nothing compared to how his heart thundered in his chest. For the hundredth time since Sophie had arrived back in his life, he asked himself what the hell he was doing. The headache attested to the fact he was nowhere near to the answer.

He wasn't the kind of man who slept with his friend's paramour. He certainly wasn't the type of man to sleep with his brother's woman. But Sophie had been his first. Not in the flesh, but he had loved her long before St. Ives had 'saved' her. Blake snorted and dropped the axe once more, the sharp crack only just distinguishable above the steady patter of rain.

If the old duke had asked Blake to find the woman he'd wronged, Blake would have brought her home. He wouldn't have offered her a position in his bed. Not as his mistress anyway.

He leaned over and hefted half a tree branch, resting it between two stumps. As he lifted and dropped the axe, rendering the useless limb down to kindling, he kept thinking what it would have been like to have Sophie by his side all these years. Even if he became a duke now, he couldn't have her. Despite Daemon having offered her marriage, they both knew it took more than even love for a duke to marry his mistress and certainly not a courtesan. It had been done but Sophie would be whispered about and the title would be eternally plunged into scandal. Generations of his future family would be tainted.

But what of her? What of Sophie? There was nothing he could do for her.

It wasn't him. A duke wasn't who he was. He was the boy delivered to his uncle as a child and beaten into a man. He was the boy who had been told so many times how useless he was that he almost believed it.

When next Blake picked up another log, water dripped from his fingertips, mixing with the sweat he would be covered in if it weren't for the still falling rain. He wished the droplets would wash away his troubles. But nothing could eliminate the truth. No matter how hard he denied it, he preferred instead the safe life he'd built.

That's what she did.

He supposed, but it was different. At least his safe illusion didn't hurt anyone. Hers hurt her family, her friends, the woman she could have become.

Blake shook his head and tipped it back, cold rain washing over his closed eyelids. Damn her and how she made him think.

"I've been looking for you," a voice called from his left.

"I've been right here," Blake shrugged, swinging the axe with more power than he truly felt.

"Sophie told me some interesting tales this afternoon."

Blake swallowed, dropped the axe and turned to his oldest friend. "Oh?"

Matthew returned his gaze--wary, hesitant, unsure of how to proceed. Blake's stomach dropped. Well, here it was, the lecture he'd waited to receive, that he needed to have in order to bring him back to reality. Funny that it should be Matthew and not Daemon.

"She told me you are Blakiston's real heir, not Charles."

His head snapped up so quickly it was a wonder he didn't fall over. "What did you say?" Matthew should have said, "How dare you sleep with my sister and then treat her like that!" or something along those lines. He should call him out, punch him in the nose or throw him in the dirt. Not this.

Matthew stepped forward. "You were supposed to be the Duke of Blakiston. How could you not tell me?"

Lie, his subconscious breathed. "I don't know what you're talking about."

"Don't give me that rot. I asked you to be the godfather to my child because you are an honest, trustworthy man, who would make an excellent role model. I didn't know then that the deception went so deep. How could you never tell me any of this?"

Blake flinched from the anger in Matthew's voice. "I didn't tell you because it isn't true. Where did Sophie hear this?"

"She heard you with your brother. Don't cover your lies with more lies. Now would be the time to tell the truth, Blake, and hope to God that this village doesn't turn its back on the one man who could have made life so much better all these years."

"It's not as easy as that." But that was also a lie.

"Tell me you aren't Blakiston's legitimate son. Tell me you were truly born on the wrong side of the blanket and I'll tell Sophie she was wrong."

He heaved great lungfuls of frigid air as his hands fisted at his sides. How dare she? From the moment she'd stepped foot in his yard, she'd tried to ruin his life. How could he even for one moment think she could be his other half?

"If you'll excuse me," he said to Matthew before turning on his heel in the mud and storming towards the kitchens. He had to make sure Sophie kept her mouth shut and her meddling to herself.

"How could you never have breathed a word about your relationship with Blake?" Sophie decided the direct approach was the only way she would have the answers she needed to complete the puzzle.

"Blake and I are friends, but I have a feeling that's not what motivates your question."

Sophie wandered around Daemon's room and folded the towel he'd left draped over a chair. What a perfect picture of domesticity they made.

"I overheard you and him talking this morning." She didn't have to look in his direction to know he'd frozen to the spot.

"What exactly did you hear?"

"Enough to know that Blake and you are brothers and that he is indeed the heir to the dukedom."

"You heard all that?" He didn't wait for a reply. "What are you going to do with this new information?"

"No, Daemon. What are *you* going to do with the information? Why are you really here and why did you purchase almost every one of Blakiston's horses?"

Daemon dropped into the chair before the cold hearth and beckoned for her to sit as well. She did so, even though her anxiety rocketed higher with each and every question that sprang to mind. There were so many.

"Charles is in deep to some very nasty men. The auction was the quickest way he could acquire the funds to flee England."

"I don't understand. Why does he not ask the Crown for help, or his friends? Surely a loan would put him back on the straight and narrow?"

"He has no friends in funds and the King has already helped as much as he is prepared to. Charles owes money to so many men, even if the estate and title could be sold, it wouldn't even be a drop in the ocean to his creditors."

"But what has this got to do with Blake? Why do you bring it all up now?"

"We've known who we are to each other for about a decade. My mother considered herself in love with the old duke until he showed his true colors and almost ruined her life. St. Ives paid no heed to her in the early days of their marriage and didn't particularly care when one of his oldest friends did. Discreetly of course. Discretion is the middle name of the ton. If it weren't for the secretiveness of the upper echelon, duels would have wiped half the aristocracy from the country."

"And you wouldn't be in the position you are now."

"Heard that too did you, minx?"

"Why aren't you angry with me?" He should have been furious, but instead he sat with his ankle on his knee, his hands steepled before his chest and a thoughtful look on his face.

Daemon shook his head, leaned forward and took one of her hands in his. "I'm not angry with you, because it is a wasted emotion. It is you who should be upset with me."

Sophie covered their clasped hands with her free one with a sinking stomach. She wouldn't pretend she didn't understand the tone in his voice. "I could never be upset with you. You have given me more than I deserved, more than I would have thought to ask for."

"What will you do now?" he asked.

"I'll wait for my niece or nephew to be born and then I'll go back to the city and pack my things. I don't belong there anymore and I suddenly find I want more than can be found in London."

"What about your friends and the infirmary. You enjoy working there."

Sophie shook her head. "In a way I always thought the clinic needed me but they only need my money. Well, our money. I can donate from anywhere in the country. I think in truth it was me who needed them. A way to stay connected with both the lives I lost. As for my friends, they only need to know that I'm safe and happy." Safe and happy in Blakiston? She wondered if that were truly possible.

"But will it be enough for you? Rotting away in the country?"

Sophie laughed at the irony, at him using her own words. It felt like a lifetime ago since she'd spoken them, so much had changed. "I believe I shall cope. Violet will need help with the baby and if she lets me, I should like to be a real aunt, perhaps even a friend."

"I think she would like that."

"What about you? What will you do about Blake?"

"I intend to set to rights the wrongs we have all wrought."

"How are you going to do that, when he so adamantly refuses to take the title?"

"He can reject the name and title as much as he wants, but he will have to make an official decision. He isn't aware of it yet, but he is already a duke. The king stripped Charles of the title last week, and is only giving him the time to flee. It's why I purchased the horses with Crown money. Charles will have the funds to start again somewhere new rather than board a ship for his sins. Blake will have the means to save the Blakiston name and build the fortune he'll need to run the estate with the King's help. It's going to take a great deal of hard work but if anyone can do it, he can."

"And if he still won't take it? He is the most stubborn, pigheaded, irrational man I've ever met."

"It sounds to me as though you care for my brother."

Before she could decide one way or another which answer to give, a banging started on Daemon's door and then it flew open to reveal Blake. A very, very angry Blake. "Well, well, well. Isn't this cozy?"

Sophie and Daemon stood at the same time, as though they'd been caught in the throes of passion. "What is the meaning of this, Blake?" Her voice came out much higher than she'd intended.

"I warned you not to meddle in my affairs," he roared as he stepped closer.

"You will not talk to her like that, brother."

Sophie almost sighed with relief when Blake's penetrating gaze switched from her own face to Daemon's.

"What did you tell her?" he demanded.

"Nothing she didn't already know," Daemon replied. He half stepped in front of Sophie so she was protected from Blake if things got out of hand. But Sophie didn't need that kind of protection, she never had.

She placed an arm on Daemon's shoulder and pushed until he once again stood beside her. "Get angry, Blake. Stomp and shout and accuse everyone else, but at the end, when the fury runs out and there's only the truth of the matter left, you'll see what a coward you are being."

He came at her, his nose level with her nose, his finger pointed at her chest, and she quailed. "I am the coward? You are the one who ran from here as fast as your legs could carry you and not once did you look back. Why do you care now? What do you care what happens to any of us when you won't be here to endure the fallout?"

"This used to be my home. One day it will be again. My brother lives here and my niece or nephew will too. How many times could you have helped the villagers with their problems? How many times could you have made life easier for your friends? My family? And I didn't run from you. You pushed me away like you do with anyone who gets close enough."

"This will never be your home! Even now after living with us and creating the illusion of making friends, you still do not belong and you never will."

"Why do I not belong? Why did I run in the first place, Blake? If you had the power of being Blakiston's heir, perhaps you could have saved me. Perhaps I would have stayed here for you had you any way to play the knight to my distress. But you didn't. You hide behind your cowardice and blame dead men for all of your troubles."

"And you don't? You flout the story that your father was going to sell you to cover for the fact that even then you were an ambitious slut. Me. I would have saved you, Sophie. I would have killed that man had there been one ounce of truth to your fears."

For a second she saw red. Her hand lifted, drew back, and then let loose, her palm connecting with his stubbled cheek with an echoing crack. But he didn't cower, he didn't show shame or remorse. His face was so close, she could see the raindrops that dripped from his clothes and hair and reminded her of their night of stupidity. How could she ever have thought he would make a difference? He could. But he wouldn't. Not in her life and not in anyone else's. "Fuck you," she breathed.

"You already did, duchess. Did you smell the hint of possibility and decide to throw a free bedding my way just in case?"

She staggered back, her hand on her chest, stinging with the urge to slap him again. Or worse.

"You mongrel," Daemon yelled as he came at Blake, fists swinging as the two went down. She'd almost forgotten he was even there.

She should have seen that sleeping with a man who thought her no better than the mud he traipsed through would come back to haunt her. His derision went so much deeper than she could ever imagine possible. To think he claimed to have once loved her.

Skirting the edge of the room, the two men pummeling each other, she gathered up her shawl and fled the inn. She needed to get out of there. She had to get back to London and her life and leave Blake and the village of her nightmares far, far behind.

"I should go and see if Sophie is all right," Daemon wheezed. One hand held a steak against his eye while the other dabbed at a cut on his lip with a handkerchief.

"She'll be fine. She doesn't need us to fuss. When she calms, she'll return, pack her things and be off."

"You wouldn't let her leave just like that, would you?" This question came from Matthew who'd arrived at the precisely the right moment to break up his fight with Daemon. Blake had anger on his side, but his brother was a renowned fighter. There was never any doubt who the victor would be.

Besides, Blake rather thought it about time he received a pummeling from one of the two men in the room. It was a surprise that Matthew hadn't placed a few kicks of his own after discovering the source of their rage was his very own sister. Like it could have been anyone or anything else.

"She doesn't need to be here," Blake sighed. "She'll take one look at that babe and tear back to London anyway."

Matthew stood and glared. "You don't know that. And I need her here. Violet needs her here. Her father hasn't given a damn about her years and her brother is busy with his own land. There are no other females in our lives, and my wife is convinced she will birth a girl. She will need her aunt."

"But will she need a frightened courtesan?"

It was Daemon who jumped to her defense once again. "Sophia is so much more than that. Why can't you see her for who she is?"

Blake stared long and hard at his brother before shaking his head. "*She* doesn't even know who she is. What can she have to offer our village? She can't return as the girl she was when she left. Too much has happened."

Matthew snorted and sat back down on the smooth floor timbers. "I wouldn't expect her to return the girl she was. She is a woman now, as well you know. The rest of the village seems to have forgiven her life choices. Why can't you?"

"She's just so damned stubborn and proud. What happened to her humility? Her gentleness and laughter? When I look at her, I don't see any of that."

"You see what you want to see," Daemon said from the foot of the bed. "When you look at her, you see a prostitute, a coward and a betrayer, but when I look at her, I see a beautiful woman. A woman, who, in the face of all the odds, is still alive and happy for the fact. Do you know what happens to girls when they arrive in London alone and terrified?"

Blake shook his head. He had a fair idea, but he hadn't witnessed any of it firsthand.

"Well, most don't even make it. The ones that do are vulnerable and naive and can be taken in by a kind word or plate of food. Greedy people take advantage of their desperation. Sophia is lucky she happened across good people, otherwise you may well have never heard from her again."

"Lucky? She should never have left in the first place!" Blake clenched his fists, the broken skin there already dried, stretched and uncomfortable over his knuckles. "She would have had a good life here."

"As Blakiston's child bride? You must have rocks in your head."

"Matthew, is it true? Did your father truly think to trade Sophie for land?"

Matthew sighed and nodded.

Every muscle in his body tensed when the color drained from Daemon's face at the same time as his brother gave his head a shake in Matthew's direction.

"You knew about it?"

Matthew inhaled, exhaled, twisted his fingers in the same way Sophie did when nervous. "First, believe me when I say I had no idea about any of it before she left. I only discovered it all from our father on his death bed. Sophie doesn't even know how much I know."

"Get on with it," Blake ground out.

"I don't know all the details, only those muttered by father in his last moments. He asked for forgiveness, but then he also asked for the land he thought he was still entitled to."

"I know she was to be sold to Blakiston, I know she was terrified and thought we wouldn't be able to help her so she left. What more is there?" said Blake

"It was all an act–Father's tears, his panic, the search parties. All the time we searched high and low for her body, he knew she was at the estate with Blakiston. The deal had been signed and done."

"He actually delivered her there?"

"Yes, and then walked away without wondering what would happen to her."

"Oh, God. There's more then, isn't there?" He didn't want to know. He was sure he wouldn't be any better off with the information burned into his brain.

Daemon took over the story from there. "For three days she was locked in the lowest levels of the house where he beat and raped her. Maybe worse. Only he and she will ever know."

Emotions battered his already fragile thoughts. All this time he'd blamed her for leaving. Blamed her for overreacting, for never saying a word to him, for taking so long to write to Matthew and let him know she was alive. All that time, she would have been terrified the duke would find her and bring her back.

"Why?"

Blake's question was rhetorical, but Daemon replied. "Before I was born, when my father paid no attention to his new bride, Blakiston fell in love with her. The fact that I stand here proves their affair. Blakiston fell in love and begged mother to marry him, to be with him and live the kind of life she deserved but she said no. Mind, that's only Blakiston's side of the story. He kept journals in those days. All the dukes of Blakiston did. Instead of farming figures and weather facts, his were full of entries of despair about the child he would never get to claim, of the happiness he would never feel again. I think the fact that she rejected him cracked him in a way. Next came your mother and she reminded him of mine. The journal entries are sporadic for a time, sometimes ranting, sometimes coherent but all lead back to my mother."

"Did he love her? My mother?"

"I don't think he didn't love her. He always had a temper difficult to leash and drinking fueled the fury. By the time he took Sophia, he was more often drunk than not. It is the only explanation for what he did."

Blake groaned again. "Do you think he took her to get back at me? Did he know how much I loved her?"

Daemon didn't react for a few moments. "I suppose that could have had something to do with it, but as far as I can tell, things only went so far wrong when she refused to say 'I do.'"

Blake's intake of breath echoed in the room. "He wanted to marry her?"

Daemon nodded again. "He looked for a bride who would make him happier than he thought my mother ever could. This was a way to get back at her."

"Did he write all of this down?" Blake asked. Did he need to burn that damned mansion to the ground to be rid of yet more evidence of depravity and betrayal?

"Like I said earlier, he thought I was the vicar come to take his deathbed confession."

Sophie had already been a duchess. His mother had been the first, but by the time he did the same with Sophie, his mother was dead. Sophie was the dowager duchess of Blakiston. Now he almost wished he had the title.

"Why didn't you tell me any of this?" Blake asked his brother.

"I did offer to tell you."

"Only yesterday."

"I guess sometimes the ugliness of the truth can hurt so many more people, you keep it to yourself and spin a pretty tale instead. She wouldn't be the first and she won't be the last."

What would life have been like for her? His own mother had fled the old duke after he'd wrapped his hands around her throat in a fit of rage. Would Sophie have been better off living on the streets in London than as the child bride of an angry drunkard? They would never know. He did know one thing. He would have been forced to watch from the sidelines as his childhood love swelled with another man's child. His father's child. If the man hadn't killed her first.

Suddenly her reactions made sense. When he touched her to remove the straw in her hair and she tensed as if he was going to throw her down on the floor then and there. It all made perfect sense. Why didn't she despise him more for the being the spawn of that man? How could she lay with him when she had been through so much?

"You have to let it all go," Daemon said. "You have to forget about the past and think to the future. Yours and hers."

"We have no future together."

"I never said together. You and Sophie are already entwined through Matthew, Violet and their child. You will always have to suffer her presence as long as you and Matthew are friends. She needs to be in contact with her family."

What had he done? Once again he'd let his out of control emotions rule the day rather than stepping back from the carnage-to-be to consider the angles. "Could I be more selfish or thoughtless?

His brother, the mind reader, said, "No, but you could start by apologizing and telling her what she means to you."

"I don't know what she means to me."

"Well, I know how much you mean to her. For that woman to have shared your bed means she cares a great deal."

"How long has it been since she shared your bed?" Why had he asked that? He didn't want to know, but he had to. He had to know if he could live with the knowledge that she liked Daemon more. Especially since *he* hadn't called her an ambitious slut. This question had nothing to do with titles at all.

"Months. Several months. We are more friends than anything else."

"I don't really think she would have me after everything that has happened."

"True, she turned me down," Daemon helpfully pointed out.

"I think she would still turn you down if you were to suddenly inherit the kingdom and become a prince," Matthew said.

"I will have to convince her."

"How?" both men asked.

"I will have to show her how much I need her and pray she believes me."

A string of violent and extraordinarily vile curses dropped from Sophie's lips as she trudged through the mud in her favorite boots, her shawl dripping from her shoulders and her hat dangling from numb fingertips. She directed another curse over her shoulder in the direction of the inn. If Blake had already been duke, the bridge would have been strong enough to carry the horse and carriage over safely and she would have already made it to Violet's to say her goodbyes.

For that's what she was doing. Only she did it on foot with the rain still falling in sheets across the countryside. No sooner had she made it across the bridge on her own two feet, had there been a roar of water carrying half an uprooted tree in its current. She'd only just made it to the slippery, grassy banks before the bridge had literally floated away before her eyes.

She prayed Matthew had a good horse in his barn that she could borrow. She'd made it to London from the house once before in the dead of night, she was sure she could do it again. From the city she would send the horse back and have her things collected. She never wanted to lay eyes on Blake again as long as she lived. But before she could leave, she had to say goodbye and tell Violet all about Blake's claim to the title so someone else could harass him in her stead. She had no doubt the women of the village could talk some sense into his thick head. Once Charles fled, they would be on their own until the land reverted back to the crown and a new man could either buy or earn the title.

If she knew anything about the King, he would already have a man in mind. She wondered if that new man would find his place here, the place that she couldn't.

"Stupid, pigheaded, stubborn idiot," she mumbled. As if the heavens agreed with her, lightening lit the afternoon's darkness and a crack of thunder made her jump. Within two steps, her nerves heightened from anger to apprehension.

Taking off in the storm hadn't been the smartest of her latest moves and when Matthew's farmhouse, the home of her somewhat happy childhood, came into view, she sighed and lengthened her stride. Her skirts pulled this way and that in the wind and her teeth chattered uncontrollably.

Why did he have to be so rude? Did the man not know how to bite his tongue and keep his opinions to himself? He certainly wouldn't last long as a duke in the capital if he couldn't learn to think before he spoke. Someone would call him out at the very first slight.

Lightening lit the sky again followed a split second later by another deafening crack of thunder. This time the sound was so loud, Sophie felt her entire body rumble. She ran the last twenty or so steps to Matthew's front door, arriving breathless and terrified of the elements. Even if Matthew did have a horse, she wouldn't be going anywhere until the weather eased a little.

She shook the excess water from her hands before knocking on the door first once, then twice then a third time with no answer. Sophie bit her lip as she turned her back to the door and peered into the distance. Matthew should be back from the village and Violet wouldn't be anywhere else but the farmhouse.

She knocked again. Still no answer.

Thunder boomed in the sky again and with a little squeal, Sophie pushed her way in, all sense of good manners gone with the howling wind.

At first she only registered that the main room of the farmhouse had changed spectacularly in fourteen years. It was hard to believe she walked into the same room. The hot glow of coals in the hearth lent the space a glow that touched on a mismatch of rugs, throws and cushions. Fresh flowers with tiny pink buds erupted from a pot on one side of the huge, curtained window and to the other side, a table overflowed with well loved books. Everywhere her gaze touched looked cozy and inviting, so different from her father's limited, rustic taste. Trailing her fingers over the back of an old day bed that appeared to double as a sofa of sorts, Sophie moved further into the house.

Just as she got to the kitchen, the back door opened and Violet hurried in, one small hand supporting her overly large stomach.

"Violet?"

"What are you doing here?" The pail of water Violet held in her other hand crashed to the floor in a bid to outdo the noise of the thunder that followed.

Sophie stepped back from the obviously distressed woman. "I'm so sorry. I shouldn't have come in, I know, but you didn't answer the door, and I...I..." She was out of excuses. "I'll leave, I'm so sorry to have entered your home."

"That's not what I-" Violet stopped talking mid sentence, leaned over her belly and let out the loudest, longest moan Sophie had ever heard.

Oh good God, no. Not now. "Is the baby coming?"

"I think so, yes...no. I don't know, but something isn't right."

"Matthew didn't come back?"

Violet shook her head, her face pale, drawn, in pain and terrified.

"No matter how you feel about me, I can't leave you like this." She couldn't tell her that unless Matthew could swim a flooded river, then he wouldn't be home any time soon.

"What are you talking about?"

Sophie bit her lip. Honesty? It was probably time for it. "I am a courtesan and I don't belong in your very pretty home."

"I never said that. Well, not those exact words."

Before she could reply, another contraction ripped through her sister-in-law and Violet bent again. This time her knees gave out. Sophie only just caught her by the shoulders before she would have hit the rough floor.

"How long have you been like this?"

"Since last evening."

With slow, sure steps, Sophie managed to herd Violet back into the sitting room where she lowered her onto a chair. "How could Matthew have left you?"

"He didn't know. First babies always take so long and I didn't want him to fuss."

And he would have been home well before dark if Sophie hadn't dragged him into her mess. Perhaps Blake wasn't the only one who needed to think before they spoke.

"Please, don't leave me. I need you."

She met the pleading eyes of a woman who didn't care who was in the room as long as she wasn't alone. "I've never actually delivered a baby, Violet." She'd had the opportunity, but always left it to the experts to take care of. What if she did something wrong? She knew the loss of a child and would not be the cause for another woman to feel it too.

"I have. I've-" Another scream filled the air and wound its way into Sophie's heart.

Once the worst of the pain had passed and Violet caught her breath again, she said, "I've attended births. You only have to do what I tell you and we'll both be fine."

There was that word again. Fine. She sure hoped so. "What do I do first?"

"Hot water and linens."

"That's it? Nothing else?"

"We don't have time for anything else..." The last word drew out as Violet's scream turned to a moan.

Sophie took her hand and let her squeeze until the worst had once again passed. It took only minutes to gather the supplies Violet told her to get, linens from the chest upstairs and hot water from a kettle on the corner of the stove, but the time that passed felt like years. Silently she prayed to whoever listened that this birth would be uncomplicated and easy for her sister-in-law. She prayed for a miracle.

Nineteen

B lake had had more than enough of the rain. He'd had enough of Daemon's smug, superior grins of victory and he'd definitely had enough of Matthew's scowls. Admitting that he'd slept with his best friend's sister wasn't the smartest move. Not that any of his actions in the previous week could boast of intelligence or even a glimmer of cleverness.

The villagers showed the illusion of happiness and prosperity, but the truth was unattractive. He'd known it all along, but he didn't want to believe it anymore now than he had two weeks, a year, even ten years ago. Sometimes the lies helped you sleep at night, helped you put one foot in front of the other. What other choice did they have?

Just like Sophie.

But perhaps in his anger at the world, at his parents and at Sophie, maybe he'd missed the point of everything. His mother had run to save her life and he'd thought her selfish when he looked back at his abandonment. Rather the truth was that she was ill and scared for her life and couldn't drag her child into the unknown with her. His father had never claimed him. Even on his deathbed and before, the old duke had tried to destroy his supposedly illegitimate child. Probably because the truth could do so much more damage than their lies ever could.

Then there was Sophie. Her betrayal had hurt more than the others because he believed her to be his salvation. Life with her would have brightened every dark day that had gone before. Or maybe that was the ultimate lie.

They could have been happy or they could have been miserable. Who knows? But he had to go to her. He had to find her and have it out with her once and for all. She had to know what was in his mind before he lost his head again. Words always seemed to come out wrong when she raised his temper to a boiling point. He used to be rational.

Perhaps he could gag her so she couldn't argue? It was a warming thought as he climbed the stairs to her room.

He knocked lightly on the door. If she was still furious with him, he would have to tread very carefully. "Sophie?" he called.

No answer.

"Please don't do this. I want to speak to you, apologize, explain what happened."

Still no answer.

Blake's anger began to grow and he took a deep calming breath before grabbing hold of the handle and throwing the door wide.

His next words fell out in a rush. "I know you don't want to see me but I have to explain. There are things you need to understa-" She wasn't there.

Cursing beneath his breath, he left the room and went back down the stairs. Maybe she was in the barn? She seemed to enjoy it there. As he stomped through the tap to the kitchen, Matthew called out to him, breathless and obviously worried.

"Sophie is gone. We found your horse and her carriage out by the bridge, but she wasn't there."

"Did you look for her? She probably went to find you. Did you check your house?"

Matthew shook his head, "The bridge is gone, I couldn't get across."

Blake didn't have to be a mind reader to know the possibilities Matthew considered.

Sophie could have been on the bridge when it washed away. She could have got there too late and done something reckless—she was certainly angry enough when she left—like swim across. "She wouldn't do that, would she? She wouldn't try to cross the river if the bridge was out."

"She could be anywhere," Matthew said. "She may have tried to go around, but why would she do that on foot?

She knows the way back to London but we don't know which way she went all those years ago. And the landscape has changed around here. With all the flooding and shifting soil, she could be in real danger."

Damn Charles and his tightfistedness. If only the cur had fixed the bridge.

You could have fixed it.

And damn his conscience too!

"You take the east and I'll take the west and we'll circle back. If you find a safe place to cross, do it and check your place. We have to hope she made it across the river or is searching for a way over somewhere else."

"The closest crossing is miles away and it's getting dark."

Blake sighed. "Then we better hope to find her quickly."

Within minutes the pair, along with Daemon, were stocked with the essentials for a search and set out into the blinding rain. Blake couldn't help but remember the other time they'd searched in the dark for a girl who didn't want to be found.

He only hoped in this instance they were more successful. Sophie would not be so lucky a second time around.

"Do you believe things happen for a reason?" Violet asked, her face pale as sweat dripped from her brow.

Sophie shook her head. "Not really. Do you think this happened for a reason? That I was out here because Matthew was not?" No need to explain that Matthew wasn't there because of her.

"No, I mean that you are here at all."

"As in alive?" Sophie asked. Were they to get philosophical at a time when Violet wore nothing more than a nightshirt and Sophie's hands were covered in her blood? There was so much blood.

Violet braced for yet another contraction, a long groan filled the air to drown out the pattering of rain on the roof. Once the worst was over, she continued, "No, I mean here, in this house, in this moment. When Matthew wrote you, you didn't reply. We thought you refused to come."

"I didn't want to put you in this position. I didn't want to taint you or the babe with my presence, but he's my brother. I could no more deny him than my next breath."

"You twist my words. It's not that I didn't want you to come. I did want to meet you. I just didn't think you actually would."

Sophie was about to reply when another contraction gripped her sister-in-law. They were getting closer, but still no baby. Only blood. With every contraction more trickled out to stain the sheet. "Violet, is there supposed to be blood?" She hadn't wanted to ask but she was ill equipped for any of this.

Violet nodded but didn't shed any light. Instead, she went on. "Why did you come?"

"I had to. Matthew asked."

"You didn't have to. Please, be honest with me. From one woman to another, why did you come?"

Sophie's hands rested against her own stomach as her heart skipped a beat. "I was pregnant."

"Was?"

"I lost the baby. I couldn't face another party, another ball, another man."

"I'm so sorry. Why didn't you say something?."

Another contraction passed before Sophie answered. "It was for the best. A woman like me has no business raising a child."

"A woman like you?"

"A courtesan. A harlot. A common prostitute."

"There is nothing common about you. You did what you had to to succeed. I see that now. That makes you unique and cunning, not common."

Sophie could almost believe Violet respected her, the decisions she'd made. Almost. "You are kind, Violet, but we both know the truth. It's why you wouldn't have me in your home."

"You're right and that is my shame to bear. I didn't want a courtesan in my home, around my baby. I am truly sorry for that."

"Thank you, Violet."

She'd been wrong about so much. About life in the country and about being accepted somewhere where people did know her name. Could she have been so wrong about Blake too? She doubted it, since he was the one who had started so many of their fights. Perhaps they were both too stubborn to see what was in each one's way? If she could change her perceptions of him, then perhaps she could change his perception of her?

"Oh, god, oh god, oh god." Violet's moans filled the air along with her blasphemy and Sophie had no more time to think about Blake or his thick head.

"Is it coming?" Sophie asked. "Is this it?"

Violet nodded and made the strangest sounds. Sounds Sophie would never in all her days forget.

She held the toweling for what felt like forever until finally a fuzzy head appeared. "Oh, I can see it, I can see the baby's head."

"What... What color is...his head?"

Through all the muck in the hair and on his skin, it took a few seconds to see but eventually she replied, "Pink. His head is pink."

Only ten minutes later and Sophie held the baby in her hands, staring at her red face as she screamed her little lungs out. "It's a girl, Violet. A beautiful baby girl."

Violet held her arms out and as Sophie laid the baby against her chest, her eyes welled and a tear dripped down her cheek.

"Thank you. Thank you for being here for me, with me."

Sophie nodded but couldn't say a word. The lump in her throat had grown so big, she feared it would choke her.

So many things were different here, where strong woman gave birth on their kitchen tables. A city woman, noble or not, would have screamed for a doctor and probably held their legs closed until one arrived.

As her hands went to her stomach again, Sophie thought about the baby she had lost. Would she have had the strength to deliver a baby in the midst of a storm? If she was the country woman she was meant to be, would she have been able to carry the baby all the way rather than lose it early? So many thoughts went through her mind, it was impossible to pin one down and concentrate on it.

"There is another baby, Sophie."

Sophie shook her head. "Not for me. I won't do it. I'll not bring a child into a world where his mother is with a different man every other season. I won't do it, I can't."

"No, I mean there is another baby to come."

Sophie snapped her gaze to Violet's and ran to take the baby from her. She put the girl on the floor on a mass of linens and covered her with a soft woolen blanket.

"How do you know?" Sophie asked.

"I can feel another. He still kicks."

The next thirty minutes were filled with Violet's screams, this baby so much harder to bear, and the occasional roll of thunder. When Sophie thought perhaps Violet had been wrong, that something had gone wrong, another head appeared.

"What color?" Violet asked, her barely there voice coming out in exhausted huffs.

"Not pink. I think, almost blue. Violet, you have to push, you have to push now."

"I can't."

"You have to. Please, please push."

She would not lose this baby. "Violet, push," she yelled.

One more contraction, one more almighty push and the body fell into her hands. Sophie didn't have to ask what to do now. She'd seen this with sheep in the years before she'd left the country. It all came flooding back as fast as the river had taken the bridge.

"He's not crying," Violet said, her voice shaky. "Why isn't he crying?"

"Give me a moment." Sophie gently placed the baby on the table between Violet's legs and placed her fingers around his little neck. Once she had the long, bloody cord away from his throat, she cleared the muck from his mouth and breathed into it with short puffs. She turned him over in her hands and patted firmly between his tiny shoulder blades, once, twice, the third time even harder.

With a little splutter, a short breath and an almighty wail, he clenched his fists and screamed his complaints long and loud, his skin turning three shades of pink.

Sophie fell to her knees on the floor, tears now flowing unheeded down her face to drip on the crying infant she clutched to her chest. "Looks like we are both stronger than we thought, little one."

"Any sign?" Blake roared to be heard over the rushing river.

Matthew shook his head and cupped his hands around his mouth. "We have to go back. We'll never find her in this."

"I'm not leaving her out here."

"You'll kill yourself looking," Daemon said as he pulled his horse to a stop in the mud.

Blake ignored the freezing sting of the rain as it pelted his head and face. He should kill himself looking for her. It was his fault that she'd left. He could have made her welcome. He could have ignored her own barbs and acted the gentleman he knew was in him somewhere. It was all his fault.

He looked Matthew in the eye, the dark making it difficult to read his friend's gaze, but he knew it would mirror the anguish he felt. "I can't lose her again."

"I know, but we can't hope to find her in this. We'll have to wait till morning."

"We did that last time and we lost her." At the time he'd thought he'd lost her forever.

"We won't lose her this time, Blake. She's a big girl and she's strong. She'll probably be up a tree waiting out the storm and wondering why she went out in it in the first place."

Blake shook his head, droplets spraying back into the still falling rain. "I can't lose her again," he said again, but more to himself and in complete defeat. Matthew was right. If they hadn't found her the first time she'd fled on a cool, clear night, then they wouldn't find her in the middle of all this either.

She was a strong woman. She was too clever for her own good. His heart sank. When they did find her, and they would, she would be even angrier with him. He was sure of it. He'd had trouble forgiving her for what she'd done to him fourteen years ago, but the tables had turned. Everything was different now.

He only hoped she found it in her heart to forgive him for being a fool.

Violet was the picture of radiance as she sighed and settled further into the mattress, her adoring eyes only leaving one cherubic face to glance to the other.

Sophie still couldn't believe it. Two babies? Who would have guessed? She suspected Violet had. "Why did you never tell Matthew that there were two babies?"

"I wasn't certain. It was only a feeling I had and he would have only fussed more."

"He may not have left your side if he'd known."

Violet half groaned, half laughed. "Thank the Lord I didn't mention it, then."

She couldn't help but chuckle, but the laugh soon turned into a yawn.

"You should get some rest," Violet told her, her own eyelids drooping despite the effort to stay awake.

"You are the one who should rest. I should get back to town and let Matthew know he is the father of not one baby but two."

"You can't go back out into this storm. Even if you made the bridge, it would be treacherous."

Sophie had forgotten about the bridge. Even if she wanted to get back, she couldn't. There was only one other way back to Blakiston and she wouldn't make it in the dark let alone the rain and flooding. "You're right," she sighed. "The bridge was washed away, so I guess it's just the four of us tonight."

"They know where you are anyway, so they won't worry."

"Uh, no they don't."

"What happened? Sophie, what were you doing on your way out here?"

She bit her lip. The woman had just given birth. How much could she burden her with? In the end, she decided everything. Violet had the right to know.

"Do you know much about Blake's history?"

"I know a bit."

"None of us really knew anything at all. His mother was married to the old duke."

"So he is the rightful heir?"

Sophie nodded. "St. Ives came to make him a duke."

"What did Blake say?"

"He refused. He is the most stubborn, fool-headed, idiot of a man. He could have made things so much better around here and instead he lied. Lied to everyone."

"He must have had his reasons."

"I don't care what his reasons were. He made a decision to fool everyone so he didn't have to take on the responsibility of the estate."

"There had to be more to it than that. A man doesn't do something for no reason, especially not a man like Blake."

"Sometimes decisions made under duress have no reason, you choose the smoother of the paths at the fork in the road."

"Is that what you did?" Violet asked in a small voice as she leaned back against the pillows once more.

Sophie sighed. It's exactly what she did. At one turn there was her father and the duke and at the other, London. She'd had no idea what living in the city would entail. If she had, things might have been different. "I made the choice between the lesser of two evils. You all pity me my life, but between the hardest of hard lives or death at the hands of a vicious man, I would always take life."

"But at the time, when you thought those were the only two choices, you neglected the third. I'm not sure if it was intentional or not, but why did you not ask Matthew or Blake for help?"

"It was too late. I never thought my father would actually go through with the deal."

"What deal?"

She'd forgotten that Violet didn't know as much as everyone else. For a second time, she poured her story out and hoped for empathy rather than disgust.

Violet gave her neither, in fact she radiated indignation. "And after? Could you not have gone to Matthew before you fled?"

"I didn't want him to have to run with me. I was so ashamed and humiliated and terrified. I would have ruined everyone's lives. He wouldn't have been able to stop Blakiston from dragging me back."

"How do you know that? Perhaps Blake would have embraced his birthright if it had meant saving you."

"He wouldn't have done that for me." As soon as the words were out, Sophie knew them for the lies they were. Of course he would have saved her. Matthew and he would never have allowed anything to happen to her, but it had taken so many years to come to the realization and by then, too much time had passed. Too much had happened.

Her mind drifted back to the night she fled—the pain she was in, the humiliation that her innocence had been taken so violently. She hadn't wanted to face anyone at all, let alone the man she would have married had he asked. And then what of revenge? What if Blake or Matthew got it in their heads to avenge her honor and wound up swinging from a rope? Yes, she'd taken the lighter fork in the road.

"He would have saved you then and he would do it now."

"I don't need saving."

"Are you sure?"

Sophie looked away from the question in Violet's eyes.

In the sense of immediate danger she did not need rescuing, but she had turned out to be her own worst enemy. Who would save her from herself? She enjoyed London. The bustling metropolis always delivered something different. No two days were ever the same and she had her life mapped out there. She had the clinic and the children they helped; she had her friends and her wealth. Everything was easy.

Except for the men.

Despite the fact her reputation was mostly gossip, she had slept with men for housing and gowns. It was a necessity she'd accepted very early on, but she was older now. She liked to think she was wiser. She hadn't made a rash choice in years.

What do you call fleeing into the driving rain?

Blake had really hurt her. She'd never realized how much the man could hurt her. Why should she stay somewhere like that with a man like him?

The question of what she would do once she returned to London still lingered. Since there was no lower legal occupation than the one already pinned to her, she was at a loose end.

"Damn," she muttered.

"He loves you," Violet put forward gently.

"He certainly has a fine way of showing it."

"It killed him when you left all those years ago. He was a wreck for months, picked fights with his uncle, Matthew, anyone who could give him a different type of pain than what you left him with. Even then, it was you he loved."

"How do you know that? I can't imagine Blake poured his heart out to you."

Violet shook her head. "He didn't tell me any of it but Matthew knew it all. What Blake told and him and what he didn't."

"And he just told you?" Wasn't there an unspoken bond between best friends? Between men? Would Blake be embarrassed to know that Matthew told his wife all of his dark secrets?

"A husband and wife have no secrets." She smiled. "Matty tells me everything."

Sophie rather doubted it. "Even if he does love me, we can't talk for more than five minutes without nearly declaring war. If I were a man, we would have chosen our seconds and had it out at dawn already."

"If you were a man, he wouldn't argue with you so. If you were a man, your leaving would have only left him angry rather than devastated."

Devastated. The word rattled around in her head. If he was so devastated, why had he never written to her? Matthew had her address in recent years. Why hadn't he come to the city to declare his love and bring her home? It's what she secretly waited for all those years of men and gambling and the never-ending night life. In the back of her mind she'd replayed the fairy tales endlessly and hated the princesses and damsels in distress for their knights. She especially hated the trusty steeds for not carrying a prince to her rescue to live happily ever after.

She'd almost given up on happily-ever-afters but sometimes, when she saw a couple like Matthew and Violet, her hope would be renewed. At least until the next blow came to knock her back to reality. Like losing the babies. For a few weeks, she had been in the happiest of places, had even begun to consider her return to Blakiston as the new start she'd needed for herself and her child. But that wasn't meant to be either. Things did happen for a reason, but the reasons were usually irrational, unexplainable, and devastating. There was that word again.

"Do you love him?" Violet asked.

"It doesn't matter anymore. He could never respect me, he could never forget the fourteen years in between and the things I've done." She looked up into Violet's eyes, her own misting with hot tears she'd held back for days. "I've done things, Violet, things I could never forget or forgive, so why would he?"

"You don't have to forget. Those years made you who you are today. You will have to forgive yourself before you can expect his forgiveness, but I suspect you don't need his. I think he's already given it to you. The arguments are his way of telling you he's still hurting but I'm sure if you could understand where the pain comes from, you can take care of it. You can take care of it, him and you."

"What if I don't have the strength?" It was the scariest question she'd ever asked out loud. What if she didn't have the strength? Would it all fall apart? "What if I can't be that strong?"

"Maybe it's time you stopped being needed and started to need. Perhaps you should let a big capable man be strong enough for the both of you?"

Twenty

B lake woke early the next morning with barely any sleep and a permanent lump stuck on the inside of his throat. The sun wasn't yet up, but it wouldn't be long and he needed to be on the road now. He dressed quickly, unaware and uncaring of what he donned. In the kitchen he made coffee. As he gulped and his stomach warmed, his gaze was drawn to the small changes Sophie had made in the short time she'd spent turning his kitchen into her domain. Everywhere he looked was neat and tidy. She'd even scrubbed the wall above the hearth, bringing it back to a warm brick color rather than the red and black grime-color it had become. He ran a tight kitchen, but he didn't get time to do some things.

She had given him so much in the past week and not all because of the bargain he'd trapped her into. After their accident, she'd stepped up and done everything expected of a publican and more. But at the end of the day, she wasn't made for this life. Running a tavern wasn't going to keep her in Blakiston and he doubted he would be enticing enough on his own. No. He had to offer her something. Something more than a farmer's wife and more than love.

In reality, with Sophie being so logical, love would not put a roof over her head. It didn't matter how he offered it, she would need more.

Would she stay for a duke if not for a tavern keeper? If it came down to it, he would sell his soul for a roof over her beautiful head.

He walked back into the tap, and using the tip of his mud-crusted boot, he kicked Matthew awake and thrust a coffee into his hands, his energy more renewed now than when he'd first woken. "Drink up and make it quick," he said. "I ride out in ten minutes with or without you."

"Is it still raining?" Matthew asked as he rubbed his eyes and sat up.

"Rain stopped around three. It'll be slippery but at least not so cold and miserable."

"Speaking of miserable," Matthew said with a small smile. "Where do you plan to start looking? It's going to be treacherous going, even if the rain does keep off."

He'd been thinking on that all night. The closest property over the bridge was Matthew's. But why she would have gone there when her brother was at the inn, he wasn't sure. Regardless, they had to start somewhere. "I'm going to backtrack to the bridge on the other side and you are going to go straight home. Check on your wife and then come and find me. The mud will be so deep on the other side that, with luck, I'll see footprints. Hopefully the other two bridges are still standing."

Neither man said it but the bridge to the south was sure to have taken the full weight of the fallen bridge and likely had been washed away as well. Hopefully, if luck did smile on them that day, the old and rotten timbers would have sank, snagged or broken up in the three miles of bends and banks before the next bridge. His hopes were pinned on sank or snagged.

"We'll take Daemon's horses."

"Will you now?" A sleepy voice asked from the doorway.

Blake spun and faced his brother, already dressed in high boots, breeches and a sturdy shirt, waistcoat and coat, the very picture of a powerful duke. "You're going to help?" he asked.

Daemon gave him a don't-be-daft-look before walking further into the room. "The Duke's horses will be faster. I had Dominic collect three of the best last night. They should be saddled and ready right about," he pulled out his fob and examined the face, "now."

"What are we waiting for, then?" Sophie could be out there, hurt, desperate or in danger. Fourteen years was more than enough time to forget how dangerous the wild countryside could be. The night they were stranded, she'd wanted to start walking back to the inn on her own. The woman had no idea.

Blake didn't wait for an answer. He turned on his heel and marched through the muddy yard and into the stable. They'd wasted enough time.

Dominic handed him the reins to a towering chestnut and with barely a nod, he swung up into the saddle and took off north. The horse mustn't have seen exercise for some time in Blakiston's yard, and sensing his eagerness, took the lead and lengthened his stride, quickening his pace until the only sound was the thunder of his hooves. The wind whipped past, stinging his cheeks.

Blake leaned over his neck, only putting the slightest pressure on the reins to keep the beast to the solid parts of the road rather than the slick mud. One of them was going to wind up with a broken neck if even one hoof was misplaced.

When the northern bridge came into view, Blake looked heavenward and gave thanks, reining in hard.

"I thought you were never going to slow," Daemon said as he brought a midnight horse to a stop next to his.

"I would rather find Sophie than die trying," he said.

"You could have ridden past her and never noticed."

Blake shook his head. "She won't be on this side of the river and the current is going to the opposite way. " He swallowed hard. "If she went in, she'll be down Matthew's end." As soon as he said the words, he groaned. He should have taken the south.

"Don't even think it," Daemon ordered. "We will find her safe and sound. That woman has more lives than an alley cat."

"I hope so," Blake muttered before crossing the bridge with care. If the water had been strong enough to take the other, then this one could have sustained damage also.

By the time they got to where the footings from the old structure stood, naked and lonely, the sun shone bright on a day of torment. He saw small boot tracks sliding about before ceasing in the harder part of the roadway.

"Thank the Lord she made it over," Daemon breathed, echoing Blake's exact thoughts.

With more hope than he dared feel an hour before, they set off again, this time in the direction of Matthew's house. There was nowhere else to go out here.

"Do you think she was wrong to react the way she did?" Blake asked as they rode. "After what I said?"

"I would have punched you, myself. Or called you out. She did what any woman would have done. But for God's sake, she should only have fled to the kitchens or barn in this weather."

"Why are you helping me now? You don't think I deserve her anymore than I do."

"It's not about who deserves whom or even how you treat each other. It's a question of whether you can make her happy. I believe you can. If you can keep your mouth shut."

But the problem wasn't going to be his mouth. Even if they found her, how could he tell her everything in his heart before she ripped his head off?

Before he could think further about the angle of his approach, she appeared. Just like that. She walked with long strides over the crest of a hill in the middle of the road on the hard packed dirt and she was...smiling. Vibrantly. The sleeves of her ruined dress were pulled up to her arms and stains darkened the front, but she smiled as she walked.

Blake kicked his heels hard to the sides of the horse until the beast surged with power beneath him. When he was close enough, he reined in, but before the animal had stopped, he kicked free of the stirrups and leapt from his back.

Blake was so unashamedly glad to see her, he threw his arms around her and lifted her from the ground. She fit in his arms as if she was made to be held by him and only him. It was a few seconds before Blake realized how he held her and went to put her back on her feet. It was only a second more until he realized she held him just as hard.

"Thank God you're all right. You could have died."

"You're here," she whispered.

"Where else would I be?"

The thunder of hoof beats brought them back to the fact they stood in the middle of the road. Daemon averted his gaze, his horse shifting after sensing her rider's discomfort.

Matthew pulled the reins hard and finally came to a stop, looked Sophie from head to toes and back again. "Where the hell have you been?"

"You were supposed to be downstream, Matthew," Blake pointed out.

"I did go that way, but then I found the remains of the bridge and the tree branches are completely blocking the bend down by the Patrick place. I figured if she had been in the water, the tree would have stopped her swim."

"How nice of you to put it that way," Sophie commented with a shiver. "As you can see, I didn't require a swim at all."

"Is that blood on your dress?" he asked, ignoring her attempt at sarcasm.

"It's not mine."

Matthew stared at her for a moment, his gaze shifted from her face to the road she had walked down. "Violet?"

Sophie didn't get the chance to answer before he'd kicked his heels to his horse's side and took off down the lane.

"Do I need to go after him?" Daemon asked.

"She is fine, as are the babies."

"Babies?" both men echoed.

"A boy and a girl."

Blake blew out a breath before speaking, "Are they all right? Jesus, Sophie, what happened last night?"

"After I left the inn, I headed to say my goodbyes to Violet and found her in labor."

"Do I want to know the rest of this story?" Daemon groaned.

Sophie laughed. "Perhaps not."

"Then I'll go and make sure your brother doesn't kill himself on his way home."

"Blake, I-"

"Sophie-"

Sophie thought Blake would do the gentlemanly thing and let her speak first but when she opened her mouth, he clapped a hand over it and shushed her. *He shushed her?*

"I have to tell you something before you ruin the moment and distract me from my purpose. Will you cease your noise?"

She nodded and he took his hand away a heartbeat before she would have tried to bite him for manhandling her. "What-"

"Sophie!" His warning was received. She nodded again and snapped her mouth shut.

"You are the most stubborn woman I have ever met. Even as a girl, you had to have everything your way. If you could have controlled the sun rising you would have told it to give you an extra hour in the day to get your hands dirty."

He was right.

"You also never listen. You hear, but you don't listen."

"Are you going to stand there and list my flaws? I'm tired, Blake, I want to get back and wash and rest."

"Will you shut up? I'm trying to tell you that I want you to stay. I want you to stay in Blakiston."

"Why?" She wasn't going to tell him she'd already decided to stay. She wanted to hear what he had to say.

"Because I don't think I could live through losing you again. Because this past week has shown me that life with you is a hell of a lot more interesting than without you."

"But we fight. All the time. Interesting isn't a word I would associate with our friendship."

Blake stepped toward her and cupped her dirt-smudged cheek. "What if ours isn't only a friendship?"

She blinked. Held her breath.

"I love you, Sophie, and I want you to stay here with me. I want you to work alongside me, sleep alongside me, live with me."

She gulped. Gulped again. Sophie racked her brain trying to think of a reason he would have to say all of the things he was saying. Was it because she'd been gone and he'd worried for her? Did he mistake fear of loss with love? The look on his face when he'd seen her was one of pure relief. Perhaps he thought he owed it to her to keep her safe? His idea of safe anyway.

"You don't have to do this." She stepped back. Instantly her cheek was cold from the loss of contact. His contact. "You don't have to try to save me."

"I'm not trying to save you. I'm trying to save me. No woman has ever lived up to your image in my mind. I stopped looking and hadn't even realized I had until you came back into my life and turned it inside out. I didn't know how miserable I was without you."

Sophie was torn. Did she believe him? Trust him? Or did she trust as she always had, only in herself and no one else. Then she wouldn't be let down, she couldn't be hurt or left out in the cold.

Blake must have taken her silence as refusal as he forged ahead. "I'll be anyone you want. I'll be a duke or a tavern owner or even a farmer, just as long as you stand beside me."

"As your what? As your maid or your mistress? Perhaps your close friend?" She had to hear the words. She wouldn't believe it until she heard it from his mouth, checked the sincerity in his eyes against the reaction in her body. What if his relief at her safety and gratitude over her help this week coerced this declaration? She wouldn't know if he offered her a life out of guilt and he wouldn't know if she accepted out of desperation.

"I want you as my wife and the mother of my children. Imagine retelling this tale to the little ones." His smile was the brightest she'd seen since they were children.

She could see in her mind the picture he painted. But there was just one problem with the vision. "There's something I have to tell you before you say anything else."

"If it's no, then I probably don't want to hear it. Do you need time to think on it? Do you need me to get down on my knees and apologize and tell you what an idiot I've been? How ashamed I am for the names I called you?"

"It's not that," she shook her head, her eyes burned with tears and the words stuck in her throat. "Before I came here..."

"Let's forget the past. Put it all behind us and never look back ever again."

"Can you do that?"

"Can you?"

"No." It was the simplest answer. Whether he stayed an innkeeper, became a farmer or took the title, her past was always going to come between them and they would be hopelessly naive to think otherwise.

"No?"

"Before I came here, I was pregnant."

"What?" This time it was Blake who stepped away from her. Exactly the reaction she'd expected from him.

"I lost the baby. And not the first one. Blake, I can never carry a child."

"How many times have you been with child?"

The disgust she'd thought would follow his initial reaction was strangely absent in his question.

"Becoming pregnant is not always avoidable in my profession."

"How many times?"

"Five. This one was to be the fifth child I would have liked to hold in my arms, heard her tiny cry..." Had someone to love and be loved by.

"I don't understand. I'm sorry for your loss, but what does this have to do with anything between us?"

"If you take the title, I won't be able to give you an heir. You'll never be a father and I will never be a mother. We won't ever have a family to call our own."

Blake raked a hand through his already mussed hair and took a deep breath. His chest hurt with the effort not to explode and rail and rant. Not at her, but for her. And mostly at himself. He should have known there was something off about Sophie when she'd looked at him from her perch in the carriage in the yard that first day. When she'd alternated between fear and fury and then resignation, he'd thought her acting skills had matured while in London. But she really had been angry and upset...hurt. Why hadn't he just let her be?

"Children don't make a family, Sophie, love and commitment do. I'll still take the title if that's what you want. After the fathers we had to walk in the shadows of, I'm not even sure I want to be one. Matthew and Violet have plenty enough babes to go around now."

"You say that now, but what about the future?"

"I'm already thirty-three years old. This is the future."

"You are the only one who can decide to take the title or not. It will be your burden to bear, but I know you can do good. Would do good."

"Haven't we made enough decisions in our lives without asking for help or considering others?"

"I thought you said you understood why I made those choices."

He took her hands in his. "I'm not judging you. I'm saying we should consider each other now. If you're to be my wife, then *we* need to make the choices here on in."

"I haven't agreed to become your wife."

"You will," Blake chuckled. He felt lighter now than he had in fourteen years. This time it didn't matter what she did or where she went. He would follow her and never let her go.

"You think to force me? Wear me down?"

Blake took her hand in his and began walking toward where the horse stood grazing quietly. He *didn't* want to let her go. Not even for a second. "I would never force you to do anything." He stared at her sideways. "Well, I may force you to take a bath. You look as though you rolled through a paddock."

"I may as well have," she muttered as her hand relaxed in his and her stride lengthened to keep pace.

"So a boy and a girl? Are they really all all right?"

"They're excellent. It was the most difficult night of my life. And the best."

"Do you think maybe you could make a life out of delivering babies?"

Sophie's nose wrinkled and she shook her head. "Never. I would never want to do it again for as long as I live."

They both laughed at that. He didn't want any of the details, but he could imagine.

As he walked alongside the animal, wondering how they were both going to fit on the narrow saddle, relishing the idea of holding her on his lap as they made their way back to the inn, the sounds of hooves reached him again.

At first he thought they might belong to Daemon, but the noise came from the other direction and the rising level signaled more than one horse.

Blake held the reins in his hand and without a word, helped Sophie into the saddle.

"I don't ride well, Blake, and this is not a side saddle."

The feeling of unease multiplied in him when a carriage and pair barreled around the bend, headed straight for the fork in the road behind where they stood. He recognized at once the conveyance and the driver behind the horses, a look of anger and desperation on his face.

He was not in the mood for a confrontation with a debt-ridden former duke.

Twenty-One

"Charles is fleeing," Sophie stated, her voice low despite the distance between them and him.

"That was the original idea."

"Where do you think he will go?"

"The Continent? The Americas? He's lucky he isn't being shipped off with the criminals. But as long as it isn't here, I don't care."

They stood and watched as he drew closer. Blake held his breath and hoped the man kept going, that he wouldn't find the need to stop.

But Blake's luck had been used up in finding Sophie and as the carriage came to a stop, Charles threw the brake on and jumped to the ground, eyes positively glinting with malice.

Blake swore under his breath.

"This is all your fault," Charles screeched, his fists at his sides as he advanced.

Blake sighed. "I hardly see how any of the blame can be laid at my door."

"If you had kept your mouth shut, the King would never have discovered the details of your birth. I would still be a duke and you would still be a nobody."

Blake didn't like the wild look in Charles's eyes but this confrontation had to come. Be it now or when the rat crawled back from the hole he would find to hide in. "I didn't tell the King anything. Do you really think he would have listened to me, anyway? I'm a nobody. Nobodies do not get heard by the King of England."

"Then how did he find out? I'll kill the man who took this all away from me."

"Does it matter? Your gambling put you here. Not the man, not the King and certainly not me. I don't even want to be a duke."

Charles roared. "It shouldn't even be a choice for you! From the sounds of it, your mother was nothing more than an ambitious slut. What did she do to get the old duke to marry her?"

The words stung. They stung more for the fact that he'd said the exact same words to Sophie only yesterday. They stung because this is how men viewed women who reached above their station. Never mind if love was involved or not. Never mind if they were beaten, raped, treated as animals. He happened to know very well his mother loved his father until he tried to kill her in a drunken rage.

"My mother and her relationship with Blakiston is none of your business. Be on your way now, Charles. There are no options left here for you."

The wild gleam grew wilder as he looked between Blake and Sophie—who sat frozen atop the horse.

"Sophie, I want you to leave now." Blake dropped the reins he held in his hands and willed her to pick them up and leave.

"I want her to stay," Charles said as he pulled an ivory-handled pistol from the pocket of his greatcoat and pointed it at Sophie.

"Sophie, go!"

But the horse must have finally picked up on the tension between the three and reared up, hooves flying through the air. Since Sophie didn't have hold of the reins, just the horse's mane, she teetered and fell.

Blake half caught her, half fell with her. The breath was knocked out of him as she landed with an elbow to his gut, her short shriek punctuating the air only to fall away.

Before they'd gotten to their feet, Charles put his boot squarely on Blake's chest to push him back to the ground. With his other hand, the deranged man pulled Sophie to her feet by her hair. She screamed again and Blake tried to right himself, but the position he'd landed in made it difficult. One of his legs was under the other and her skirts still lay across them. If he moved, he would become more tangled.

"Get your hands off her," he growled.

"Or what?" Charles snickered. "I have the gun and you have nothing. Just the way it should have been."

"You're mad," Sophie puffed, still trying to catch her breath. "You can't possibly go anywhere new from here. Blake is going to be duke."

"It's never that simple," Charles said, tightening his grip in her hair until her scalp smarted and tears filled her eyes.

She met Blake's gaze, his eyes flicked to the right. He wanted her to run. Well, there was no way. He'd said it himself. They were in this together and together they would get out of it. She just had to distract Charles so Blake could get to his feet.

"I'm telling you, I can't see how this will work. If you kill Blake, you will go to prison. Perhaps if he had been a nobody, you would get away with it, but not like this. Not with the line of succession in question."

"Oh, there's no question. While this son of a bitch holds the title, I'll go back to being the heir until he spawns a brat."

"And then you'll be the nobody," Blake grunted.

Charles pressed his boot deeper into Blake's chest and leaned forward slightly.

"Never!" he spat. "I will not let it get that far."

"But you can't kill him," Sophie pointed out again. If she could shove him hard enough with her shoulder, he would fall and then Blake could wrestle the pistol from him. It was risky but it was their only chance. "I'll tell everyone that you killed him and you will be transported."

"No one is going to believe you, whore," Charles laughed, sending shivers down her spine.

"Daemon will believe me."

"Not if you're dead too."

This time it was Blake who laughed. "How are you going to get away with two murders? This is why you were never a successful gambler. You don't think things through."

"But you have already set the scene for this little drama," Charles said. "You two have done nothing but tear into each other since she arrived. There isn't a soul in town who won't believe she killed you in a rage. She has quite the temper, you see."

"Matthew won't believe that, and neither will Daemon."

Charles laughed again. This time the sound rose as hysteria took over. "I'm going to tell him that Blake forced himself on you and you killed him."

Sophie smiled down at Blake. "Now that, neither Daemon nor Matthew will believe. They already know the truth of our relationship."

Charles tensed, wild eyes once again flicking back and forth between Sophie and Blake. "You bedded him?"

Blake's smug grin gave him the answer.

"Where did I get the gun?" Sophie asked, not sure they'd done the smartest thing just then. Charles would only get angrier, since he wasn't able to charm her himself. She had to keep him talking until she found her moment.

"I don't care where you got the gun," Charles yelled. The sound echoed and for a second Sophie hoped Daemon or Matthew would hear the commotion and come back and rescue them.

"Is it yours?" Blake asked. "Because if you took it from the house, the authorities will know of its origins."

"She could have taken it from the house at the auction."

"I never went to the house." She would never set foot in that house again. Ever.

"Yes, you came there to meet me. You wanted to thank me properly for rescuing you on the road that day."

"I don't think so," Sophie said adamantly. But perhaps that angle would work for him. She was a courtesan. All he had to say was that she was soliciting a new protector and it would put her in the house. Even with all of the witnesses at the inn, his word would mean more than all of theirs put together. But then again, his credibility was cracked. As was his mind evidently.

"What have I got to lose?" Charles said with a shrug and a smile.

Sophie took that moment, when his grip relaxed in her hair and his boot still pressed into Blake's chest, to brace her legs and push with all her might.

Charles overbalanced and the gun dropped dangerously close to Blake's body, but then he was falling. He couldn't regain his balance, but neither did he let go of her. In a tangle of arms and legs, Sophie fell over Blake's feet and into Charles's chest. The impact knocked his hand loose of her head until he could wrap his arm around her and hold the reclaimed gun to her cheek. "That was not smart," he hissed, spittle flying everywhere.

Blake was on his feet in a second, but stopped at the sight of the pistol pressed to her head.

"Let her go, Charles. This has nothing to do with Sophie. It's between you and me."

"Oh, no. There are more players in this game than the three of us. St. Ives has the ear of the king. If I'm to lose my position, then he must lose too."

"That is why you wouldn't leave me alone? You were trying to steal me from him?"

"If you were a typical slut, I would have offered you more money than him, but it's clear you are different. I haven't yet worked out what motivates you."

Certainly not money, but she wasn't going to tell him that. "If you kill us both, Daemon will hunt you down. He won't rest until he finds you."

Charles began to laugh again. "I'm counting on it."

It didn't make sense. Was he after all three of them for getting in the way of his title or was there more behind his hatred for Daemon? Perhaps he was shooting the messenger, literally. Sophie gulped. The cool hard metal of the gun made her cheek hurt and the rumble of Charles's laugh at her back made her want to retch. She suddenly felt as though she would turn into an aristocratic lady after all and faint.

The notion held appeal. Since her back was to Charles and he couldn't see her face, she closed her eyes for a few seconds and then opened them wide. Blake shook his head. She held out her left hand and counted one, two, three and then with a forced groan, she dropped like a sack.

Charles was caught off guard and wasn't strong enough to hold her up with one hand. For a second his arm tightened painfully about her throat as he cursed but then he was forced to drop her. Sophie hit the ground and rolled away from the maniac. A flash of dark boots filled her vision as Blake jumped over her and slammed his body into Charles's. The gun flew from his hand to land in the dirt not far from where Sophie tried to catch her breath for a second time. Without hesitation she launched herself at the gun, picked it up in two hands and, aiming it into the sky, pulled the trigger.

The shot was deafening but it did make Charles pause, obviously waiting for pain. Blake had been in enough hand-to-hand fights to know never to hesitate.

He squeezed his arms around his distant cousin to roll him and started punching. He saw nothing but red that this bastard had held a gun to a woman. To his woman. When pain exploded in his knuckle with a vicious crunch against Charles's cheek bone, he should have stopped, but how could he? If the bastard got up, he would be a danger to them all again.

Charles gave as good as he got and Blake was surprised. For his sliminess and slight stature, he would have thought the man wouldn't have much of a fight in him.

Blake took a hit to the chest followed by a flyaway fist to the side of his head that put stars in his eyes. It shook him long enough for Charles to get the upper hand and roll him onto his back. He took more blows to the head but the way they sat, Blake couldn't get his arms back far enough to swing. His own punches weren't doing enough damage. Suddenly Charles was gone, the pressure on his chest eased, but his head hurt and his vision darkened. Out of the corner of his eye, he saw Sophie's skirts flash.

By the time Blake lurched to his feet, Charles had rearmed himself with a small, but wicked-looking knife.

"Can't face me like a man?" Blake huffed as he wiped blood from his lip with the back of his dirty hand.

"I'm a duke. I don't have to fight like a man."

"You think they aren't one and the same? Being a duke and a man?" As they swapped words, they moved in circles, their shoes leaving imprints in the mud.

"Only if there are two types of men," Charles said with a wild swipe.

The time for small talk was over. He went to step forward, but at the last minute threw his body left, his hand wrapping around the handle of the knife, around Charles's fingers to pull on the blade, his other arm he pushed across Charles's chest but then his leg folded and they went down again. They landed with a thump, with a whoosh of combined breath. Only Charles wore an expression of complete bewilderment.

Both men looked down at the same time, at the hilt sticking out of the chest of the former duke of Blakiston.

Charles drew a shaky breath, opened his mouth, closed it again.

Blake scrambled back, back in the direction of Sophie's screams. Horse's hooves vibrated against a ground that suddenly seemed so close. Try as he might, he couldn't right himself. Just as he was about to have a second try, two pairs of hands reached out for him. Sophie's were soft and warm, Daemon's large and strong. Then the world darkened until everything was black. He stopped hearing their voices. He could no longer feel their comfort. Even as he thought the thought, he could no longer hear the beating of his own heart.

Sophie didn't look away from Blake's face. She should have said yes. When he'd asked her to marry him, she should have said yes. Why had she hesitated? In the face of losing him, she didn't care where his intentions were when he asked her to be his wife. Fear of loss did feel a hell of a lot like love. It made her stomach flip-flop and her heart race so hard and fast she thought it likely to burst from her chest. Maybe it was the same way he felt when she disappeared? Twice. Only this time she'd been found safe and sound, and he only had part of the night and the morning to worry for her. Last time he'd had months and even when he knew she was alive, his fear and grief had twisted to anger. It was little wonder the feelings he'd had for her all those years ago hadn't dried up and turned to hatred.

And he'd said he loved her. Those three little words instilled more shock in her than any other moment that had gone before. In her darkest nightmares and brightest dreams, she had never held out the hope that someone would love her. She'd clung to her ideals, her decisions and choices, and never let anyone get close enough to truly feel for her. The one man she tried to hold at arm's length, the one man above all others she thought would never forgive her the things she'd done—he was the one to fall in love with her.

Somewhere out there in the heavens was a deity with a twisted smile on his face.

Before Daemon could hoist the still unconscious Blake over the saddle of his horse, Sophie pressed her lips to his and whispered, "I love you."

Twenty-Two

As a strange warmth spread over Blake's body, his limbs felt a little less heavy. He could hear a voice getting louder but could see nothing. He wanted to see her. To know she was real and not a figment of his imagination. He hoped the fact that his head felt as though it would explode meant that he was still alive.

Slowly, so slowly it hurt, he opened his eyes. His vision filled with night dark hair, eyes the bluest of blue twinkled back at him and the scent of apples filled the air.

"Am I dreaming?" he asked, not sure what was happening. Was it heaven that she was there or would it be hell when she walked away? He'd asked her to marry him and she hadn't said yes.

She hadn't said no either...

"Does it feel like a dream?"

He nodded. "It's beautiful like a dream. You're beautiful."

She laughed again, the sound calming him, making him smile in return. "Nothing about this day is like a dream."

Hadn't she said the opposite only a few minutes ago? Was that a few minutes ago? "What happened, Sophie?

Where are we?"

"We're at Matthew's house. Charles is dead. It seems there's a title with your name on it if you want it."

"And will you be my duchess?" He knew without a doubt he didn't dream now. He took her hand in his once again and spoke again before she had the chance to. "That day when I asked if you wanted to be a duchess, I had no idea then that you already were one."

For a moment her face disappeared from his vision and she tried to pull her hand from his. He held on tight. "I know what happened all those years ago."

"How can you not hate me?"

"I did," he admitted. She sighed. "But that was before I had all of the facts. And I could never hate you for something you had no control over."

"And now?"

In her eyes were all her hopes and dreams for the future. He sat up, took both of her hands in his. "Now I want to make you my wife. Not a duchess or an innkeeper's woman. I want you for me. I want to feel your skin against mine. I want to wake up next to you in my bed every day for the rest of our lives."

"And if I say no? What if I decide I'm not strong enough for country life? What if I decide this life is not for me and go back to the city? What will you do then, Blake? Will you forget about me once and for all?"

He shook his head. "Never. If you go to the city, then I go to the city. If you take passage on a ship headed for the Americas, I'll be there right beside you. There is nowhere you can flee this time, sweeting, that I won't find you."

"Yes."

His hands tightened around hers. "Yes?"

"Yes."

"What about-"

She put her fingers to his lips to silence him. "I love you. Let's worry about the details later. You need to rest now."

That was the last thing he needed. "There's only one thing I need right now." He reached for her, wrapped his arm around her lower back and pulled her onto his lap.

"What's that?" she asked with a giggle.

He kissed her long and hard, poured his heart and soul into it. "I think it works better if I show you..."

The end

A note from the author

The idea for Sophia's loss came mostly from an article I read in a magazine many moons ago. The lady had suffered nine miscarriages before being diagnosed with a folate deficiency, resulting in miscarriage generally before nine weeks gestation. One of my closest friends suffered three miscarriages before the doctors picked it up with her (or her husband in their case).

In a study conducted by researchers from Sweden's Karolinka Institute in conjunction with the U.S. National Institute of Child Health and Human Services (NICHD) and published in 2002 in the *Journal of the American Medical Association* proved that women with less than 50% folate levels had increased risks of early pregnancy losses.

Folic acid, also known as folate, is a vitamin necessary for proper cell growth and embryo development. Folate deficiency also has been associated with placental separation during pregnancy, pregnancy-induced hypertension, and low blood supply to the placenta. These effects may in part be responsible for the increased risk of miscarriage.

In 1998, the FDA began requiring food manufacturers to fortify certain grain products with folic acid. Many breakfast cereals, rice, pasta, and most breads are now an excellent source of the vitamin, as are beans, leafy green vegetables, and citrus fruits.

But in the Regency era, can you imagine how many women would have suffered from low or no folate and endured miscarriages and delivered babies with birth defects? It's not like the diets of the rich and famous in London would have been loaded with healthy greens. Folate deficiency can also affect men and regularly does even in the 21st century.

While I can predict a very happy future for Blake and Sophia (with a diet change and greens from their very own garden) and I do like to think they would have been blessed with a huge family and lived happily ever after, however since magic babies and miracle pregnancies are rare in real life, so they should be rare in the stories we read which is why I'm leaving the rest to your imagination...

Bronwyn.

Printed in Great Britain
by Amazon